# THE
# FORTUNATE
# FALL

D0814060

1.) health
2.) methcare
3.) clothes
4.) Books
5.) Puja

# THE
# FORTUNATE
# FALL

RAPHAEL CARTER

TOR®

A TOM DOHERTY ASSOCIATES BOOK
NEW YORK

This is a work of fiction. All the characters and events portrayed in this novel are either fictitious or are used fictitiously.

THE FORTUNATE FALL

This book is printed on acid-free paper.
Edited by Patrick Nielsen Hayden

A Tor Book
Published by Tom Doherty Associates, Inc.
175 Fifth Avenue, New York, NY 10010

Tor Books on the World Wide Web: http://www.tor.com

Tor® is a registered trademark of Tom Doherty Associates, Inc.

Library of Congress Cataloging-in-Publication Data

Carter, Raphael.
    The fortunate fall / Raphael Carter.—1st ed.
        p.    cm.
    "A Tom Doherty Associates book."
    ISBN 0-312-86034-X (alk. paper) (hc)
    ISBN 0-312-86327-6 (pb)
    1. Women journalists—Russia—Fiction.    2. Genocide—Russia Fiction.
        3. Virtual reality—Fiction.    I. Title.
    PS3553.A78278F67        1996
    813'.54—dc20                                                    96-2656
                                                                        CIP

First hardcover edition: July 1996
First trade paperback edition: May 1997

Printed in the United States of America

0   9   8   7   6   5   4   3   2   1

**for Pamela Dyer-Bennet
who turned out to be real**

# THANKS

to Rich Veraa, who was first to read it;

to Patrick Goodman, who delivered take-out and helped vet the continuity;

to George Willard, who posed for a statue, and provided lessons in parachuting and costumery;

to Beth Friedman, who taught the nanobugs how to drink;

to Patricia Wrede, who provided a critique so perceptive I suspect she may be God;

and to Larissa Printzian, who told me the story of Ivan Durachok, and may live to regret it.

# 1

## VIRTUAL OR IMMEDIATE TOUCH

Love not the heavenly Spirits, and how their love
Express they? by looks only? or do they mix
Irradiance, virtual or immediate touch?

—Milton, *Paradise Lost*

The whale, the traitor; the note she left me and the run-in with the Post police; and how I felt about her and what she turned out to be—all this you know. I suppose I can't complain. I knew the risks when I became a camera. If you see something important enough, your thoughts become a coveted commodity: they steal your memories and sell them tied in twine. Now you may find my life for sale in certain stalls, on dusty street and twisting alleyway; it is available on moistdisk, opticube, and dryROM. There are places on the Net where you can make a copy free, although the colors may have faded to sepia and the passions to pastel. You have taken my memories and slotted them into your head. And you have played them through, reclining on a futon in some neon-streaked apartment, reliving my every sensation and thought from the hour underground with the whale.

If you paid extra for the moistdisk, you have more than just that hour. You can peer around each thought to see the memories implied in it, the way you'd turn a hologram to see what lies behind the rose. You can freeze-frame at the moment I first saw the whale, and follow the associations back—to the argument over *Moby-Dick* the night before; to the first time Voskresenye said the word, in the café on Nevsky Prospect; to the dolphins that made me clutch my mother's hand with fear, at the amusement park when I was six years old. You have searched me and known me: and when at last you put the disk away, you thought of my mind as a sucked orange, dry of secrets.

But what you saw, heard, touched, remembered, does not quite exhaust my meanings. With the moistdisk in your head, however bristled you may be with sockets, what you see is only the moment of experience, frozen forever. It excludes any later reflections upon the event—as the hologram of a rose in bloom excludes the flower's swollen ripening and black decay.

I will give you my thoughts since that time, but not on moist-disk. I will not let you explore the twining pathways of my thoughts as I explore them—not again. I will hide instead behind this wall of words, and I will conceal what I choose to conceal. I will tell you the story in order, as you'd tell a story to a stranger who knows nothing of it: for you are not my friend, and what you know is far less than you think you know. You will read my life in phosphors on a screen, or glowing letters scrolling up the inside of your eye. And when you reach the end, you will lie down again in your indifferent dark apartment, with the neon splashing watercolor blues across your face, and you will know a little less about me than you did before.

# one

## ASHES, ASHES

**O**kay, what's this scent?"

"Roses," I said.

"And this one?"

"Citrus. Grapefruit."

"All right. What about this?"

"Cow shit."

"Close."

"Okay, horse shit."

"Bull's-eye. Olfactory systems are go. Let's do hearing."

I was standing by the River Chu, in Kazakhstan, staring at a little hill from which three naked chimneys rose. I stood alone; but a thousand miles away, in Leningrad, a woman I had never met was testing my senses. When she had finished, she would slide herself into my mind, like a rat into water. As my thoughts went out live to the Net, she would screen them through hers, strengthening my foreground thoughts and sifting out impurities, so that—if she was any good—the signal that went out on News One would be pure and clear. And when she drew herself out of my mind again, five minutes later, she would know more about me than a friend of thirty years.

"I think it's an E flat," I said.

"Yes, but what instrument?"

"Brass."

"Be specific."

"Do I look like a conductor?"

"It's a trombone. You can tell by the glissando. Now what's this?"

I had never met this Keishi Mirabara. I had no idea what she looked like. But Keishi was a screener, so for her, our acquaintance of half an hour was already long. Hooking up mind to mind, the way they do, they can only scorn the glacial rituals the rest of us use to form friendships. By the end of the day, she might already hate me—not with some casual dislike, but with a deep, dissective hatred, such as is otherwise only attained after decades of marriage. It's bad stuff, their hatred. Their love is worse: a surge of emotion that comes at you flood-fast, overwhelming your own feelings before you're even certain what they are. And the poor camera, who can reach out to another mind only with mute eyes and vague bludgeoning words . . . well, it's like being an amnesia victim, coming home a stranger to someone who's loved you all your life.

"All right, stop me when this stripe is the same color as the sky."

"Now—no, a little more—yes, there."

"You're coming through faded, then. I'm going to split your field of vision. What you're seeing will be on your left, and what's coming through here will be on your right. Tell me when the colors are the same. Ready?"

"Ready," I said. I gave it only half attention. I had done this all before.

Keishi had come in to screen for me only that evening, when my last screener, Anton Tamarich, disappeared on the day of a broadcast. It didn't surprise me—screeners go burnout all the time—but it left me stuck going live with a screener I'd never worked with before. It's the beginning of any of a dozen camera nightmares. You're working with a new screener who falls asleep at the switch just when you remember something you heard once about how to make brain viruses, and a Weaver possesses the man you're interviewing and kills you on the spot. Or some especially compromising sexual fantasy flits through your head and out into the Net and is the scandal of the week. The untried screener is the camera's equivalent of having your fly open.

It was scary enough that—though I'd never thought I'd say it—I missed Anton. I hadn't liked him, but I'd liked working with him. He was an informer for the Post police, and he hated me. I knew where I stood.

"Say the words that come into your head."

"Excrescence. Trapezoid. Spark. Blanket. Bolus. Rust."

"Verbal, go. Okay, Maya, I'm ready for link-up. Say when."

I walked halfway up the hill, arranged myself facing the river, and started to prepare myself for contact. After all these years of having strangers in my head, it's still not easy. I scratched my nose, adjusted the camera moistware in the temporal socket at the side of my head, and made sure for the tenth time that I really did not have to go to the bathroom.

"Relax, will you?" Keishi whispered in my ear, from Leningrad. " 'So Your Camera Has To Pee' is chapter two in the Basic Screening textbook, and heck, girl, I'm up to chapter four already."

At that moment gallows humor was not what I needed. Fear shifted in the coils of my intestines, like a restless snake. I would forget my lines. I would trip on a buried cobblestone and half the Russian Historical Nation would feel me break my nose. I fixed my eyes on the ground and began to hyperventilate, fighting for control.

And Keishi, knowing that anything she said would make it worse, did the only thing she could do to help. She plugged in her screening chip and patched into my mind.

There's a sense of presence when the screener comes on line, a faint heat, a pullulation. Keishi's feedback was clear and warm and reassuring, the strongest I've ever felt—as though someone had wrapped a blanket around my head. ("That's me," Keishi agreed. "An electric babushka.") Maybe this would work out after all, I decided, knowing she heard the thought.

"Ten more seconds," she warned me. "Five. Four. Three . . . and you're *live*, girl." I felt the "up" drug flood my visual cortex, making me strain my eyes to separate the river from the rolling hill behind it. Keishi fed the hours of interviews and research that Anton and I had done into my memory, so that the five-minute Netcast could imply a whole week's work. And you came on line, a shadow audience that always stood behind me no matter how I turned my head.

"This is what's left of Square-Mile-on-Chu," I said aloud, panning slowly around from the river. You said it with me. In a single body, with the same volition, we strode forward up the hill. "Three crumbling chimneys and some scattered stones, half sunk into the ground." I had reached the middle chimney now; I walked around it, running my hand over the cobblestones to transmit their tiled smoothnesses. "Typical Guardian construction: cobblestone instead of brick because of the thousands of hours of slave labor it took to gather the stones, carry them up here, and fit them together. The more labor-intensive, the greater the status."

I panned around to view the river again, then carefully leaned against the chimney, feeling it cool and lumpy against my back. "It's as idyllic a scene as you'll find anywhere in Kazakhstan. You could spend hours in this place. Nature bounces back, you think, whatever humans do. The hills are leaved with grass, and laced with branches, growing the same as ever. The birds have long forgotten what happened here, if indeed they ever noticed, and are building their nests now. And the river flows on, just as it did when the word Guardian meant a good thing."

I walked down the hill, slowly, letting the sun warm my back that the stones had made cold. It was an aggressively beautiful spring day, tyrannically perfect: the kind of day that spurs the suicide to action by its mocking contrast to her own despair. *Lull them, Keishi,* I subvocalized. *Make them* feel *it.*

"I'm lulling, I'm lulling," was her reply, as laconic as the mood I wished to set and as the day itself.

Walking slowly in the mild breeze, I approached the lake, reached it, and did not stop. Without removing my shoes or rolling up my cuffs or bracing myself against the touch of the water, I walked off into the muck. Skirls of shock and disgust mingled with the cold—your shock. Feedback to the limbic system, say the manuals; what it means is that what you feel, I feel. And vice versa: I took the feeling and intensified it, hurling it back out at you.

"It is a beautiful day in Kazakhstan," I said, "and you are calf-deep in the ash of human bodies." A second long wave of mute horror as the ash and mud cemented in around my legs, entrapping them.

"The Unanimous Army came through here in the fall of 2246," I said when the audience had quieted. Calling on my imagination chip, I drew a sound of marching out of the white noise of the river. Then I looked up at the shadowed hillside and began to sculpt its waving grasses into men. "Imagine a solid column of humanity, twenty abreast, and so long that if you wanted to cross their path you'd have to camp here until dawn tomorrow. They have no uniforms, but wear whatever they happened to have on when they were absorbed: overalls, cocktail dresses—some are naked beneath makeshift coats. But all have the same round black chip, the size of a ruble coin, in their left temples. From time to time a memory unit passes, like the nameless man we met last week—" and here Keishi lifted a curtain from the memory "—people whose minds the Army erased and filled with its data, so the memories of the others could remain inviolate. The memory units can no longer even walk, so they are carried along—but upright, to confuse snipers. At this distance they are lost in the crowd, and you will never know them."

By now the Army was almost as clear as reality, thanks to the imagination chip in my right temporal socket. Keishi flashed the word "re-creation" at the bottom of my field of vision, so credulous channel-flippers wouldn't call the station thinking that the Army had returned.

"The first quarter-mile of the Army consists of people who are weak or dying or otherwise of little use. Their only purpose is to walk blindly into everything and see if it will kill them. Now that they've marched through the Square Mile without harm, Sensors start to break away from the column: Eyes, Ears, Noses, Fingertips, each with its respective sense enhanced and all the others numbed. They swarm over the Square Mile in thousands, sniffing and prodding and tasting. They take nothing, but now and again they smear something with a fragrant paint they carry with them, or with urine or blood.

"When the Sensors return to the march, the column slows and spreads out to the width of the Square Mile. And when it has passed, hours later, everything in the camp—the barbed wire, the burnt wood, even the concrete from the foundations—is gone, digested into that great worm of meat that once was, and will soon again be, human.

"By November, every man, woman, and child over five in Kazakhstan had been taken up into the One Mind and was marching on Occupied Russia. And in 2248, when the Army software detected victory and suddenly erased itself from all its component minds, more than half the people in the world found themselves at least a thousand miles from home. It was a time of global confusion, during which millions starved or were murdered. Not many people were concerned with seeing to it that places like this were remembered."

"But is that the whole explanation?" (*Okay, let's wind it up,* I subvoked.) "Or is there a deeper reason? The Holocaust and Terror-Famine both haunted the consciences of generations, yet the Calinshchina is barely remembered—why? We'll have some answers for you next week, in the third and last part of our series."

*And then it's back to fads and scandals for the both of us,* I subvoked to Keishi, who chuckled politely in reply. I closed my eyes, calling up my quite beautiful and utterly fictitious Net-portrait, and signed off: "Maya Tatyanichna Andreyeva. Of News One hearth, a Camera."

No sooner had the audience fallen away than Keishi said: "I can't believe you gave that whole speech standing in the water. I filtered out most of the cold and wetness, but even so, it wasn't easy to keep their minds on history while water was seeping into their underwear."

"If I'd walked out of the water and stood around dripping," I said, sitting down on the grass to take off my shoes, "it would have been even more distracting."

"You could have saved your swimming lesson for the very end," she said. "You could—" but I had pulled the Net chip out of my head, cutting her off. The chip was long and white, with many metal legs; cupped in my hand, it looked like some pale, crawling thing that you'd find living under a rock. Vermin. I slipped it into a pocket and began to scrape the ash off of my shoes.

# two

## THE PLATYPUS

This was closed to you, even on moistdisk. Keishi was careful to block certain things from the Net-cast—not that it mattered, in the end.

I was folded into the single front seat of the electric car I'd rented in Alma-Ata. Thanks to the rental company's paternalism, the car would go no faster than 100 kph. At that rate I was four hours from the trainport, then three more hours by bullet train from the empty cathedrals and copper towers of Leningrad. Kazakhstan crept past me in spurts of brush and patchy fields. There was nothing for my eyes to do but look ahead for the five-kilometer markers, distracted only where the scarred land condescended to support a token sheep.

A yellow light flashed in the corner of my eye. "What?" I said irritably.

The answer scrolled across my eyes: FEED NANOTECH.

"All right. Cancel alarm."

SECOND WARNING.

"All right, I said." The letters meekly disappeared.

I took my flask out of my pocket and shook it. Almost half full, and I could get a refill on the train. No problem. I dug the telltale out of my duffel bag and pressed it against the back of my neck. It hummed as it read my implant, and clicked a few times, thinking. Finally it chimed, and I pulled it away. It said I needed fifty-three millilitres—just a booster. My nano population was steady as she goes. I opened the flask and, pinching it between my knees, dug into my duffel for a graduated cup.

The shout of a siren interrupted my search. The car pulled itself over to the side of the road.

"What? What's wrong?"

"Alcohol detected," the car informed me primly. "Drinking and driving goes counter to company policy, as well as the laws of the Fusion of Historical Nations."

"Oh, right," I said. I touched the telltale to the dashboard, but there was no answering chime.

"It's right there," I said irritably. "Can't you read?"

"Drinking and driving is not permitted," the car repeated. "There are no exceptions to this policy."

"Look," I said, "I'm a camera. I've got more nanobugs in my head than a corpse has worms. They're the *old kind.*" I was speaking very slowly and distinctly, as if this might help the car to understand me. "They live on ethanol. If I don't give them some, they'll starve, and they'll get all clotted up in my blood vessels, and I'll have a stroke and die. What do the laws of Kazakhstan have to say about dying and driving?"

"*Drinking* and driving," it corrected me, "go counter to—"

"Company policy, yes, all right. The company was supposed to tell you this before we left. Do you understand me? *I won't get drunk.* The nanobugs will eat the alcohol. I'm not going to wrap us around a tree—even if there were any trees around. Do you see any trees? I don't see any trees."

"Accidents are possible at any place and time. Drinking and driving—"

"All right, I heard you," I said. "I'm overdue to feed the bugs already. If I don't drink some nanojuice within a couple of hours, I will, at the very least, be in a coma. And when that happens, I promise, if there's even one tree in this whole damned Historical Nation, I'll find it and wrap your pretty little bumper—"

The alarm light in my eye flashed again. "Yes, I know," I said. "What do you think I'm trying to do?"

A message scrolled by, just above the horizon: CAN I BUY YOU A DRINK?—KM.

"Mirabara?" I said. "How did you find me?"

ONLY PERSON IN KAZAKHSTAN WHO WOULD ARGUE WITH A CAR, she answered. MIND IF I HELP?

I sighed and said, "Do I have a choice?"

SURE YOU DO. LET BUGS DIE. OTHERWISE, IMAGINE A PLATYPUS.

"What?"

HUMOR ME. VISUALIZE PLATYPUS.

I stared at the car's hood ornament and tried to imagine a platypus curled up around it. Gradually the animal gained solidity, and I made it wake up, yawn, and defecate on the hood.

NOW MAKE IT A WEASEL.

I shrank the platypus into a weasel.

CHANGE IT INTO A WHALE.

"A whale won't fit on the car hood."

SMALL WHALE, she suggested. Then I heard her voice behind me: "Never mind, I'm here."

In the back seat was a cloud of static, gradually taking on human shape. As I watched it in the rear-view mirror, it sent out a tendril to the dashboard.

"Company headquarters has just informed me of a change in policy," the car said breathlessly. "Drinking and driving is now allowed. No—I'm sorry, strike that—" it paused as though listening "—drinking and driving now *encouraged.* Also—" as it pulled back out onto the road "—speed limit throughout Kazakhstan has now been doubled. Tripled if you happen to be wearing a black shirt, and—" it squealed with excitement "—you are!"

The accelerator fell under my foot. The speed indicator sprouted an extra digit, and turned red.

"Visualize bat out of hell," she said. I glanced into the rear-view mirror, which showed me only a strip of forehead; by craning my neck a little I managed to see one eyelid, harboring an orb of static. Then I looked back at the road, which was passing at an alarming rate.

"All right, Mirabara, I understand how you slipped the text in through my camera chip, but how are you giving me visual?"

"Through your imagination enhancer."

I frowned. "That doesn't hook up with the Net."

"Not usually. But it'll call out to News One's stock library if it needs to draw something you don't have a clear memory of."

"Oh. Like a platypus."

"Exactly," she said. "By the way, you'd better not take any assignments in Australia for a while. It's a little confused about egg-laying mammals—thinks they all look like me. Oh, and they're a lot bigger than you were imagining. See?" She reached forward and deposited a platypus on my lap.

"Hey!" I tried to brush the animal away, but it was insubstantial; my hands passed through it. "Will you get rid of that? I'm trying to drive."

"Oh, all right. Spoilsport." She made the animal disappear. "You'd better drink your nanojuice now."

I poured out the vodka—100 proof, strictly regulation; I hate having to do math before I drink.

"Hey, nice flask," she said admiringly. "Right out of an old movie."

I shrugged. "Keeps me from getting caught without when I'm out on assignment."

"So," she said dismissively, "would a crusty old plaid thermos out of a lunch box. And a thermos would keep it cold, so you could put nutrient mix in it. But that flask does something much better."

"What's that?" I asked, unwarily.

"Makes you feel like Sam Spade."

I dropped my voice half an octave and drawled: " 'All we've got is that maybe you love me and maybe I love you. . . . ' "

I stopped; the pleasure of quotation had carried me past caution. She gave me a brief speculative look, but let the implication pass.

"Not bad," she said. "Best Bogart I've heard in a long time."

"Flatterer." I've been to Japan, so I knew she was putting me on. The Japanese profess to think that Classical America was the high-water mark of world civilization—mostly to spite the Africans' love of Egypt. A good Bogart can get you promotions in Tokyo. Me, I don't even like Bogart. I just watch *The Maltese Falcon* for Peter Lorre, and *Casablanca* because the thought of people wanting *out* of Africa is so agreeably deranged.

"Not that I'm not enjoying this little chat with the back of your head," Keishi said, "but do you mind if I come up front?"

I looked around at the interior of the narrow electric car. "There's nowhere to sit up here except my lap."

"Tempting as that offer is," she said, "I think I'll make my own accommodations." The right door of the car shimmered and receded, and a new seat ballooned into the extra space. The car flickered a little as it morphed, but when she was finished, I couldn't find the line where real car ended and illusion began.

I looked away, disquieted that my reality could be changed so easily. "Aren't my intrusion lockouts good for anything?" I asked.

"Oh, they're good enough to keep you safe from the general rabble."

"But not enough to make me safe from you?"

She clucked her tongue at me. "Girl, that's not a software problem."

At that moment a car passed us on the highway, which, in Kazakhstan, was a rare enough event to command my full attention.

"Why are you doing that?" she asked softly.

"Doing what?"

"Looking away every time I look over at you."

"I am not," I said irritably. "I'm trying to drive, that's all."

"Oh, yeah? What color are my eyes?"

"Mirabara, I don't even know what color *my* eyes are."

"All right, then, what color's my hair?"

"Black."

"You just guessed that because you know I'm Japanese."

"Do you have any idea how many blondes there are in Japan now?"

"Quit changing the subject and look at me."

It really was a beautiful day. April: time to start cleaning. That insulation would have to come out of the windows. And the bathroom was really disgraceful—

"Pull over!" Keishi was shouting.

"What? What's wrong?"

"You blacked out, that's what. Now pull over before you get yourself killed."

"I feel fine," I said resentfully, but I stopped the car by the side of the road.

"Maybe too fine? Maybe drank a little too much nanojuice?"

"You saw me. I drank exactly what the telltale said. When exactly did this alleged blackout happen?"

"Right after you turned around to look at me. I think I'm insulted."

"Very funny," I said, but I looked down into my lap. I was beginning to suspect what had gone wrong.

There are two ways of creating a virtual image. If you want, you can send video to the optic nerve, but that takes a lot of bandwidth. If all telepresence worked that way, we'd have sixty channels instead of six thousand. So most channels barely send any video at all. I saw a demo once in which they patched some soap-opera channel through a video screen, and all you could see was a few pale ghosts swimming in static. It looks solid to you because your implants secrete what cameras call "down," which makes your brain, well, gullible—"lowers your thresholds," I think is the phrase. No, I don't know what thresholds they're talking about, either. They say it's like the way dreams work, if that means anything to you.

To make sure you see what you're meant to see instead of just dreaming at random, the moistware sends signals to some gizmos called neuromodulators, that sit in the part of your brain that recognizes things. And the neuromodulators guide your mind, as it amplifies the patterns it's being fed.

This is not an exact science. Sometimes the mind will amplify a purely random pattern in the static, or make the right pattern into the wrong thing. That's why on the low-bandwidth channels, you sometimes get misrecognitions. The camera sees the Prime Minister, and you see your Uncle Vanya. The camera sees her first love, and you see yours. In a case like mine this presents certain problems, as you can imagine.

Now, News One does go out in full video, precisely because they don't want Mr. Yablokov to turn into Dyadya Vanya during a speech. So while I'm transmitting, my nanos secrete "up," which somehow makes my eyes work harder so you get a better signal. Sometimes a new screener will give me too much up, and I'll go agnosic—look at things and not know what they are. But Keishi was coming in through my imagination chip's feeble Net-link, and that is a *very* low-bandwidth connection, lower than even the most obscure channels. To get an image that way, I'd need a lot more down than I was used to. Since I'm a camera, the bugs would keep the down corralled in certain parts of my brain, which explained why I could still more or less drive; but my visual cortex must have been swimming in the stuff. Any moment now, the road might turn into a river, the grass into seaweed, the sheep into shellfish. Small wonder if I mistook Keishi for someone else.

Unless. What if it wasn't a misrecognition? What if she *was?*

I glanced at her, minutely so she might not notice. I could have seen her for no more than a fraction of a second, and yet I felt my mind skid—with a moment of panic, like slipping on ice—back to the thought of the insulation in the windows. And this thought, which had gone through my mind a hundred times and was familiar to it, brought on a pulse of nausea: as on those mornings when the throat forgets all previous intimacy with the toothbrush and, gagging, rejects it.

*You're wrong,* I told myself forcefully. *She is Keishi Mirabara, a screener, a stranger, and not what you think.*

But if she was?

"Turn around," she said. "Let me take a look at your pupils."

"I said, I'm all right. I'm just a little tired, that's all."

She leaned toward me; I twisted away. Finally she drew back and frowned. "I think I see the problem." For a time, silence. Then she said, "It's okay, you can turn around now."

"What did you do?" I said, not moving.

"Told your nanobugs to clean the fatigue products out of your system. It'll keep you a few hours. There's a long-term solution—called sleeping. You should ask the Net about it."

I suspected that the excuse of fatigue was as much a lie in her mouth as in mine. But having advanced the explanation myself, I could hardly deny it now. Slitting my eyes, as though that could protect me from the sight, I turned toward her—

And felt waves of relief. ("There now," she said, "that's better.") She was twenty years too young to be her—to be one of them—to be what I had thought. Maybe I really was tired, and imagining things. Or maybe it was too much down. And she really was alarmingly beautiful; maybe it was only that.

No, wait. Strike that. I took a second look: she was indifferently pretty, perhaps, but taken for all in all, she was far too much Central Casting's idea of the Japanese Black émigré to attract anyone but the shallow. You know the type—young, overeager, and a little bit more fashionable than it is fashionable to be. She even had the statutory name-you've-never-heard-before. If this were a vid, first we'd have the history lesson about how the Unanimous Army stranded thousands of American Blacks in Japan, and then she'd start telling me how she tried to get to Africa but they turned her away at the border because she wasn't pure enough of blood. Though, come to think of it, she looked as if she might have been; the East had left few traces in her face, except to lighten it. She could easily pass for an African.

"Well, don't bother thanking me," she said as I pulled back out onto the road.

"Thank you," I said with exaggerated courtesy. "Now will you please tell me what the devil News One thought they were doing sending me an NCG to go live? I could have been eaten up out there."

"What's an NCG?"

"New College Graduate," I said. "You know, a redshirt. Cannon fodder."

Keishi gestured at the car she had refashioned. "Have you ever had a screener before who could do this?"

"Horsepower is one thing. Experience is another."

"I've got that, too. Over ten years of it."

"Mirabara, you aren't old enough to have ten years' experience in anything."

"I'm not in flesh, Maya. Virtual images don't age unless you tell them to, you know. So I'm a little older than I choose to look—is that a crime?"

I had to admit, it was a likely enough explanation for someone like her. "That's different, then. I suppose I might take off a few years myself, if I had the choice."

"Really?" she said with bland surprise. "What for?"

"You don't have to be sarcastic about it." I had only been trying to be charitable.

"I'm not," she said. "I can't imagine why you'd change a thing."

"I said, that's enough."

Keishi chuckled, leaning back in her seat. "You're a difficult
woman to compliment, News One."

"I don't need your compliments," I said, more harshly than I'd
intended. "What I expect out of a screener is a clean signal, period.
I don't need flattery, or companionship, or witty repartee—"

"Or help with recalcitrant rental cars?" she said mildly.

I fixed my eyes on the road and tried to will myself not to
blush. There was no sense apologizing now. I'd been hostile
enough to make her ask for repartnering, and that would be the
end of it. And even if she didn't ask, they would send me someone
new within the week. They don't pair men with men or women
with women, for obvious reasons. The more so in my case. It was
a mix-up, probably; her name looked like a weird transliteration
of Keiji, a man's name, and someone must have made the wrong
assumption. If her assignment to me wasn't a mistake, it was a
test—or maybe both, since every screener is a test, in one way or
another. When you run into one like Anton, who only works for
the Postcops, you try to hold onto him. Most of them work for the
Weavers, and the Weavers are a lot more dangerous.

"So," she said briskly, "we've gone over what you want from a
screener. What do you want from a research assistant?"

"Why do you ask?" I said with a sense of dread.

"Because I saw the request for an RA you posted. And I'd like
to do it."

"Oh, Mirabara," I said, grasping for any polite cliché, "I don't
know that that's a good idea. I don't think we're really ready to be
living in each other's back pockets just yet. These first few months
of a partnering are always hard. . . . "

"We don't have to work that closely. After all, I've been mind-to-mind with you—I've got a pretty good idea how you'll respond to things. Just give me a direction and turn me loose. If you want, I can even do fill-in recordings and make it look and feel just like your style."

"You can do that? You're wired camera?" When I got into the business, you could either be a camera or a screener, never both; when they wired you, you were tracked for life. It was nice. It cut down on the understudy effect. But I'd heard of people wired both ways, screening each other, a two-way connection. There were even some who left the link on all the time, merging their minds forever—people who had ceased to be human, by any reasonable definition of that word.

"Wired camera?" she said. "Girl, I'm wired everything." And suddenly her face was bathed in light. An invisible Net-rune, no less. The tech in that head must have been worth more than the whole Kazakhi GNP. It was tempting. But it would be intolerable.

She must have seen "no" in my face. "Look," she said, "we'll be seeing each other less than if I just screen, because I can work independently. And if I'm doing some of the camera work, we won't have to go mind-to-mind as much."

"Look, I just don't think—"

"If you want," she interrupted, with bitterness in her voice, "you can send me instructions by Net-text and you won't have to see me at all."

I looked at her and, despite myself, felt sympathy. She seemed not far from tears. It was my fault—mine and the bastard's who invented this technology. It's his plotline we're forced to repeat. For the camera, a stranger with the key to all your secrets. For the screener, feeling closer than a sister to someone who does nothing but push you away. And as I thought of this, I felt a grim determination to see things through with Keishi. There was a kind of poetry to it—her irreverence, my hostility. We deserved each other.

"All right," I said, "we'll try it. But there's one thing you need to know."

"What?"

I glanced over at her. "Do you know how I got this assignment?"

"No," she said, her eyes narrowing with curiosity. "And I wondered. No offense, Maya, but you're not exactly typecast."

"I applied for it," I said. "I put in a proposal."

"What possessed them to accept? Sunspots?"

"They didn't accept. I got back a curt little Net-text saying that they had no plans to do a story like that at this time. They were just going to let the anniversary go by."

"Let me guess. You hacked the News One computers and inserted the assignment."

"No," I said irritably. "Are you kidding? News One is a fortress. I couldn't pull off a thing like that. I don't think anyone could."

"*I* could," she said smugly.

I looked at her skeptically out of the corner of my eye. "Be that as it may. I took a more low-tech solution. I was interviewing the camera who broke the Shimanski scandal—typical incestuous News One bullshit; I think I've interviewed more cameras than I have anyone else. That's what happens when you slip this far down on the food chain."

"A predator who feeds on other predators is at the *top* of the food chain," she pointed out.

"Only if she takes them live. This was scavenging, and I wasn't even the first jackal at the corpse. So I got down to question number six on the Universal Interviewing-Another-Camera Script, which is, and I quote, 'What's your position on invisible wiring and cameras without Net-runes? Is it really ethical to put someone on the air without his knowledge, or—' "

" 'Or is it an unwarranted invasion of privacy?' " Keishi chimed in the last words.

"Exactly. I see you've watched telepresence at least once in the last ten years. Of course the only political topics they let us cover are the ones that will never change anything—they are not going to go back and scar all the new cameras just so people will know what they're dealing with. So this idiot I'm interviewing, who's been asked the same question a hundred times in the last week, makes doe-eyes at me out of his perfect face and says, 'Well, my goodness, Maya Andreyeva, you really ask the serious questions.' "

"Oh, God."

"My reaction exactly. And I thought, I can't go on like this. I just can't do it anymore."

"What did you do?" she asked, with a peculiar tenderness.

"Well," I said, "it had to be sudden, or Anton would see it coming. So I just reached out with my foot and pushed over the table between us, and while Anton was racing to cover up the sound and create the image of a table and cover up the idiot camera's shock, I said: 'Well, that'll certainly be useful next week, when I'll be doing a story in honor of the anniversary of the liberation of the Square Miles. Um, a three-part series, actually.' And it went out on the Net, and News One decided to run the story rather than have people wonder."

"Didn't the filters screen it out?"

"Why? The Calinshchina isn't killfiled."

"So it's not," she said appreciatively. "There's a Weaver that keeps track of it, but Weavers don't care how you pursue your career goals."

"That could have called a Weaver?" I said in sudden fear.

She looked at me strangely, as though my reaction had been unexpected. "Maya, if a whiteshirt were going to come for you, don't you think she would have done it long ago?"

"Of course," I said hastily, realizing I'd misstepped. "I'm just being paranoid, that's all. Occupational hazard."

"After all," she said slowly, "the Weavers have the whole Net to control. Why would one single you out?"

"Yes, you're right." I kept my eyes on the road, trying to make my mind as blank as possible.

She watched me a little longer, then let the subject drop. "So," she said. "The point of your story is that News One is pissed at you, and that you're the last person I should hitch my fortunes to. Well, you're not going to get rid of me that easily."

"No," I said. "The point of my story is that my objectives and News One's may not always correspond. You can back them, or you can back me. And if you're going to back them, I don't want you around."

"I see." She turned her eyes on my feet and did a slow pan upward.

"What are you doing?" I said.

"Deciding."

"I don't have time for games, Mirabara."

"Oh?" she said, and chuckled. "Well, don't worry. It was never even close."

We drove on, in a conspiratorial silence.

At the next five-K marker she added: "On one condition."

*Here it comes*, I thought. "What kind of condition?"

"I know you're not used to our Japanese informality, but you're driving me crazy using my surname all the time."

I winced in apology. She had asked me to call her Keishi, and I had done so, in my thoughts. But I was reluctant to pronounce the name, with its diphthong, its doubtful gender, and its indeclinability. At least "Mirabara" had a feminine ending, whatever its bastard origins.

"If you really can't bring yourself to just call me Keishi," she said, "I could make up a matronymic. Keishi Eikovna."

I laughed. "That sounds like a patronymic. You want people thinking you're eighty years old, be my guest."

"Well, what do you do with names that end in o, then? My mother's name was Eiko."

"Russian names don't end in o."

"Well, whose fault is that?" She frowned and tried again. "Ei-kichna?"

"Better not try," I said, and hazarded: "Keishi?"

She smiled on the attempt. "Close enough. If you could bring yourself to hold that first vowel for more than a femtosecond it might sound a little bit less like a sneeze—" she saw my irritation "—but, yes, certainly, you may bid me by that name. How may I serve Your Eminence?"

"For a start," I said, "pull out everything available about the Holocaust, the Terror-Famine, and any other miscellaneous horrors you can think of. I'm looking for popular media, mostly. Then dig up every broadcast and Net-text about the Calinshchina. And sit down for about a megascops-hour and think about the similarities and differences—not between the events, so much as between the reactions to them. Then put it all on a chip I can slot in over breakfast tomorrow. Can you do that?"

"That, and have time for about four hours' sleep besides."

"In that case, bring it to me at the Leningrad trainport. I should arrive there around two this morning. And quit bragging, it's not attractive."

"Only if you quit trying to intimidate me," she said. "I'm not afraid of work. I told you, you can't scare me away that easily."

She smiled and her image faded, then returned. "Oh, one more thing. Stick your camera chip in your wrist socket for a second. I want to tweak some things—you're not getting the color fidelity you should be."

"I don't have an adapter."

"You do too, it's in your duffel. Don't you know you can't lie to your screener?"

"I like my colors the way they are," I said.

"Now you're grasping at straws."

"No, I mean it. Most cameras nowadays make all their colors

super-bright. The muted colors from the old moistware remind people that I'm a veteran, not just a mayfly that some idiot has wired."

"Like me, you mean?"

"Doesn't one of us have some work that she's neglecting?"

"Oh, all right, if that's how you want to be about it." She faded again. When only Cheshire eyes remained, she said softly: "It will work out, Maya. I promise it will."

"This," I said, lapsing back into Bogart, "could be the beginning of a truly appalling partnership."

I heard her laughter, and the clinking of her earrings. The car's extra seat disappeared.

Earrings! Honestly! It struck me only then: how like her, to follow fashion right off the cliff into that quaint disfigurement. In my day when you poked holes in your head it was to expand your mind, not just for decoration. Except, of course, for the people who had fake sockets drilled, so everyone would think they could afford a real set. As I drove toward Alma-Ata I wondered idly what those people were doing now that the real status was in being wired invisibly, like Keishi. Wearing hats, I supposed. And carrying around fake totems with fake chips plugged into them. I ought to do a retrospective.

Vanity. I took out the rest of my chips—all but two—and drove to Alma-Ata quite inviolate, my head accepting input only from the holes that Nature drilled there.

It was a quiet drive, and would have been restful, if not for one thought I could not put aside. No doubt it was only a trick of my memory, which I had every reason to distrust. Or too much down and not enough bandwidth. But when Keishi had first appeared and I had seen her forehead in the rearview mirror, a featureless strip of anonymous skin—I was almost sure of it—that skin had not been black.

**(Centipede)**

(I did leave two chips in my head; one was a dream coprocessor. Whatever you've heard, dreams don't reveal your hidden desires— if they did, I'd never be allowed to dream. They don't reveal solutions to your problems, and they don't foretell the future. They're just the fumes your brain exhales as it digests the day's new memories and mulches them into the old. A dream coprocessor increases the efficiency of that process, improving memory. Which is a good thing on the whole, although from time to time I wish there were a button for "forget." One that *I* controlled, I mean. The dreams you get with a coprocessor are bloody, vivid, and obscure, like second-rate German Expressionism.

On the bullet train to Leningrad I briefly slept, and dreamed she stood before me, holding something in her hand: a centipede. She held it out to me. I must have refused, for she drew it back, laughing. And then I saw that she was wearing a cloak with two hoods, one lying empty on her shoulder. But no, it was not empty. Her second head lifted itself slowly, and its eyes were flashing incandescent bulbs in metal sockets.

I woke with the tunnel lights reddening the inside of my eyelids, dark and bright, flashing, flashing.)

# three

## A FASTER CABLE

**I** had expected that she would be waiting for me, but she wasn't. I walked out of the gate into the trainport, past a shop full of T-shirts, snow domes, and cheap telepresence tapes of the city's attractions; past a kiosk of black moist-novels and garish blue and yellow drydisk magazines; then into the trainport bar, which was, I thought, entirely brighter than it should have been. When I gave the bartender my order, he looked at me with alarm. "Vodka and what?"

"Compost. Vodka and compost. You haven't been here long, have you?"

"No, ma'am," he said sheepishly. "The servo's broken. I'm sort of an emergency replacement."

"There's a lot of that going around. Let me guess. You probably have ten years' experience too. You're a virtual ghost the same age as Prime Minister Yablokov."

"Excuse me, *tavarishcha?*"

"Comrade," no less. This one was as young as he looked. "All right, look. Compost. Noun. A mixture of micronutrients for the nourishment of aging nanobugs. Named for the taste—"

"Oh, you mean NanoSweet?"

"That's what the manufacturer is pleased to call it, yes."

The bartender chuckled. "I'll just need to see your readout, *tavarishcha.*" Oh, goodie, I'd made a friend.

I touched the telltale to the back of my neck, and showed it to him when it chimed. The number was higher this time; Mirabara must have fried quite a few bugs remodeling the rental car. That was fine with me. At least the drink would taste like alcohol, even if it didn't feel like it.

Ten minutes later I'd drunk the last vile drop, and still no sign of Mirabara. I gave her another five minutes while I drank a cup of coffee, then got up to leave, resolving to fill out a repartnering form before I went to bed. I was almost out the door when a bell chimed softly and a speaker above the bar singsonged: "M. T. Andreyeva, hearth News One, clan Camera, insert a white courtesy plug please. Maya at News One of Camera, white courtesy plug."

I found the rack of plugs conveniently located right where people had to stand to look up at the arrivals screen. You'd think a trainport would be quiet at two in the morning, but, this being Leningrad, there was a crowd. By the time I got through to the phone I'd used three different obscenities a total of seven times, made at least two lifelong enemies, and possibly broken one toe— not mine, someone else's. Served them right for using the monitor when they could get the same data faster from the Net.

When I looked at the plug I felt a wave of nausea. The cable was crusted with reddish-brown spots—catsup was the least disgusting theory—and the plug itself was greasy with someone's hair oil. I didn't relish the thought of having it a centimeter from my brain. Why do they always give you an audio plug, anyway? A microphone and speaker would be just as good and far more sanitary. Kickbacks from the manufacturer? There was a story in there somewhere.

I looked wistfully through the press of bodies at the snow dome store, where I might beg a disinfectant. But that would mean fighting my way out again through sweat, perfume, body heat, and gutter exclamations. Besides, they probably wouldn't have it. I settled for wiping the plug on my shirt, to replace some of the unknown dirt with dirt I was on intimate terms with, and slid the disgusting thing into my minisocket. Then I remembered that the minisocket was sitting right on top of Wernicke's area, so if the plug infected my brain with something, the first thing I'd lose would be the ability to understand speech. Oh well, I thought jauntily, it's too late now; and besides, how often do people say anything worth listening to, these days? You could almost get along without that skill.

In this cheerful state of mind I thought out into the cable and said: "This had better be good."

The answer was terse and delivered at a volume just this side of a shout: "Slot up for God's sake, agoraphobe." Click. It was Keishi.

Sighing, I made my way back through the crowd, less rudely and therefore more slowly than before. I settled back down at the bar, took out my Net chip, and put it on the counter in front of me.

"Would you like something else, *tavarishcha?*"

"As a matter of fact, yes," I said, leaning forward. "I would like to get well and truly drunk. I know it's probably against company policy, but you wouldn't tell on me, would you?"

He shuffled his feet uneasily. "Drinking beyond your ration can be very dangerous—especially—" He broke off.

"Especially at my age. So you know that, do you. You know, you remind me of a car I met once. Look, overfeeding them just this one time won't kill me. Even if they *have* evolved out of their bug birth control program, they can only reproduce so fast."

He gave me a pained look. "I'm sorry, *tavarishcha.* We're not allowed."

"Oh, all right then. If you can't, you can't." I started to turn away, then looked back at him appraisingly and said: "Of all the seedy two-bit brains in all the Historical Nations in the world, she patches into mine."

He searched my face, puzzled. Then he smiled the smile of someone finally making out the elephant in a child's drawing. "Oh, is that supposed to be Bogart, ma'am?"

Just as I'd suspected. I ordered coffee to make him go away, then picked up the chip from the counter and slotted it in.

"Behind you," she said.

I turned around on the stool. "Fashion risk, Mirabara?" Keishi was wearing a Leningrad University T-shirt that must have been twenty years old, and at most had been washed once in all that time; white slacks stained gray and rolled up at least six inches; wisps of greasy hair escaping from a broad-brimmed hat. She looked like a hard-core wirehead, the kind you see trying to kiss the horse in Senate Square.

"I saw the way you looked at my earrings last time. I thought I'd try a different effect."

"Maybe something a little less radical," I said.

She shrugged and morphed back into the clothing of the day before. "It's just a virtual image. Actually, this is what my body's wearing today in real."

"Then what was it wearing yesterday?"

"Nothing."

"All right, if you don't want to tell me . . . "

"I just did," she said, raising her eyebrows.

This reminded me that *my* body was sitting in a trainport bar carrying on a conversation with thin air. I glanced warily at the bartender. He returned the look without surprise and said, "More coffee, ma'am?"

"No, I'm all right," I said. He seemed blasé enough about it. "Anything for your friend?"

I looked at him incredulously. "I'm not a lunatic, I'm virtual conferencing. And even if I were a lunatic, I wouldn't need you to humor me."

Keishi's voice chimed from the speaker above the bar: "Please excuse Maya Tatyanichna, she is a little confused about modern technology this morning. I'll have a coffee, too, please."

"And your Netname?"

"Keishi Mirabara, of hearth—"

"Put it on mine," I interrupted, before she could say "News One." I don't like being recognized.

"Thanks, but it doesn't matter," she told me. "I'm hearth Whisper—Margay clan, you know. I only use News One bang Screener as a hathook, for expense accounts. But thanks."

"What are you here for, Mirabara? With a high-class address like that, why do you need a job?"

"Green," she said frankly. "Margay doesn't take the Robot Dollar."

"*Bozhe moy*—last capitalists on earth refuse the dole; sensorium at eleven."

"They have to," Keishi said. "Most of their hardware's from Africa—Whisper itself runs on a Dahlak. They have to have money they can convert."

The bartender pulled a sky-blue cable out from under the counter, cleaned the plug carefully with peroxide, and handed it to me. When I hesitated he said, "it goes in your wrist, *tavarishcha.*"

"I know a wrist plug when I see one." I looked at Keishi, then sighed and plugged it in. At least it was clean. "You do know that you're completely insane. If you can materialize half of a car, you can easily whip up some virtual coffee. But instead you're paying trainport prices for it."

"It's a matter of etiquette," Keishi said, picking up the cup that had materialized before her. "It would be inconvenient if someone else were to sit in the bar stool where I'm manifesting. So I'm paying for the privilege of occupying space that could hold a real customer."

More information than I'd wanted. "So where are you physically, and where's my research? You said you were going to have it for me by now."

"My flesh is at the archives and so is your research, for now," she said, rubbing her eyes. "When I gave you that estimate, I was planning to get everything through the Net and send it straight into memory, bypassing my conscious mind to save time. But it turns out that most of the material on the Holocaust was never uploaded. Some of it's on paper and the rest is on something called microfilm. So even though I could uptake the information at around ten megabaud, that doesn't do me any good, because my eye muscles can only move about a hundredth that fast. Then I had the bright idea of looking at it through a videophone camera, only to find that the hardware wouldn't go over a refresh rate of sixty frames per second, and I couldn't even turn the pages *that* fast. And this microfilm thing is insane—it takes longer to thread the damned spools than it does to read them. So the bottom line is, working straight through, I can have it for you by noon tomorrow. Um, I mean today, since it's past midnight."

I looked at her with a new respect. "I'll give you one thing. You know how to work."

"Well," she said, "somehow I got the idea that if I worked my ass off for you, you might start taking me seriously."

"What makes you think I don't take you seriously?"

She looked at me as though I'd solemnly informed her that the moon was made of green cheese. Right. Never lie to your screener.

"All right, it's true," I said. "I didn't at first. You look so young that it's hard to. But I'm working on it."

"Age is easily fixed." She morphed older, the skin of her face curdling, silver corrupting her hair; then smiled at my horror, and switched back to an age just a few years older than she'd been before. "Better?"

"Not so you'd notice," I said. "But it doesn't matter."

She added a few more years and glanced at the mirror behind the bar. Then, satisfied, she drank down the last of her coffee, holding the cup in both hands. "I'd better get back to the library," she said. "I've got a deadline to meet. Besides, now that I'm almost your age, I'll have to add an afternoon nap to my schedule."

"Make sure you get someone to burp you afterward," I said, smiling despite myself into my coffee cup. "How much data do you have so far?"

"Nearly everything for the Calinshchina. I've got about three-quarters of what's out there on the Terror-Famine, and maybe half on the Holocaust. Add it all up, and the minimum descriptive algorithm is about a megaturing."

"How many bytes is that?"

"Well," she said, "you really can't express moist memory in bytes, because it's not a string of ones and zeros and there's no single way to convert it into one. See, if I converted it all back to the forms I found it in, it would be one number of bytes, but if I just recorded the connections of each neurode in the network it's stored in, it would be a completely different number. It's like those bone-head British cameras on Science News who give you the *weight* of a space probe. The probe would have one weight on Earth and another on the moon, and besides, those are just potentials—it doesn't actually weigh anything, as long as it's out there between the stars. Space probes have mass, moist memories have minimum descriptive algorithms. Measuring it in bytes wouldn't tell you anything."

I nodded. "So," I said, "how many bytes is that?"

Keishi sighed. "About a trillion."

I laid my hand on her arm. The virtual software let me feel the fabric, but could not make her arm solid, so my hand passed through skin, vein, and bone. "Mirabara—*Keishi*—get some rest," I said. "I've never seen a terabyte of research on one chip in my life. You must be exhausted. You know, I didn't even think about it, but what a horrible assignment. That telepresence, especially. It must have really put you through the wringer."

"Actually," she said, "the books are worse. I can send the telepresence straight to disk, so I don't have to look at most of it. And it looks like the telepresence is all by cameras, not the survivors themselves. Some of the books are by people who were there, and—" She shivered.

"Now, that's funny," I said. "Why shouldn't there be telepresence from survivors? There were thousands, weren't there? You'd think that at least one of them would have put it on disk."

"The Army took over all the camps," Keishi said, "so the survivors were enlisted. And most of them didn't already have sockets, because they were prisoners. The Army had to give them sockets. Now, when you've been drilled by an Army soldier in the middle of a field, with a rock to the head for anesthesia, further implants. . . . "

"Oh. Yes, that makes sense," I said. "Too bad; I thought I was onto something. No moist memory either, I suppose?"

"Of the survivors themselves? Not a single disk."

"Well, it can't be helped. Anyway, what I really need is that megascops-hour of making sense out of it. But get some sleep first and do it in the morning—I mean, the afternoon—when you're fresh. How long will that take you?"

"I can do the 'hour on the train home from the archives, and have the chip waiting for you when you wake up."

I looked at her in disbelief. "You can do—that's what? three hundred and sixty million scop?—on the train home? Keishi, how fast are you?"

"For simple stuff like this, a couple meg. It should take me about half an hour."

A few hundred scop—Standard Consciousness Operations—go into the making of a typical word of interior monologue. An unaugmented human brain does maybe a thousand such ops per second, a kiloscops. Keishi was talking about thinking two thousand times that fast. That's raw processing speed, mind you; the wet-memory interface is much slower. So it's not quite as incredible as it sounds. It's I-saw-an-alien incredible but not I-am-an-alien incredible.

"You were wired in Japan, then?"

"No," she said. "On Zanzibar."

Oh—African tech. In that case, go back to the I-am-an-alien thing. "How'd you manage that?"

"Under the Law of Return. My skin's just dark enough to make me Presumptively African—yes, I know, what a term for it—so that got me in long enough to dive for the nearest knife while they decided to reject my blood sample."

"I'm surprised the Africans don't keep a better lid on their tech."

"Oh, it's illegal all right, but they don't enforce the laws. They love watching us dissect their chips, not understand a thing about them, and build exact replicas that don't work."

I thought for a moment. "You know, I could do that for the last segment, if all else fails. How world politics are still determined by the Army's actions. Try to figure out why they left so much of Leningrad and Tokyo, and didn't get past the Sahara at all."

"Easy question. The Sahara's too hot, Leningrad's too cold, and . . . oh, I don't know, one of the hackers who made the Army probably had a grandmother in Tokyo or something." She smiled at me. "But in the Netcast, you talked like you already knew what you were doing next week. It *was* a little transparent, you know. You weren't trying to lie to your screener, were you?"

"No, just to the audience."

"Oh. Well, that's all right then. I always patch up lies in post-production, anyway. Just be sure to tell me if you ever want them to *know* you're lying." The bartender nodded toward her cup; she shook her head and dematerialized it. "So when I've got the research, what do we do next?"

"Then we look for an interview."

Keishi raised her eyebrows. Oh—she'd tricked me into saying "we." Well, it wouldn't matter. We'd be reassigned soon enough.

"Then I'll call you in the morning. You should sleep in. Shall we say around noon?"

I hesitated, nodded, then turned to the bartender and asked for the bill. He laid a matte black card before me on the bar. When I

pressed my thumb into it, gold script numbers appeared, display-
ing the usual breakdown—this much of your cup of coffee was produced by human labor, and the rest is owing to the labor of robots,
so we suggest you pay so much in green and the rest in red. I always read that stuff; it's interesting; but I don't go by it. It's not always accurate, anyway. For example, they'll tell you that your steak
dinner is ninety percent robot-made, but they get that by count-
ing animals as robots. And my Netcasts count as a hundred percent human, though my head's as much metal as bone.

I touched the right side of the card, to pay all in red. Old
habits—I like to use the robots' earnings first, and hold on to what
I've produced myself. Actually, of course, the Robot Dollar is just
as good as the Reconstructed Ruble, unless you're going to go to
Africa, and what are the chances of that?

"Confirm," I said to the card. *Thank You, Maya Tatyanichna Andreyeva*, it scripted.

The bartender picked up the card and glanced at the back,
where my name and Net address were displayed. "That page earlier—it *was* for you. You're on News One."

This didn't seem to be a question, so I didn't bother answering.

"I've seen your Netcasts," he said. "Not this history thing—
that's a little dry for me—but I saw your piece on that bastard Shimanski. You really told it like it is."

I grunted noncommittally. After an awkward pause he blurted
out: "You don't look much like your Net-portrait."

"It keeps me from being recognized by *duraks* whose fathers
never taught them any manners," I snapped back, out of reflex. But
I could not help looking past him at the mirror behind the bar. I
look in the mirror every morning, of course, but there are certain
things my eyes have ceased to notice. In that mirror, I saw the five
palm-sized holes drilled in my head, capped with black adapters
into which the brightly colored modern chips were plugged. I saw
the Net-rune in my cheek, a scar of garish luminescence slashing

down from eye to jaw in swoops and angles. I saw the places where the hair has never grown back right since surgery, and the bumps and bulges in the left side of my skull where implants nestled in the connective tissue, like baby spiders hidden in the tangle of their egg sac.

"I saved you the trouble of killing him," Keishi said from behind me. "Over the next thirty-six hours his body parts will be arriving in twenty different Historical Nations in the luggage of unsuspecting passengers."

I stole a glance at the bartender. He was alive, but involved in a heated phone debate which he seemed to be getting much the worst of.

"Don't punish him for pointing out the obvious," I said.

She put her chin on my shoulder—not an easy feat for a virtual ghost—and looked my reflection in the eye. I hated the smoothness, youth, perfection of her face next to mine. "How many people know your face, Maya?" she asked me gravely. "A few hundred? Well, a hundred million know you from the inside out. They know who you really are, not just what you look like. What's a face but Nature's blind kludge at a way of letting minds communicate? You have a better interface than that, a faster cable. You've evolved beyond the body. The face is a sheath for the mind. It's nothing—it's *maya*, illusion," she said, smiling. "Forget about it."

I could think of nothing that she could have said that would have been less comforting.

She drew back. "Besides," she said, "a lot of people think scars are sexy." And she drew her finger along my cheek and around to the back of my head, over Net-rune and camerasoft and bare occipital socket. If she had been there in her body, my ruined nerves would have felt nothing. But because she was a virtual ghost, a thing of air and shadows, I could feel her soft, warm fingers just as if the flesh were whole.

# four

## To Make Much of Time

I woke at ten that morning to a
pounding on the door. I answered it holding my bathrobe closed
with one hand, with what hair I have matted or standing on end;
hastily thumbed the offered card; and accepted the package. The
box was a triangular prism a meter long, such as roses are sometimes shipped in. If Keishi had sent me roses, we were going to have
to have a serious talk. I sat down in the little passageway between
inner and outer doors, which in winter keeps the warmth inside the
house from mixing with the cold outside, and opened it.

It was not roses. The box had three separate flaps, one for each
side. I opened the first and found a set of kopek-sized chips, already
plugged into the adapters that they'd need to fit my old style ruble
sockets. Both the chips and the adapters were a medium brown and
no thicker than a fingernail. When I pried one out of the foam and
held it up, it slowly changed color and lustre until it matched the
skin of my hand perfectly, even mimicking the pores. Oh, of course;
a brown default color because they were African. It was probably
the skin color of some drone in quality control—inspected by café
au lait. If I put the chips in, then from a few feet away, maybe even
close up, you'd hardly know I'd been drilled at all.

The second flap revealed another set of adapters and chips, just like the first set, but teal blue instead of brown. I touched one and it displayed a palette; when I chose a color at random, the whole set of chips turned a dusty rose. The chip asked if I wanted to explore textures, but I touched the box marked "no."

Behind the third flap was a blaze of gold: some chips inscribed with hieroglyphs, others painted with jackal-headed gods and lapis scarabs, all in holographic bas-relief. Ooh, Egyptian kitsch. It was African, all right. I read the card:

> *Even though the mother country thought her girlchild was too white, I still have connections there. Nice to use them for something halfway legal just this once. Wear these if you ever decide to quit camera work and take up modeling—you've got the bones, girl.*
>
> *Mirabara.*

With roses I would at least have known for certain. This gift was ambiguous. Certainly it was no ordinary *podarok*. She had spent sweatcoin on this—not robot labor, given in red to every citizen, but her own work in green Reconstructed Rubles. And at that, the gods only knew how she'd gotten them to take it; even red money is about as hard as a three-minute egg, in Africa. Connections, my ass—she had called in a favor for this, I would have bet on it. And getting an African to owe you a favor is slightly less difficult than putting God in your debt.

It might have meant nothing more than overactive thoughtfulness—not an uncommon vice in screeners. Or it could have been a truly world-class effort to curry favor. But there was a chance it was more than that, and no chip in the world, or even in Africa, was worth that kind of trouble.

I looked more closely at the chips, to see what she'd given me. One chip in each set was a memory wedge, and the skin-colored one had a moistdisk stuck into it—a cylinder actually, even less disklike than its Russian cousins. I plugged it in and found it held my research. That, at least, I need not refuse. Most of the others were just copies of what my head already held, some in more up-to-date versions. Then there were a few extra basics, such as four fluency chips with a total of sixty-four languages, most of them African. And there were a few things I didn't recognize at all, chips popular in Africa, I guess: an intuition enhancer, a myth co-processor. No, don't ask me what a myth coprocessor does. Makes you act like a hero, I guess.

I took a deep breath. Face it, Maya. You want these a lot.

I took the box into the bathroom, where sunlight filtered dimly through the paper wadded up between the double windows. Got to take that insulation out, as soon as this series ends, I thought. Maybe take a week off and do all that stuff. Yeah, right. I set the box on end on the counter, where it promptly extended a pedestal and rotated itself. Typical. The girls in Nairobi had more industrial capacity than common sense. I'd be lucky if I could leave the room without it hopping out after me.

I put shrink-seals over my sockets to protect them—my sockets are guaranteed waterproof, of course, but a guarantee can't restore a scorched forebrain—and showered, hastily because I was getting close to my Strongly Suggested Sustainable Water Usage for the month.

When I had dried my hair and gotten dressed, I opened the box and started to slot in the chameleons. They matched my skin color even better than before, but once I had a couple of them in, my head started to take on a sort of chemotherapy look: patches of sparse hair interrupted by tracts of bare skin. I tried brushing a lock of hair over one of the chips, and they got the idea and mimicked it, but their hologram engines could only produce so much depth. The look would make more sense if I shaved my hair off, which would be fashionable enough, but I wasn't ready for that yet. So I switched to the colored set, slotted them in, and chose a dark blue from the palette the chips superimposed on my field of vision. Then another problem stopped me. There was one chip I could not take out without risking a number of complications, starting with moderate to severe brain damage and getting worse from there. I'd have to leave it in, but I didn't want Keishi to know I was wearing it. I needed to cover it up somehow.

I went to the bedroom and dug a strip of gray and yellow fabric out of my chest of drawers. It was supposed to be the scarf for my Truth Awards suit, but since I'd worn the same outfit to the last five years' ceremonies, I was probably due for a new one anyway. Or I could just not go, though it was always kind of fun to sit around with all the other Swiss-cheese types and hate the smooth-heads who were walking away with everything. I took the scarf back into the bathroom, folded it down, and tied it around my head so that the frontal socket was covered. Then I menued the chips' color to a gray that matched the fabric. I stepped back and checked the effect in the mirror.

The transformation was amazing. Ten minutes ago, I'd looked like a typically encrusted old-time Netcaster. Now I looked like a dangerous lunatic with no fashion sense. Stop me before I accessorize again.

*All right, News One*, I thought, taking off the scarf, *you may not be a megascops, but you're a reasonably intelligent person. You can figure out what to do about that damned suppressor.*

Apparently I'd thought the magic words. My face faded from the mirror, to be replaced by a map of Africa on which the god Osiris was stretched out, as on a crucifix. I recognized the Diaspora motion logo—the one the Africans had on their banners when they took Egypt from the Guardians. This was the full-length version, beginning all the way back with the slave trade. I tried saying "escape" and "cancel," but it wouldn't, so I leaned back against the towel rack to wait it out. The continent was stabbed by ships, and hemorrhaged men; the fertile soil dried up and cracked into countries. At the same time Osiris was torn into parts, which were scattered.

Then the flow reversed: men came back to Africa in planes and ships, the borders healed, and Osiris began to gather himself together. His-Majesty-in-Chains appeared in person to sew Egypt back on—with thread, not missiles as you might expect—whereupon Osiris was at last restored. Behind His Majesty, the two other Known Kings of Africa were briefly visible: a shining tower to represent Its-Ethereal-Highness, and for Only-A-Man, a face that changed from male to female, adult to child. At last Osiris opened his eyes; the deserts exploded with green trees and waving wheat; and the Wall of Souls was raised around the continent, like armor. It's a hell of a mogo. Myself, I wouldn't have gone to war for it, but that's me.

The map of Africa didn't disappear, only faded, until it was as subtle as a watermark on paper. I was expecting something else to show up in the mirror, so I watched and waited. Then suddenly someone was standing beside me: an Egyptian god—Horus, the one with the hawk's head—pressing so close that his beak was only inches from my eye. I was startled, then entranced. He was breathtaking. In the little painted portrait on the chip, he'd looked smooth and cartoonish. But the virtual image overwhelmed me with its bloody realism: feathers accurate in every fibre, some split and notched as if by battle; beak the color of bone, sharp as glass; a yellow raptor's eye without a trace of mercy, in whose lids the throbbing veins were clearly visible. So *this* is why people become pagans, I thought; this cold, this inhuman regard. The same reason we listen for messages from the stars.

The alien god fixed me with a yellow stare and said—in an absurdly inappropriate Moscow accent—"All Series 6000 moistware is equipped with automatic neural dampeners for the changeout or removal of suppressor chips without the use of chemical anesthetics. Since you have already inserted at least one Series 6000 moistware package, you may safely remove your suppressor chip from its socket. If you do not replace it with the corresponding Series 6000 moistware within thirty seconds, a timed phaseout of the dampening function will automatically initiate. Series 6000 moistware is guaranteed to prevent any and all neural damage from suppressor chips, including those that have been implanted as a punitive measure by the agents of fraudulent and tyrannical First World warlords, and this guarantee is backed by the full force of the treasury and army of His-Majesty-In-Chains. We conclude this communication in the confidence that Series 6000 moistware will provide full satisfaction and exceed all reasonable expectations."

And he vanished. For a moment of stunned silence I could only think that if I had known an Egyptian god was going to manifest himself in my bathroom I would at least have scrubbed out the toilet bowl. Then I was clawing the 6000s out of my head and saying aloud, "All right, Maya, don't panic, it's just a standard message, they all come with it, it doesn't mean anything—" but I was not convinced. And I took the chip that looked like an encyclopedia, stuck it in my occipital socket, and asked the Net what it was.

The Net's answer was immediate. Keishi had indeed perfectly duplicated what was in my head. And one of the chips in my head had the cover of a DejaVu Instant Encyclopedia chip, holding something it was never meant to hold. In exchange for that thorn in my pride, Keishi had given me a chip that bore the DejaVu logo in faint white outline, but contained the very moistware that had sat disguised in my frontal lobe so long that the pins must have rusted solid to the socket. It was a chip of the model which Post-Soft Limited had named, apparently without a trace of intentional humor, the Nun 500. It was a device that blocked all memories from ten years of my life, and eradicated even the most minute sexual impulse. And the Nun 500 did not come with any set, nor could she have bought it off the shelf—not in this package. She must have had it custom made, or possibly configured it herself, bending over it for fevered hours in some tiny rented workspace, with scales of sweat sloughing off her brow, her eyes rolled back into her head, and both her wrists and both her temples tied by cables to a robot arm with vision more acute and touch more delicate than any flesh.

She knew.

# five

## AS A WIFE HAS A COW

**I** have played this scene over and over, with the moistdisk slotted into the back of my head, until the pain has almost—not quite—worn away.

I waited for her in the living room, pacing, too restless to sit down. When she manifested, I saw the videophone swivel toward me. She was looking through its camera so she could see me as I was, not just a default image generated by her moistware. When the camera focused on my face, she looked at me with surprise that quickly turned to disappointment. "Is something wrong? You're not wearing your research."

"I transferred it to this." I tapped a memory-wedge at my temple, not holding the single African moistdisk, but a battery of Russian ones that I'd dug out of various drawers—looking like a roll of toroidal candies in assorted flavors. Six held her research; the seventh was quietly recording our conversation, in case I needed evidence of what had happened.

"Oh," she said. "If there's something wrong with the 6000s, you know, they're on warranty—"

"I know," I said shakily. "A little bird told me."

"I see." She looked puzzled, but did not pursue the line of questioning. "So, are you ready to find that interview?"

"Keishi, I think I may have misled you, and if I have, I'm sorry. I've been working alone much too long to change now. I know you put a lot of work into that research, and I appreciate it, but that's all I really need. I'll take it from here."

"Nice speech," she said flatly. "How long did it take to write?"

"Keishi, I'm serious—"

"You think I'm not?" She turned away suddenly, walked over to the videophone table, and leaned against it. "So when should I plan on screening your first interview, or do you just want me to stay on call?"

One more hurdle, and it would be over. I said with an effort: "I'm going to record to a disk for now and have it screened later. And . . . I'm going to file for repartnering, Keishi. It's nothing personal. Or rather, I mean, it is personal and not professional. I'll give you the highest rating. But I don't think it's going to work out. Between us."

Her eyes and the vidphone's eyes watched me together, like two cats. Unnerved by her silence, I blurted out: "I mean, after all, Anton will be back soon, it's really not fair—"

"Anton has been Net-silent for two days," Keishi said. "He probably rejected his bugs in some back alley, and they'll have to bring his brain home in a sausage casing. Don't *try* to tell me this is about him."

Her eyes stared into mine, unflinchingly, but the vidphone glanced at the rosebox on the table. "This is about that encyclopedia of yours, isn't it? That's why you're not wearing the moistware I gave you."

I felt myself silhouetted by the accusation, like a deer by headlights.

"You really thought I didn't know," she marveled. "Maya—I wish I didn't have to be the one to tell you, but I don't see any other way. Every screener you've had must have known. Screening out sex is the main thing we do, after politics. People use suppressors, but even so, you get memories, traces. When somebody comes through completely blank . . . well, it's not hard to guess why."

"How much do you know?" I asked, trembling as though she'd touched me.

"I know you're wearing a suppressor chip that you haven't had out for a very long time. And that making it look like an encyclopedia is a typical Postcop trick. And that when I look into your memories, there's a hole you could drive a ten-year marriage through. All of which means that you've had some good tea in your time, though you don't remember it very well."

"What are you going to do?"

She looked at me in exasperation. "I'm going to tell the whole Net, make a huge scandal, ruin your career, and get you disappeared, what do you think? Maya, I'm not going to 'do' anything. I would never have brought it up if you hadn't forced me to."

"Thank you." I sat down, relief stinging my eyes. "I should have known. I guess I'm a little paranoid—oh, all right, I'm a lot paranoid. A felon on News One has to be. If one hint of my past made it out on the Net, I'd disappear, you know, *kak korova yazikom menya slizala.*"

"Like a what?"

I smiled, grateful for the change of subject. "As though a cow had licked me with its tongue. Meaning completely. The way you do when you run afoul of the Weavers."

"I've never heard that expression in my life," she said. "It never fails; just when I think I'm finally assimilated. Hang on, let me get that down." She took out her totem, a faux-granite obelisk, to put her fluency chip into learn mode. Then she set the totem down on nothing; there must have been a table there where she was, but to my eyes, it simply hovered in the air.

"That might not be a good idea," I said. "If it's not on the fluency chip, it's probably because someone doesn't want it there. The Postcops might throw you a tea party just for having it in RAM."

She raised an eyebrow. "Agent 99, I live for danger."

I sputtered—relief was still making me giddy—but recovered in time to produce a creditable "Oh, Max."

"Really, Maya, I don't care what you do," she said with (so it seems to me now, playing it back from the disk in slow motion) a studied indifference. "Speaking strictly under the Cone of Silence, why don't you just take the damned thing out and put in a real encyclopedia? You can count on the 6000s to prevent any brain damage—His-Majesty-In-Chains does not make idle guarantees. And I can fix your Netcasts to look like it's still in place. You can have your memories back. And . . . and the rest of it." She shrugged. Her body was pretending to examine the tabletop, but the vidphone's eye was pointing right at me. "It's something to think about. We don't have to talk about it now."

I looked at her in horror. "You're a cuckoo."

"What?"

"You're a Postcop. Or"—and a blade of ice slid into my heart— "are you a Weaver?"

"What makes you think that, Maya?" she said in a tone that was not at all what I'd expected. "How could I be a Weaver?"

"Anton Tamarich is drinking tea, and you're his cuckoo," I said. "No *wonder* I've never seen you except in virtual. You're sitting in some control tower, running, what is it, my sixth loyalty check, or are we up to seven now? Don't you people ever give up?"

"Oh," she said, looking down. "I see. That's what you think. Maya, it isn't true."

"Come on. I know the drill by now. You just gave me a textbook incitement to violate parole—nice and hypothetical, nothing that would look too pushy on the disk. Perfect, in fact. You're a lot better than that idiot they sent last time, I'll give you that."

"Whatever I may be, I'm not a Postcop," she said.

"Really? Let's see—" I sent out a query to the Net "—your résumé says you graduated from Leningrad University. Lapshina is still dean of the department there, isn't she? I've known her since before you were born, if you're the age you look. If I were to call her up . . . "

"By all means."

I moved toward the videophone. She was still standing in front of it. When she wouldn't move aside, I reached through her for the touchplate.

"Oh, God." She sat down without bothering to materialize a chair; it was an eerie effect. "I was hoping you were bluffing." Of course I had been, but I wasn't going to tell her that. "No, she won't remember me and yes, my résumé is a fake. But it's not what you're thinking. Maya, the degree takes four years at a minimum, and there's no way to expedite. Do you have any idea how absurd that is for a multimegascops?" She had talked herself out of fear and into anger. "The Net makes universities obsolete. Anyone with a bandwidth over room temperature can learn how to screen from the Net in a few hours. All those years of university training—they're not trying to give you knowledge, they're trying to control it. They're weeding out the ideologically impure."

"Incitement to agree with slanders against the government. That's very inventive. You must be up against a bitch of a quota." I picked up the box of moistware and threw it at her image. It sailed through her and clattered against the wall, spilling out flesh-tone and gold. "Take your rosebox and go home, cop."

"What are you going to do?" she said.

"I'm going to apply for immediate repartnering. If they'll take it without a reason, fine. If not, I'll put down unprofessional conduct, which would be true even if you were just an overeager megascops."

"You don't even trust me enough to give me one chance to prove that I am who I say I am?"

"I quit believing in trust twenty years ago, over one hell of a cup of tea."

On the disk her face clouds for an instant. Watching it now, freezing the moment, zooming in, I wonder if her enhancements sped up emotion, as well as thought. Was this the brief catch in the throat it seemed to be, or was she crying in there for hours, in her silicon cage? Or—I cannot help but think it—was that sob a cover, under which she plotted the next phase of her deception?

When I unpause the disk, she says quietly: "You'd have to have absolute proof."

"Yes."

"Then I'll give you your trust through a cable," she said with sudden vehemence, "since that's the only kind you understand."

"You must be joking. I'm not going to give you a direct line to my brain."

She lifted her eyebrows incredulously. "You really think you can keep me out, if I want in?"

If I had been able to stop the disk then, as I can now, I might have seen this as the product of rejection and despair. But at the time, I could think only one thing. Keishi Mirabara scared the hell out of me.

I reached for my Net chip, but too late. She had grasped her totem in her fist and thrust it into my head, a symbol of the invisible connection she was making through the Net. (Now, replaying it in slow motion, I can feel a tingling as the granite spire passes the skull, but only silence as it moves through layer after layer of unfeeling brain.) Then all at once her mind was *there*, out at the end of the virtual cable, and it was impossible not to stretch out to it, impossible not to touch those memories, so much clearer than my own. And gradually, gently, passively, her mind gave up its secrets.

"Am I a cop, Maya Tatyanichna?" she said at last.

"No. I guess you're not."

She drew the totem out. "You believed it, though, didn't you? You didn't have a trace of doubt. You really don't trust me."

"Keishi, why the devil should I trust you?" I nourished the anger I felt, knowing that nothing else could make me say what I had to say. "I've known you for two days—no, not so much, not two. The ink isn't even dry on our partnering assignment. I don't know you and you don't know me. You think we have a connection because of all the things you've sucked out of my mind by screening, but that isn't real. Trust comes when you've worked with someone for years; it doesn't speed up just because you can think fast, and it doesn't materialize when you stick a cable in someone's head. What you get from screening me isn't friendship, it's data. We're strangers."

She looked down to hide the moistness in her eyes. "Yes," she said, "I guess we are."

And she vanished—leaving me feeling like I'd just told a child that her mother was dead, not because it was true, but just for fun. But I had to be ruthless, yes, ruthless. For with the Net linking our minds, she had not been able to hide it. Keishi Mirabara was in love.

# six

## THE WORD

That night I went over the research, with Keishi's thoughts haunting my mind.

"Most images of the Holocaust come from photos taken during the Allied liberation of the camps," she said once, "but the Square Miles were liberated by the Unanimous Army, which did not take pictures, and whose component selves did not remember the experience." And again: "The Nazis had only a few years to carry out their pogrom. The Guardians had nearly fifty, and they had the whole world to do it in. In fifty years you can raise new generations that have never known anything but tyranny. You can destroy not just a people, but all memory of a people." By nine o'clock the next morning—late evening by my body clock—my mind began to wander, her voice intruding on my free associations in a surreal counterpoint. Soon my thoughts turned to what I'd felt from Keishi through the cable, and the moistdisk announced: "The homosexual prisoners of the Nazi concentration camps were not released when the camps were liberated. Not only were they returned to prison, but their time in the camps was not counted toward their sentences. Compare Calinshchina."

"Christ," I said.

"Yeah, that one's a bitch, isn't it?"

I'd grown so used to hearing her voice in my head that I forgot to be startled. She was walking toward me through the slanting sunlight in the hall; a black fedora cast a diagonal shadow across her face. She wore a mask of eggshell-thin ceramic, after the African fashion, matte white. When she smiled, the mask copied her expression, but its features were not hers. Her image was so vivid that I thought it must be real, until I noticed that the milling dustmotes were indifferent to her presence. Had she been flesh, they would have swirled about her as she walked, as if recoiling from her touch.

She came to the doorway and stopped, leaning against the wall and watching me to see what I would do. She was wearing a Word: a gold cartouche on her lapel that, from time to time, would pluck a single word from her thoughts and display it. That's the fashion, too—a random, drop-by-drop exposure that always struck me as faintly obscene. At the moment it said *inversion*, for no reason I could think of.

"You've got to quit barging in on me like this, Mirabara."

"I seem to have this problem knocking," she said, passing her hand through the wall. "But I'll ring the videophone next time."

"That would be nice. Just in case I'm in the shower or something," I said, and *inversion* faded into *soap*. "So is this just general neighborliness, or is there a special reason for this visit?"

*Foodchain* flashed on the Word as she said "Depends. You want to do an interview?"

"Who?"

"Pavel Sergeyevich Voskresenye."

The moistdisk instantly supplied an image. I was reading a tattered old book at impossible speeds. I closed it with a snap. The spine said: *Victims of the Square Miles*, by P. S. Voskresenye. It was one of the first books published during the early Reconstruction, and a cornerstone of Keishi's research.

"Voskresenye is alive?"

"He's got a pulse and a Netname. Beyond that, I wouldn't expect much. At his age he ought to be half fossilized."

"What's his real name?"

"That's what's on the records: Voskresenye."

"Not Voskresen*ski?*"

"Nope, that's what it says. 'Mister Sunday.' And it gets better. He's operating as Pavel of hearth <null>, clan Darkness-at-Noon."

"What the hell kind of a clan name is that?"

"A fake one," she said, and waited.

"More than that," I said. "There's plain fake, and then there's *obviously* fake. If he just didn't want to be found, he'd have plain fake. But Darkness-at-Noon is obviously fake. He wants everyone to know that he doesn't want to be found. It's a challenge."

Keishi smiled, a teacher pleased with her slow but faithful student. I turned to the videophone and repeated the Netname. White letters appeared on the screen: "Connected. Video unavailable."

"Pavel Voskresenye," I said to the blank screen, "this is Maya Andreyeva, a Camera at News One hearth. I'd like to set up—"

"Meet me in grayspace," said a voice from the videophone, followed by the flashing message: CONNECTION BROKEN.

"Why would an old man out of the Square Miles want to meet in grayspace?" I said warily.

"Maybe he figures it's your home turf. Maybe he remembers."

And that was possible. Back in 2297 I covered the Binary Biodiversity Act, the law that put life into grayspace. It was an African idea: since most computers are partly idle most of the time, why not use the extra processing capacity to evolve new algorithms? The Fusion was mistrustful, naturally, but the idea was too good to pass up out of spite. So the unused space—the grayspace—on thousands of computers was stitched together into two kingdoms: moist grayspace, dry grayspace. The dry side was seeded with random code, and the moist with random neurodes.

For the first couple of years everybody was happy, and I got to say all sorts of pretty phrases about a new age of cooperation between the FHN and Africa. After all, they'd given us such a good deal: we could have anything in grayspace that we recognized as useful, and they'd have their pick of the rest. I don't need to tell you who got the better end of that bargain. And so, instead of getting more stories on African politics, as I'd hoped, I wound up going back to grayspace every couple of months to check up on the aborigines and grouse about African trickery.

I still wonder: what did the Africans want? Were they as naïve as we were, hoping for a faster sorting algorithm and better robot vision? Or did they *want* to fill up grayspace with feral intelligences, and if so, to what end?

"I hope I haven't thrown out my myrmichor," I said. But I knew just where it was, nestled in foam in a plastic box on the top shelf of the bedroom closet. The myrmichor plugs into the occipital socket, the parietal, and both temporals, so I had to take out all my other moistware, except, of course, the encyclopedia. After some fumbling I got it strapped on: a baroque headdress covering the whole back of my skull, looking like a set of external vertebrae.

"Why don't you plug your camera chip into your wrist," she said, "so it'll be there if you need it?"

"What good would that do? It won't work in my wrist."

"I can get to it through your wrist socket and patch it back into your temporal lobe. Just in case he says something you want to catch." As she spoke, her Word panned from *slithering* to *hope*.

"This is strictly background, Keishi. I'm not going to use it directly. No one cares what Pavel Voskresenye looks like in grayspace. What is it with you and that camera chip, anyway?"

The mask grinned. "Okay, you caught me. I was going to modernize your colors. But subtly, subtly. You would have liked the results."

"Just leave my colors alone."

"Whatever you say, chief." *Bolus* appeared on her Word in elaborate script letters. "Are you ready?"

"Keishi, you are *not* going with me."

"Oh, come on," she said. "It's an old dream of mine. When I was in school I glued the cover from a textbook onto my Net chip so I could watch you in history class. When the Mars landing was up against reruns of your show, I watched your show. I've dreamed about going into grayspace with you since I was twelve years old."

"I was on the Net when you were twelve? Excuse me while I crawl off into a corner and decompose."

"Oh, quit being so sensitive," she said. "Just let me tag along. It really means a lot to me—it's like getting a chance to ride with the Lone Ranger."

The Lone Ranger, no less. The things a classical education does to people's minds. I wasn't going to have the energy to fight this out, I realized. "All right," I said, "Just don't get in the way."

"Perish the thought." *Cross*, said the Word.

I didn't trust her for a second, but I said: "All right, you've been here more recently than I have; should I put on my shields?"

"Depends. What kind of shielding have you got?"

"I don't know. Whatever they gave me, fifteen years ago."

"Oh, good God. Petrov shielding? The kind without camouflage?"

"I said, I don't know what it's called."

"Looks like you're encased in a gigantic Christmas tree?"

"That's the one."

"Leave it off, then. It'll attract predators for miles around. I guess you left before the aborigines discovered stealth technology."

"Stealth? What kind of stealth?"

"Well, to begin with, you should turn the sensitivity and contrast on your myrmichor all the way up, if you want to see anything."

"Terrific." I hadn't even met Voskresenye, and I was already starting to dislike him.

*Take me in*, I thought to the myrmichor, and it began to feed images into my optic nerve. It wasn't loading me into grayspace yet, only sticking a periscope into it, so I could find a nice safe corner where I could upload in peace.

But everything I saw looked quiet and safe, even when I turned up the controls as far as they would go. I was using the classic interface: the size of a neurode shows how many connections it's got; colors indicate how many times it's fired since you've been watching; you blink to reset. But no matter how long I held my eyes open, and no matter how much I played with the depth of field, nothing would strobe down the spectrum to red. There were long branching synapse-chains, like veins or vines, that would slowly turn golden; drifting baleens in violet and indigo against the black; but nothing that looked capable of locomotion.

"All right, then," I said. "Let's do it right here." The myrmichor touched my brain, and began to upload me.

I read somewhere that *myrmichor* means "being carried away by ants." I don't know if that's even true, but when I hear the word I always think of a video I saw once, of an ant cutting a circle of leaf and carrying it off in her mouth; and then the camera zooms back, and you see there are a million ants, and the tree is almost bare.

It's actually a little bit more organized than that. First the bugs divide your mind into parcels that are almost independent—I always picture paper growing up between the wrinkles of the brain, like the membrane between cloves of garlic. The ants descend on each clove in turn, carry it off to grayspace, and reconnect it. As this happens, you briefly lose certain capacities; sight, mostly—I was blind for a long time, and when the sight came back I was agnosic, and then paralyzed.

At least there was no aphasia, and no obvious loss of memory;

the myrmichor only had to upload a part of my mind. In Africa, where the Net will hold souls, people upload nearly all of their brains into grayspace, neuron by neuron. In the real world, if you do that you lose your sensory qualia: colors are reduced to wavelengths, emotions become mere data, and in short, you get de-souled. So we leave most of the brain in the skull, and only move the parts that need to run at Net speeds. I don't know the details of what uploads and what doesn't, but you can tell that some of your memories stay in the skull. If you try to remember how your breakfast looked, you can do it easily; but if you try to remember how it tasted, it seems to take hours, as if your mind had to send off to Moscow for the information. And all the while your eyes are darting around, hyper-alert to the least movement. As in a dream, where your pulse is racing but your legs won't move at all.

Even having a little bit of your brain in the Net is an unpleasant sensation, though. You feel half dead, half petrified, as if you'd been given artificial legs. It feels—tinny, false. It's impossible to describe. If you've got nanobugs in your head, try it and you'll know. If you've only got an implant, then for God's sake don't upgrade for grayspace; it's overrated.

The myrmichor chimed to signal that the upload was complete. I moved my muscles experimentally, trying to get used to my new body. The body feels different in grayspace; something to do with the organization of the sensory and motor cortices. I didn't really read that part of the manual, though I remember the illustration: a little homunculus arched over a cross-section of the brain, with its face upside-down above the rest of its body and its tongue above that—which is about what it feels like. The Africans draw this as the sky-goddess Nut stretched out over the world, which is not how it feels, at least not in Russia.

When I'd finished uploading, I looked around me. Where was Keishi? She should have loaded faster than I did; her myrmichor was newer. But all I could see was rain—little yellow sparks of life, falling randomly into the dark, that could animate what they touched. Most were being eaten up by driftweeds, the grayspace equivalent of plants.

All right, then, I thought; if she didn't want to come, that was fine with me. I didn't have time for games.

I called up a hardware map and, sure enough, there was Darkness-at-Noon—visible, I suspected, only to me. I began to swim in its direction.

Then my vision went red. I blinked it back, but it was red again the moment my eyes opened. I turned, but it was all around me. I tried to break through, but I was trapped. Some driftnet spider, combing the waves, had entangled me. Reaching back into my body, I groped for the manual abort button.

"Cancel that!" Keishi said. "Relax, News One. It's only me."

My mistake had been looking for something my own size. She was all around me, spread out in a thin layer of cortex from which towers of enhancement rose. I had, of course, known before how fast and dense her mind was, but only now did I truly feel it. Beside her acres and arches and spires of mind, mine was a mere clot of neurodes. As I searched for her, I had been moving through her, like a tumbleweed through an abandoned city.

Then the city came to life, collapsed its towers, and gathered into folds around me.

"Keishi, what are you doing?"

"Umm, I'm sort of engulfing you," she answered distractedly.

I felt her mind seep into me, taking up my unused spaces, and then seal itself around me like a shell.

"Keishi, this isn't funny."

"I'm trying to protect you. Stealth technology, remember? You're shining like a lighthouse; half of grayspace can see you."

"There's nothing there to see me."

"Contrast, News One, contrast. Just because you can't see it doesn't mean it isn't there."

When I protested again, she said impatiently: "Here, look!" and folded a layer of herself over my eyes. All at once the space around us, which had been a field of undistinguished neurodes, took on odor, taste, and texture. I felt tremblings, tramplings, stirrings round me. It was like the bottom of the ocean, where strange cave-jawed fish, impossible in light, are nourished, and pearl and weed have been developing for years, unseen of man. I saw a shark sniff Keishi's tendrils, turn bronze in fear, and scull away; and in the distance some lopsided creature spasmed, drowning, tangled in a knot of fishing line.

"You could have shown me this before you did it," I said, but so halfheartedly she didn't bother to reply. Instead she moved forward, instantly attaining an impossible velocity. I was frightened at first, but then began to lose myself to the experience. I swept past sharks and spiders, and rocketed through tangler webs, invulnerable because I was armored in her; so that I began to dread the thought that we would soon reach Voskresenye, and she would have to stop.

We passed a border between computers. I couldn't see it, but I felt it slow us down, like breaking through a sheet of paper. "This is Whisper," she said. "My hearth." It looked just like the rest of grayspace; yet, somehow, the confidence was comforting. "We'll just be going through one corner of it, though—yes, here."

Ahead of us, sharks were moving in slow motion.

"Oh, devil take it! I thought Swazi would be the fastest way—it's a Dahlak—but it's overloaded. Some idiot must be compiling an AI. Well, it's still quicker than backtracking."

We passed through into the slower hearth. Our thoughts didn't slow down; the speed of neural nets isn't affected by load in other parts of the system. But our motion ground to a crawl.

There was no sense trying to look ahead of us—everything there would be as slow as we were—so I looked behind us, where things would be faster. But Whisper was as black as night. "Did you take away that new interface?" I said.

"No, it's still there."

"Then why am I blind?"

"The regulators are way backlogged on 'see' commands," she said.

"That never used to happen. Motion would get slow, but you could always see."

"That was back when most abos were still blind, so demand for sight was low. Now almost everything has vision, and the rules committee won't increase the regulator standards. Just thank God you weren't here ten years ago, when the abos were collecting eyes like kids collect marbles. One argus could bring a whole hearth to its knees. God, I'm glad they're extinct. —Burst your eyes, Swazi, if you can't keep your grayspace running right, then give it the hell away. Fucking public hearth admins. . . . " She crawled and fumed, mostly in Sapir.

The sharks back in Whisper were starting to fade into view, their movements fast and jerky, like bad time-lapse. One or two dipped into Swazi, tempted by slow-moving prey, but most kept their distance. The abos know you can't compare speeds across the boundary between computers. Gradually, they were dispersing.

Then as the sharks became brighter, I saw that some of them were not just pacing at the border. Some had their mouths stuck into Swazi, and were spinning out great woven sheets of neurodes, larger than a tangler's web.

"What are they doing?" I asked.

"That's right," Keishi said, "you don't know about webfish either. They're a convertible shark that takes advantage of slow-downs. They stay at the border, where the vision is still fast, and send out sticky strands one neurode wide. Since the strands are so small, they move faster than everything else. And when the slow-down's over, they reel in their catches. It's sort of a brainless strategy, but it works. That's why arguses had so many eyes, too— they'd deliberately backlog the regulators until everyone was equally blind, and then they'd fish by touch."

"What happened to them?"

"The hearth admins screamed about the overloads, so the rules committee decided to limit the number of vision calls per abo. The arguses lost all their eyes, but they developed a symbiosis with these huge clouds of aphids that each had one eye, and those were even better at slowing a system down than the argus had been. Finally some bright hacker cooked up a program called Millipede, that would run around faster and faster the less it could see, so that no matter what happened, motion was always backlogged worse than vision. That made the argus strategy obsolete. Made huge traffic jams, too, until the ecosystems all reorganized to cope with it. —Thank God, here, this is Veles."

We broke through another membrane, and Keishi began to pick up speed.

"Just in time, too," she said. "Swazi is about to freeze up. We'd have had to unplug and start over."

As we moved away I saw Swazi behind us begin to turn silver. Swazi had been unable to maintain its part of grayspace, and, finding no one to take it over, was storing it all on a moistdisk, frozen in time.

A boom of sound disturbed my sightseeing. I looked forward. Some long, lithe creature, like an eel, was swimming for its life, with an immense shark behind it. It jumped over us, booming; the shark followed, close enough to touch. At the last instant, the eel ducked into Swazi and was silvered. The shark tried to follow it in, but bounced off. Pacing in Veles, it fretted and fumed, like a cartoon lawman stopped by a painted border.

"Oh, clever thing!" Keishi said. "Beautifully timed!"

"What good does that do it?" I asked. "Eventually that part of grayspace will be reactivated. If Swazi can't find time to run it, someone else will."

"Yes, but the eel will still have its momentum and the shark won't," Keishi said. "Besides, by then the shark may have lost interest." Then she was silent for a long time. I was about to ask another question when she said thoughtfully: "Although, I don't know, some sharks are damned persistent." She slowed a little, as if she might go back to chase the shark away. But she shook the impulse off, and we swam on through Veles.

"This is nice," I said. "The water—I mean, grayspace is clear here. No weeds, no debris."

"Veles is reliable. They've held on to this section of grayspace for weeks without a serious slowdown. So the gazehounds and sharks keep things pretty clean. Yes, it's nice. Nice if you're armored."

A school of spheres came toward us from above, enveloped us, and matched our pace. Then they turned silvery, reflecting us. It was like seeing your image in a thousand hand-mirrors.

"What are those?" I said.

"Doppelgangers. They won't hurt you, they'll just imitate you."

"Like mirror-fish?"

"Not really. Mirror-fish just imitated for camouflage. Dopplers do it to learn better algorithms, to take back to their queen. They won't get much from us, though—we're optimized for a different universe."

"I thought that kind of imitation was what shielding was meant to prevent. Algorithmic quarantine, and all that. You know, 'Imagine the destruction of native culture that would ensue if you dropped a radio on some unsuspecting tribe of Bushmen—' "

"Oh, that's an excuse. Bushmen, my ass. They only said that to piss off the Africans. If you dropped a radio on a traditional village, they'd bloody well use it to grind flour—they'd see it in a way appropriate to their world. No abo's going to duplicate a human; we're sloppy and inefficient, by their standards. The Weavers made all that up to keep people out of grayspace, because they were afraid grayspace would be impossible to control. But it didn't work out that way. As you can see, right up ahead."

The dopplers had gone; I saw nothing. "Where?"

"Dead ahead. Do you see her?"

"Who?"

"Look carefully—there." She made an arrow in my visual field to point it out to me: a barely visible disturbance in the neurodes, moving slowly, like the shadow of a hawk against the ground.

"What is it?" I said.

"Weaver."

"Why are we staying here? Why aren't we running?"

"Stay calm, News One. It's just a tendril. She can't see us at this distance."

"Why risk it?" I said. "Let's just go."

"Sit tight a minute," she said, creeping toward it. "I want to see the rest of her."

"Keishi!"

"Hold on." And we were moving again, twice as fast as before. Beneath us was a vein of shadow that gradually widened and silvered, a creek becoming a river. Then suddenly it was a delta, and an ocean, and we were rocketing up away from it, until we could see all its twining tendrils and its spinning core. It looked like something you might see on the slide of a microscope; and then again it looked like a galaxy, something impossibly vast. I felt a rush of vertigo—a fear that I had lost myself, that I would never return to my body. I had to carefully concentrate out of the Net, and focus on the slow inflation of my lungs, to prove to myself I was still real.

"Let's see which one she is," Keishi said, and blew out a stream of bubbles.

"Are you insane?"

"Relax. The stimuli are so low-level she'll hardly even notice them. And she couldn't trace them to me if she did. I just want to see which one she goes for."

The bubbles circled the shifting and spiraling Weaver. At length one of her tendrils flicked idly, like a hand absently grasping a teacup, and a bubble disappeared.

"Aha," Keishi said respectfully. "This one sweeps for a brain virus called Parafango. Minor, but not as minor as I thought. —But then, this wouldn't be the original. This virus killed three or four Weavers, before they finally made the nastiest strains extinct."

"Who wrote it?"

"No one, it's indigenous. It's a timid little herbivore that learned to protect itself in grayspace by hiding in a human brain. Perfectly harmless, as long as you're here. But if it gets downloaded into your flesh brain—well, they wiped out the one that trashes the arcuate fasciculus, thank God. So much for your Bushman's radio; do you really think the Weavers could fight abos like that and still worry that *we'd* invade *them?*"

Her derision made me nervous, but the Weaver was still grazing unperturbed.

"Have you ever seen one before?" she asked.

"A Weaver? No," I said. And then: "Not that I remember."

"I'm glad you got the chance, then. Isn't she beautiful?"

"Beautiful?" I said scornfully. "Necessary, maybe. I don't want another Army any more than anyone else. But Weavers, beautiful? They scare the hell out of me."

"Beautiful *and* terrible," she said. "Like a snake, or a tiger."

"Squids and spiders come to mind."

"Oh, don't be so literal. Doesn't she remind you of—damn!" she cried out suddenly. And we were speeding through the Net again, in full flight.

"What happened?"

"She almost saw us," Keishi said, slowing down. "It's okay, she's not pursuing. She was just curious."

"That's what you get for taking risks like that."

She ignored the warning. "This," she said, "is Darkness-at-Noon."

I first saw Voskresenye as a tiny knot of neurodes, about the size of mine but more irregularly shaped, like an apple with some bites out of it. Grouper fish of some kind, not dopplers, were schooling around him. As Keishi circled him at a distance, I saw that the lump of neurodes was thickly cabled to a vast dark bulk that loomed above us, dwarfing even Keishi. It was like a storm-cloud that takes up the whole sky. The eye shrank from it. How the hell did a man that old get wired like that?

"How interesting." The voice came from the little knob of cells I had first seen. "A delegation. Does one address Leviathan, or the seed in his stomach?"

Before I could answer, Keishi said "I was going to ask if you were the blimp, or the ugly dwarf in its gondola."

"Keishi!" I cried out, shocked. But Voskresenye was not offended:

"I expected someone unenhanced, so I extruded something her own size for her to talk to. I hardly expected that she would come riding an elephant."

Keishi swam a little closer toward him, and spoke a stream of static.

*What was that?* I subvocalized.

"Sapir."

*I know it's Sapir*, I said irritably. There are only two computer languages that have native human speakers, and KRIOL sounds different. I know Sapir when I hear it; I just never got past the seg-mentive case. *What did you say?*

"If you put in your new language chip—"

*The audience doesn't want to deal with Sapir any more than I do*, I said. *Will you just tell me?*

"It was a superimposition of several comments involving his sexual preferences, his mother, and his bandwidth."

*Keishi, for God's sake*, I said. But by that time, she and Voskresenye had already exchanged more words in Sapir than I could hope to count. *What's he saying to you?*

"Umm, let's just say that only a few years ago it would have been anatomically impossible."

Then Keishi said something that made Voskresenye laugh and turn away.

*What? What was that?*

"Sorry, no way could I translate," she said. "Some insults just don't make sense unless you can specify a waveform with a single word."

Voskresenye's eyestalks swiveled toward me, and he spoke again.

"I'm sorry," I said. "I don't speak Sapir."

"He asked you to confirm your Netname," Keishi said.

"Oh. Umm, confirm(Maya, News One, camera)," I said, pleased to discover that in grayspace the palatal click for left-paren didn't hurt my mouth. A pattern of colored lights appeared between us.

"Is it safe to say my pass phrase?" I asked Keishi.

"Yes," she said. "I've got you covered."

I had a moment of amusement when I realized she meant this literally. A million kilometers away, my body stirred and whispered: "Give up your past desires, and leave the poor world to its fate." The colors rippled in response.

"Confirmed," Voskresenye said, after a brief pause. "Gol an ix (KRIOL)?"

"I don't speak native KRIOL either," I admitted, feeling thoroughly outclassed. "Only interpreted."

"Well, I can tell you one thing," Keishi said. "He speaks a very high-class KRIOL. Judging by the number of parentheses he elides, he's been talking to computers that could parse Russian if they felt like it. He split the verb from its argument, too, and he used the pronoun 'ix' without a restrictive definition. He's been talking to AIs; I'd bet on it."

*Thanks,* I said. I wasn't sure what use the information was, but better to have Keishi feeding me trivia than heckling Voskresenye.

To my relief, Voskresenye switched to Russian. "Even so," he said, in a tone of pleased surprise, "you speak KRIOL. How quaint. Nothing has quite the appeal of a dead language; it's no accident that most of the world's great religions have been conducted in them."

"KRIOL isn't dead," I said.

"Not in Russia," he said dismissively. "It is in Africa, where it matters."

I seemed to have completely lost control of the conversation. To gain time I said—not very originally—"You are Pavel Voskresenye?"

"Yes," he said. "And I know who you are. So, the formalities being over, you may now proceed to the jugular, if you can find one."

"Don't you love it when your reputation precedes you?" Keishi whispered in my ear.

"I wasn't thinking of you as an opponent, Pavel Sergeyevich," I said. "Why are you treating me like one?"

"I have lived a long life," he said, "and I have made so many friends and so many enemies that I can no longer remember which is which. So I treat everyone as an enemy. It saves memory which can be used to better purpose."

I blinked. Lucky that Keishi had changed my interface, or I would have had to wait for him to reappear. "And why grayspace?"

"As I've explained, I have many enemies. Grayspace is not secure, not anymore, but it is more secure than vidphones; if someone happens to be listening in, it should be relatively easy to detect him."

"So ask him what he's got to hide," Keishi prompted.

I had been about to do just that. I nearly changed plans out of annoyance with her; but no, she would take that as a triumph. "Anything you say to me is going to wind up all over the Net, one way or another," I said. "What's the danger?"

"The danger, Maya Tatyanichna, is that if I tell something to a camera, the obvious way to prevent its becoming common knowledge is to kill both that camera and me before the Netcast can begin. Once the information is already on the Net, of course, that solution is useless. One must still fear revenge, but revenge is a less powerful motive than necessity."

"I see." I paused as if considering this closely, and subvoked: *Keishi, just for fun, see if there's a psychiatric record on this man.*

"There's not," she said. "Which isn't to say that there shouldn't be, but there isn't."

*Well, it was worth a try.* Aloud I said: "We somehow skipped the part of this conversation where I tell you why I'm here, and I think you've gotten the wrong impression. All I want to do is ask you a few questions about the Calinshchina. I don't see why there should be anything sensitive about that. It's part of a series that's been on News One for two weeks already. If someone wanted it suppressed, wouldn't they have done it by now?"

"Asking questions about the Calinshchina," he said, "is like pulling on a tangler's web. You can pull them all day and find nothing. But if you choose the wrong one, you never know what sort of twitching horror you may bring to light."

"I see," I said, again. Voskresenye had a knack for crafting answers that frustrated all my follow-ups; I couldn't pursue the question without risking the attention of a Weaver. I went to a canned question:

"In your book you give hundreds of survivors' stories, but you leave out your own. Why? Which Square Mile did you survive?"

"I was imprisoned at Arkhangelsk," he said, and even in grayspace, where there are no facial expressions, I could sense bitterness tinged with amusement. "Whether I *survived* is a matter of some debate."

"What do you mean by that?"

He paused, then replied ironically: "What records there are insist no one survived Arkhangelsk. I have allowed the misconception to persist. I would not wish to diminish Mr. Calin's crime by subtracting even one death from his body count."

It was another of his slantwise evasions. Yet I could feel myself warming to him, and if I did, so would the audience. I decided to consider this a screen test, and not worry about pinning him down. Later I'd go over the disk, analyze his strategies, and develop a response.

"There is no disk, remember?" Keishi whispered. "If you want to put your camera chip in—"

*Forget it*, I subvoked flatly. *Record this yourself, if you want.*

To Voskresenye I said, "Wouldn't you rather tell people about the millions who died, instead of just adding one to the ranks of the forgotten?"

"Naturally." His tone was nonchalant.

"Pavel Voskresenye, why don't we remember?"

The stormcloud that hung above our heads shifted uneasily. "That is a question that wants answering in a dark place where no one can listen, with all the chips out of our heads. Will you meet with me?"

"I was going to ask the same thing," I said, and added to Keishi: *but not for the same reasons.* "Where do you live?"

"Meet me tomorrow, precisely at noon, by the Bronze Horseman."

I frowned. "I'd rather record you on your own turf. In your home, if possible." I hate doing interviews in public places; it's not fair to the screener to make her edit out gawkers. Then, too, a house is an extension of the self—a shell the soul secretes; like faces, they leak information.

"Perhaps later," he said. "For now, the Horseman. I must ask that you come alone, and isolated from the Net. You may have an encrypted channel to your screener—I have just given her the specifications—but no more. Bring a vehicle; I will direct you to the site of the interview from there."

"You're maybe taking her to the Batcave?" Keishi said. "You want I should blindfold her?"

*Keishi, behave!*

"It is a most ill-mannered elephant."

"She's a loaner. My real screener's in the shop." I had been about to ask him for a different meeting place, but after Keishi's outburst, it seemed petty to press the issue. "How will I recognize you?" I asked.

"I assure you I am unmistakable. I look forward to our conversation, Maya Tatyanichna. Now if you will excuse me."

"Until tomorrow, then."

"Tomorrow." He looked up, toward where the rest of Keishi's body towered over me. "Good-bye, elephant. Such an oddity—an elephant raised by wolves."

"Yeah, same to you, buddy."

"Keishi!"

But perhaps he did not even hear her; he had already moved away, the blimp swiftly reeling in the dwarf as he receded. A single grouper, streaming toward us from the dwarf's direction, was about to overtake us—

Then I was back sitting in my living room. Rather than swim back to where we'd started, Keishi had simply pulled the plug.

It always takes me a long time to recover from going into grayspace. The parts of your brain that get copied into grayspace aren't silenced, they're just cut off from the rest of the brain. Isolated, they dream; and though the myrmichor overwrites the dream, there's always something that remains, just out of reach. I can't help trying to grasp it, though it always slips through my fingers.

Keishi, however, was awake at once. "What an asshole!" she said.

"I think he'll be all right," I said when I felt whole again. "He's got presence—it's a strange kind, but he's got it. If I could feel it even in grayspace, it should come through beautifully in the Netcast. This could work out."

"Well, if he screens well, he screens well. There's no arguing with that," she said grudgingly. "He's still an asshole," she confided to the vidphone. Then she inclined her head and said slyly, "Have you thought any more about—"

"You know," I interrupted, "you can't keep doing this forever."

"What?"

"I know you think now that you've got something on me, you can do anything you want. And you're right, there's nothing I can do. But sooner or later, News One's going to catch on."

She rested her elbow on nothing and leaned her head against her hand. "Haven't we had this conversation already? At least once? It's like a bad video game: if you leave the castle and go back in, the Guardians are resurrected and you have to fight your way through all over again. I thought we established that I'm not a cop, or a spy, or a blackmailer. I thought we'd finally reached some understanding—"

"Of what? Of what you showed me yesterday? What does that have to do with disrupting my interviews?"

"Oh," she said. "That's what you mean." Her image shrugged; the Word scrolled down from *treachery* to *flame*. "It's a whole different etiquette in grayspace, Maya. People always insult each other—it's practically impolite not to. I mean, it worked, didn't it? You got your interview. I can't always explain everything. Sometimes I have to just follow my instincts—"

"You don't have instincts yet," I said. "You haven't earned them."

"Oh, God, not this again. I thought I took care of this before—"

"You took care of it by lying to me, yes. You can't expect me to stick to that now that the lie's been uncovered."

"Scratch 'video game,' " she said. "Insert 'soap opera.' " She turned aside, and I thought she would leave. Then she wheeled back around and said in a burst of energy: "Why do you have to make this so complicated? Why won't you understand—"

"Because I can't," I said.

She made a vague searching gesture, as though about to argue the point, then hesitated. She fixed her eyes on my encyclopedia. Doubt crossed her face like a shadow. "No," she said bleakly, "you can't. Of course you can't. I don't know why I ever expected anything else."

I took out my Net chip, and she vanished. For a while I sat with my hand on the moistdisk, lest she should, by some miracle, find a way in through that. She didn't. I moved my hand around to the front of my head, and rested it against the familiar warmth of my suppressor chip.

I want to say that it's horrible. I want to tell you that being suppressed makes every moment of existence a torment, because maybe that would help—but it would be a lie. In fact, the most horrible thing is how easy it is to slide into contentment, how hard it is to nourish anger or regret. If you lost the sense of smell, say, or taste, you'd grieve for it; but if you were born without that sense, you'd never miss it. You'd almost forget there was such a thing as smell, until someone reminded you, and even then you'd only half believe it. That's how it was for me—the sense was gone, as though it had never been. For the first few years after suppression, I kept myself in misery by sheer effort of will, trying to imagine, every day, what it was that I had lost. But in the end, it became too much trouble. I gave in to the inevitable. I forgot.

It must, I supposed, have been terribly strong, for me to risk so much. Did it come over me by surprise, like a storm uprooting everything? Or was it always there, enriching my perceptions—as when Keishi covered my eyes, making the dark world bright with salts and textures? I didn't know. In those early years, when I imagined desire, I used to think of it as an energy that clings to objects— an electricity, that sparks and dies in every rustling of a dress, and that lives deep among the wires beneath the skin.

But those were only words. I could no more bring back the feeling with them than a man desouled in grayspace could remember the smell of a rose. I had forgotten. I had grown complacent.

And now she came into my life, and offered me all of it back— and I must refuse it. Because it would mean being dependent on her forever. Because I could never ask her to leave. Because when it was over between us, or when her enhancements aged into obsolescence, some automatic spy would sniff me out and we'd both disappear. It was impossible. I liked her—it was not that; might have liked her a lot under other circumstances; but it was impossible. The false intimacy of the screening chip had ruined any chance of friendship, much less love.

If only, I thought, I could meet her in some other place, where the Net did not reach, and where the only cables were the roots by which the grasses passed along their ancient thoughts. If only we could meet there as if for the first time, and talk together as two strangers talk: locked into our separate skulls, as though nothing had been said between us.

**(The Helmet)**

(Dreams don't contain symbols. Where would they come from? Not from some collective unconscious—we're not born cabled to the world-mind, that's a myth. Not from your own mind, either; symbols are hard enough to invent when you're awake, you're not going to come up with them fast asleep. So if something in a dream looks like a cross between a vidphone and your cat, it's not because your cat is like a vidphone; it's because you're too sleepy to make up your mind. If Mr. Yablokov turns into your father, it's not because he reminds you of your father, it's because there's no continuity director.

That night, I did not dream of Keishi. Instead I dreamed, over and over, that I met Pavel Voskresenye. He was an old man, sitting in a wooden chair. Blood was leaking from a small hole in his temple. As I watched from a coign of vantage, he reached up and guided down an enormous helmet which, when he locked it into place, engulfed his head completely. But it was not a helmet: it was a brain, from the back of which there trailed a spine a hundred meters long, like a skeleton in a museum. The rest of him sat motionless, but the spine began to twitch, drawing all my attention toward it. It shuddered, then rippled sinuously like the body of a snake. At last, with an effort that wrinkled his brow, the spine raised itself and arched forward over his head, like the tail of a scorpion.)

# seven

## KHRISTOS VOSKRESYE

**P**ut in your code chip."

*All right*, I subvoked, fumbling it into my head. *Are we scrambled?*

"Yeah, we're locked up tight. I still don't see the point, though."

*Neither do I, but we might as well do what he says. It can't hurt anything.*

I'd come early and waited for a parking place near the Horseman to open up, so I could watch for him from the car. Now I was having second thoughts about the whole plan. He'd probably counted on recognizing me from my Net-portrait, in which case we were in trouble. And there was little hope of his being unmistakable: on that sidewalk, no one could have been so outlandish as to stand out.

Or so I thought until I happened to glance in the rear-view mirror, and saw a man of about the right age, wearing a heavy black overcoat that was wildly inappropriate for the early spring sweater-weather. I half-opened the door for a better look. His head was full of sockets of every possible design, and he was not only wearing a coat, but gloves—black and lumpish. He was unmistakable, all right.

"Voskresenye?" I called out.

The man looked at me as though I were mad. *"Voistinu voskresye*—but not today!"

Oh. *Khristos voskresye* is an old Easter greeting meaning "Christ is risen." *Voistinu voskresye* is the answer—"truly he is risen"—but of course, it wasn't Easter. Well, it wouldn't be the last time I'd make an idiot out of myself in the name of journalism. For a moment I was afraid he'd think I was a wirehead trying to steal the car—I've got enough sockets to look the part—but he passed by without further comment, disappearing into the crowd.

Then the passenger door seemed to open by itself. I flipped open the cover of the Electrify switch and had my finger on the toggle when he hissed, "It's me—Voskresenye!" and climbed into the seat with a peculiar crab-motion, still crouching down.

"What the hell are you doing?"

"No time. Pretend you've given up on me and drive away."

One of the advantages of driving a car of Reconstruction vintage is that they generally put in a few concealed weapons. There was a ceramic flechette gun behind a panel just beneath the driver's side armrest; a tap with my left hand, a quick grab with my right, and I'd have it. I would take the gun, make him get out of the car, drive away, and produce some nice boring conclusion to my series on the Calinshchina. I would take the assignments I was given, and I would die in my sleep.

Then I looked at his face, and my hand wavered. He had one of every kind of socket ever made, from the round Army standard to the tiny modern squares, but the ones at his temples were like nothing I'd ever seen before: oval, with three concentric rings of pins inside. And the jagged scar that went all the way around his head was beyond the clumsiness of even the most disreputable Moscow hack. He'd been modified by the Guardians.

I turned my sigh of resignation into one of frustration and slumped my shoulders to mime discouragement. After another thirty seconds of craning my neck I muttered, "The hell with it, then," found a tiny chink in the wall of traffic, and threaded the car into it.

"You shouldn't have called out my name," he said, straightening up. "I know you didn't know, and it can't be helped now in any case. But I don't think we've fooled anyone. We'll have to try to lose ourselves in traffic."

"Voskresenye, why are we acting like fugitives?"

"I know how all this must seem, Maya Tatyanichna. But I am not paranoid, nor am I being overcautious. On the contrary, it is reckless of me even to risk speaking to you. I am widely accounted a most desirable person to have at one's tea party. Ask your screener."

"He's telling the truth," Keishi said. "He's been wanted by the Fusion of Historical Nations since before it fused."

*What for?*

"Oh, treason, terrorism, conspiracy to overthrow the government. Little things like that."

I thought wistfully of the flechette gun and the chance that had evaporated when I decided not to use it.

*Why didn't you tell me this before?*

"It never occurred to me to check for warrants on someone his age," she said with chagrin.

Twenty years of good behavior, sunk by a stereotype. Now I'd get to test the old maxim about Postcop tea. The first time you drink it, they say, you soon forget it—that part I'd already proved. But the second time, the saying goes on, you remember it the rest of your life.

"Give me one good reason why I shouldn't make you get out now," I said.

"Because it's too late. They already know we're together. I just saw the bulletin go out."

*What are my chances if I kill him and say he tried to carjack me?* I asked. *No, don't bother, I know the answer. Don't mind me, I'm just struggling against the inevitable.*

"I assure you that your reputation will not be damaged as a result of this meeting," he said. "I have made extensive preparations to avoid endangering you. When the day shift clocks out, I will erase the information from their chips before the next shift slots them in, and purge all external records. At six o'clock this evening, you will be as clean as you were yesterday."

"And if he doesn't do it, I will," Keishi said. "I'll power-down their whole network if I have to."

Keishi was wired beyond the Post police, but even so, it didn't seem remotely plausible. And while they both sounded confident, I wasn't sure how much to credit that. The overenhanced often come to believe they can hack their way out of anything. Sooner or later, life proves them all wrong.

"I'm not making this up, Maya. I can do it."

*I believe you,* I subvoked without conviction.

"The first thing," Voskresenye said, "is to lose any surveillance we may have attracted. Take a right turn up at the light."

"Where are we going?"

"I'll know when we get there."

I wasn't reassured, but saw no reason not to go where he suggested. As I made the turn I said, "Just so I know what I'm being disappeared for, what exactly did you do? Plant a bomb or something?"

"I planted something much more dangerous. An idea. —Here! Turn into this parking lot. —An idea, but it didn't go off. Secondhand explosives; you can't trust them. Park there, next to that gray car."

I pulled in next to a car that was a perfect duplicate of mine, except for being a slightly darker shade of gray. The owner must have parked it indoors. Kruchonykh never sold a gray car, you understand; they just turn that color.

He got out, and though his movements were neither as fast nor as acrobatic as they had been when he scuttled into the car, they still didn't fit with his age. For a moment I wondered if he was a younger man in some sort of make-up. But no, it was more than that. There was something inhuman about the way he moved, about its smoothness—fast precise movements with no diagonals, like a toy robot.

I followed him around to the back of the car and started to ask what he was doing, but he put his finger to his lips and looked into the sky. "There . . . and there . . . " he murmured, then said to me: "Stand over to your left a little, and keep talking."

"What sort of idea?"

"Oh, some nonsense about human beings having inalienable rights. Or was it that the Earth is flat? At my age one begins to forget these things."

He had removed my license plate, using a tiny electric screwdriver produced from one of his coat's many pockets. "About a foot to your right, if you please," he said. Then he went to the car beside us, and started switching plates.

"Will that work?" I whispered.

"Speak freely; no one can hear us now. And yes, it should. You're between me and the closest spy satellite; the other one's too far to see much. Back to where you were before, please." He put on the new plate, then moved back to the other car and laid his hands on it. Its dashboard lit up, except for the security section, which remained dark. "All right, friend," he murmured to the car, bending down to press his cheek against its hood, "who do we belong to? Ah, registered to Maria Petrova and Ivan Petrov, a man and a woman . . . and they're both here. Perfect. That makes everything much easier." He straightened back up and brought one hand to his head. I heard the car's phone begin to dial itself.

On the second ring someone picked up the phone. "Petrova."

"Maria Petrova," he said in a creditable imitation of an early-model Kruchonykh voice, "this is an automated call from your Kruchonykh KL-37. There has been an attempt to steal me. I have already electrocuted the offenders and alerted the appropriate authorities. Please proceed to my vicinity as soon as possible to fill out the police report."

"*Bozhe moy*—how many were there? Are they alive?"

"The hooligan or hooligans are dead. No further information is available at this time. Thank you for choosing Kruchonykh." The phone went dark. He turned to me and said: "That ought to do it. The promise of carnage rarely fails to bring people running."

"Won't they just call the cops and draw attention?"

"It doesn't matter if they do or not; the cops already know we're here." He touched the car again and its motor started. "The satellites have infrared, so their motor has to be about as warm as ours. The Postcops will figure they started it remotely, if they notice at all. —You were asking about my checkered past."

" 'Conspiracy to overthrow the government'?"

"Oh yes, that. A youthful folly. That was when I thought that liberty in the Fusion was being destroyed by people, and not by impersonal forces. I tried to embarrass a few of those people. But I discovered that in the Historical Nations you will never run out of tyrants. Depose all you want, they'll make more. By the time I realized who my targets should have been, I had become much too old for such antics. 'If youth knew, if age could.' "

"If you don't mind my saying so, you look as though your age can."

"Aesculapius and Hephaestus have been kind to me," he said, "but there are limits."

"He means medicine and technology, the pretentious old bat," Keishi put in, before I could ask.

I was about to ask another question when he said: "Don't look now, but here come the Petrovs, every petty-bourgeois inch of them. Now, the satellite takes pictures at a rate of one every four seconds, so when they're four seconds away from the car—say, when they reach the bumper on that Honda there—get in as fast as you can. Ready?" He adjusted the side mirror as the couple approached. Then at the appointed moment we both jumped in.

"Look," he whispered, pointing to the side mirror. "They're standing by the car and talking. They're us, and we're them. He's even wearing a sweater, so he'll only be a little brighter than me in infrared. We've done it."

Maria Petrova noticed us and rapped at the window. I rolled it down.

"Excuse me, *tavarishcha*. Did you see anyone near this car?"

"No," I said, "but we heard the alarm call you. It must be on the fritz."

"Those Kruchonykh alarms are crap," Voskresenye said in a crotchety old man's voice. "They'll do that every time. It's a miracle we weren't electrocuted. Just you trade that pile of garbage in on a Stepanova. You mark my words."

I rolled my eyes. "Oh, Sergei." To Maria Petrova I said, "Sergei is an engineer for Stepanova. He gets like this."

She looked back and forth between us, seeing the difference in ages—then decided to smile. "I understand. You should hear Ivan on the evils of Japanese software."

Having affirmed my membership in the international sorority of suffering spouses, I realized, I could now drive away without arousing comment. "Sergei, let's go home and quit bothering these nice people," I said, and to Petrova: *"Proshaite, sestra."*

As I backed out I heard Ivan say, "But *she's* driving a Kruchonykh!"

"Of course I am!" I called out the window. "I'm not stupid enough to drive anything my husband designed!"

Voskresenye chuckled as we drove away. "Most impressive. You missed your calling. You should have been an actor."

"I am," I said. "Or at least, I was until today. Are we clean now?"

"Once more for good measure. Stop anywhere along here."

I did, and he switched the license plate again, this time with a small green convertible that he said was between sensors.

"*Now* we're clean. By the time anyone figures out what happened, we'll be miles away, and they'll be tracking the wrong vehicle."

"And Maria Petrova drinks tea?"

"No. At the most, a Postcop asks some questions and they get an extra dose of surveillance for a while; nothing worse. Even if we were being watched, which we may not have been."

"And meanwhile, I sink deeper and deeper."

"Not at all. As of six o'clock, that's always been your plate number. I have already set up the logic bomb."

"He's telling the truth. I saw him do it," Keishi said with grudging admiration. "Under all that rusting hardware, the man's got street."

I looked toward Voskresenye, and then around at the spot just behind me where I always imagine the screener standing, and shook my head. "So are we clean enough to make it out into the countryside, to someplace unsurveilled?"

"We're clean enough, but that's the wrong place to go. It's too obvious, and a plate search on cars leaving the city wouldn't take them long. What we need is a place within the city where we can be certain we're unobserved."

Keishi's voice rasped from the car speaker: "Like a nice big semistable bubble right on Nevsky Prospect?"

"Exactly," Voskresenye said, nodding.

"What's a bubble?" I asked.

"A temporary surveillance-free zone. Head back downtown, if you please. Park us near the Admiralty, and we'll walk."

"Why do you want to go back downtown? Isn't that the first place they'll look?"

"Who would expect us to circle back to the place where we were first identified?"

"Anyone with an ounce of imagination," I said. "Anyone who's ever read an American detective novel."

He nodded. "You mean, anyone but a Postcop. Besides, they can look all they want; they won't find us."

I looked at him skeptically. "And what good does this bubble do us?"

"It gives you a chance to interview me."

"Are you putting me on?" I glanced from the road to his face, which was unreadable. "You think I'm not in deep enough tea already, I should try Netcasting the life and times of a wanted criminal?"

"We can limit our discussion to the Calinshchina," he said. "Your screener can alter my features, and elide any mention of my so-called terrorist activities."

I thought for a moment. *Keishi, can you make this 'cast clean? I mean a hundred percent, no traces whatsoever?*

"In my sleep, girl."

I decided that if she could make the Postcops forget about me, she could give me a clean Netcast; and if she couldn't, then it wouldn't matter. I might as well go ahead and get the story I was risking my career for. Besides, I was curious.

"All right," I said grudgingly. "In for a penny, in for a pound."

"That's the spirit," Voskresenye said brightly. "Nothing like a good cliché to help you to a wise decision."

As I opened my mouth to answer, I heard a siren behind us. "Oh, God. Please tell me that's an ambulance," I said feebly.

"No. It's a yellow-and-black," he said. "Turn your head, as though you were looking for a place to pull over."

"I hope you've got a backup plan," I whispered, complying.

"That's not for us. He's chasing a speeder or something."

"Look," I said, "you're wanted, you were seen, I was heard calling your name, now a Postcop comes out of nowhere. It stands to reason she's looking for us."

"Listen." The wasp's siren dopplered past, not even slowing.

"You see? The Postcops are unimaginative, predictable, and overdependent on machines, but they are not stupid. In a matter of this importance they would not be so unsubtle as to send a wasp. If they come for us in a car, you may rest assured it will be unmarked and Net-silent."

"How comforting."

"You could not be safer than with me, Maya Tatyanichna," he said with quiet amusement. "The Hanged Man is not in my cards. I am told to fear death by drowning, which has happened once already, and will happen once again—but not just yet."

The traffic was now so thick that I had to devote all my attention to driving. At last, just a few blocks away from where we'd started, he silently pointed out a crowded parking lot. He had me park the car with its rear bumper to a wall, so the license plate would be hidden from the security camera.

"Our bubble is some kilometers away," he said. "I apologize for making you walk, but that way, if they do find the car—" he tapped its hood smartly, making the dashboard lights wink "—we'll have some warning."

As we walked I asked him what the terrorism charge on his record was for.

"The charge is actually 'informational terrorism,' " he said.

"What?" I turned to face him, fear constricting my throat. "*Informational* terrorism? That's not a Postcop crime. That's under Weaver jurisdiction."

"It happened a long time ago," he said. "The Weavers have long since forgotten."

"Weavers don't forget."

"They most certainly do," he said. "Unlike the Postcops, the Weavers are entirely rational; that is their only point of weakness. If they are confident that you cannot repeat your crime, they will not seek you out. You need only stay offline for some years, and you will be entirely gone from their minds."

*Should I believe that?*

"Sure," Keishi said. "A Weaver sees a healthy chunk of the whole Net every day; they can't remember all of it. For most things they rely on sense and reflex, not on memory."

"How did this charge come about?" I asked Voskresenye.

"Some decades ago," he said, "I was involved with a group of dissident hackers who wrote a virus designed to seek out the computers of every financial and governmental agency in the FHN. Only computers, you understand, not minds—otherwise it would have been far harder to get past the Weavers. It hid there until a certain day, then encrypted every byte of data it could find and self-destructed, leaving a series of ransom demands behind it. In effect, we were holding the information hostage."

*Why doesn't that sound right to me?* I subvoked.

"Ask him how he put an unbreakable code in the space of a virus," Keishi whispered in my ear. "A virus would have to be small, to get so widespread without being detected. You could fit in a key a few thousand bits long, maybe, but you put a couple of teraflops on that and it'll crumble."

I paused to reorganize the question in my mind, then repeated it to Voskresenye.

"Oh, it did crumble," he said. "It crumbled very quickly. We were astonished to discover that in some places it had held out as long as forty minutes."

"Then what good was it?"

He looked at me out of the corner of his eye, not moving his head—almost, I thought, as though he couldn't. "You might better ask, what good would it be otherwise? Do you think the Weavers negotiate with terrorists? What concessions will they give as ransom? Would they not instead hunt us down and kill us, even if it took a thousand men to take each one? If we had succeeded, it would have sealed our fates—such a simple trick as temporary disappearance would never have thrown them off, if I had done enough damage for them to take me seriously."

"So you failed deliberately?"

"We invented a false purpose, and deliberately failed in that, yes. This was to conceal our true purpose."

"Which was?" I prompted.

"To build a network of back doors into the computers that we infected. We knew that when they decrypted the data, after such a short time, they would not bother to check that what they recovered was the same as what they had before—especially since they had intercepted several copies of the virus, and made sure that their only function was to encrypt. We had only to hope they would not find the few copies of the virus that were subtly different from the others; and they did not. So the programs they restored had points of entry that had not been there before."

"These back doors—wouldn't they have found them eventually?"

"Certainly. But they remained in place only a few weeks. They were only meant to provide us access to the lowest levels of the system, a toe in the door. From there we could strip away the root passwords, letter by letter and bit by bit. And once we had root access, we could create all the back doors we dared. In that way, and by not doing anything that would alarm the Weavers unduly, we've managed to keep one step ahead of them ever since. The descendants of those original back doors are still being maintained. That's how we're able to create the bubbles."

"Who do you mean when you say 'we'? The people involved in this virus project?"

"Their current equivalents. All the members of that team have long since been disappeared, and those that followed them, and those that followed the ones that followed. You can evade the Postcops a long time, and the Weavers a short time; but in the end, they always catch you."

*Keishi, crack the surveillance camera and give me a direct shot of his face*, I subvocalized. I wanted to see his reaction to my next question. When the window opened up in the lower left-hand quadrant of my field of vision, I asked him: "You say a person can only evade the authorities a few years, yet you've apparently been doing it for decades. Why have you survived where so many others were caught?"

In the window he raised his eyebrows. "Why, skill, of course." Then he laughed: "All right, then, good wiring." And then the window closed and he said, "Off the record? A combination of abject cowardice and pure luck. But don't let it get around."

The window opened again on a face without expression, save perhaps a hint of mischief at the corners of the mouth.

*Can he hear everything I say to you?*

"Absolutely not," she said. "He didn't hear you ask me for that crack, he saw the crack. Your thoughts are cabled to me on quanta; if he looks at it, he changes it and I can tell. He can't break that unless he can revoke the laws of physics. The very first leg of the trip is by radio, and that he could hack in theory, but it's coded with megabit primes and not even he could break that. Besides, I'm keeping close tabs on what goes on inside that crummy little cranium, and if he tried to crack us open, I'd see it in a second. Believe me, Maya, he's good, but I'm a whole lot better. And when I say we're tight, we're tight."

When she was finished I said, exhaustedly, *Keishi?*

"Yes?"

*Next time I ask you a yes or no question, give me a yes or no answer, OK?*

"OK. Umm, I mean yes."

*Thank you.*

Keishi's lecture had forced an awkward pause in my conversation with Voskresenye. To end it I asked why he hadn't tried scrubbing the data, instead of encoding it.

"Because by that time I had realized that destroying data wouldn't have weakened their grip. I needed a bigger bomb."

"What kind of bomb?"

"It has not been set off yet. Perhaps it does not exist. —Here we are; this is our bubble."

"Where?"

"Right in front of you."

We had come to a little open-air cafe on Nevsky itself, crammed with customers and visible to hundreds of passers-by. Overlooking it were two surveillance cameras mounted on lampposts. The cameras were at least twenty years out of date, since we could see them; but that didn't make them any less effective.

"You must be kidding," I said. "I'm not going to sit here and discuss your career as a terrorist where a thousand wired people can see us. Not to mention those cameras. I thought you were taking me someplace unsurveilled."

"At the moment, this is the most secure spot in the Russian Historical Nation. If you will kindly refrain from looking in my direction for a moment, I will demonstrate."

I was a little edgy about turning my back on him, but I would have felt foolish saying so, so I averted my eyes.

"Thank you. Now, dearest elephant, can you tell me how many fingers I am holding up?"

My face went numb, and for a moment I thought he'd done it. But it was Keishi's voice that came from my mouth: "There's no need for games. As long as you're in the bubble, I can't see you unless she looks at you. You're secure."

*Don't* ever *do that again*, I subvocalized, gasping for air as the sensation in my face returned.

"I'm sorry. But he did ask, and I can't get at any other speakers—"

*I am not a speaker. Keep your mind to yourself.*

"I said I was sorry."

*Later! I don't want to hear another word from you until this interview is over.*

"Why don't you just send me to my room?"

I imagined myself filling out a repartnering form, and she responded with silence.

"Trouble controlling the elephant?" Voskresenye said. "In the circus they use hooks, I think."

"I'll have to look into that," I said.

"Are you now confident that we can safely talk here?"

"I believe we're safe from cameras," I said. "But what if someone overhears us? The Postcops may not be able to pick that up, but Weavers can."

"A legitimate worry. I will be keeping tabs on the minds in our vicinity; however, you might wish to have your screener double-check. It can't hurt, and it would surely take most of her brainpower, so it might keep her quiet."

"Tell him I could watch everyone in Leningrad and never miss the bandwidth!"

I pictured myself thumbing the form and handing it in. *Keep an eye on them, but don't say a word unless you see something. I mean it.*

We found a table in the shade. As he sat across from me, I noticed that he was sweating under his out-of-season overcoat. When water and menus had been brought, I said, "Why don't you start by telling me why you're dressed for snow in this weather?"

"I will explain; but first I suggest you have your screener alter my features. The events I will retell may be safely Netcast, but my face may be familiar to the Post police."

"Go ahead, Keishi," I said, and then subvoked: *Don't tell me how you're doing it, just do it.*

His face morphed through a series of subtle changes that, collectively, left it unrecognizable.

"Maybe you should take out the sockets, too," I said. "They're pretty distinctive."

"I'm afraid they are essential to the story," Voskresenye put in. "However, there are others still alive who are socketed much as I am, so it should not matter."

"All right then. Now, about that overcoat."

"Since when do you cover fashion?" Keishi whispered; I ignored her.

"It is uncomfortable, yes, but I did not wish to call attention to myself. And while an overcoat in April might draw the occasional glance, I think you'll agree that this would be substantially more indiscreet." Screening his hand from the sidewalk with a menu, he took off one glove to reveal the structure of metal and insulated wire that covered his hand. Steel slid against oiled steel to lift one of his fingers, and the tangle of wires on his skin shifted uneasily with the motion.

"Without this . . . device, you are paralyzed?"

"Nearly so, yes. I can move a little, but I cannot walk. And without the wires, I'm quite atactile. My mind and my body no longer talk to each other the way they used to; like so many couples nowadays, they prefer to interact through a machine."

"May I ask . . . an accident? A degenerative disease?"

"Yes, and yes. An accident with a degenerative disease named Derzhavin."

"Aleksandr Derzhavin?" Unassisted, I would not have known the name, but Keishi's moistdisk had woven itself so seamlessly into my memory that I could not keep a note of horror out of my voice. "You were a victim of Derzhavin?"

"Victim is such a loaded term," he said, calmly replacing the glove. "I have a great deal to thank the man for, including much of my current bandwidth and all of my continued mobility at my advanced age. No, not his victim. In the beginning I was his experimental subject, then his lab assistant, and eventually—" and here I heard the whirr of clockwork as he picked up his water glass "—a great deal more."

"I thought Derzhavin did his experiments on Kazakhs, not politicals."

"Kazakhs and the mentally retarded. And by the time I met him, I fit that latter description very well. Read the marks for yourself." He pulled up his coat sleeve.

As I looked for the Guardian tattoo, I saw that the steel rods that controlled his hands were connected to a hard black shell that started just below his wrists. *Keishi,* I subvoked, *give me four hundred percent, quick.* When the magnification kicked in, I could see the rows of copper needles that anchored the carapace into his skin.

"You understand the code?" he prompted.

I canceled the zoom and looked back at the thirty-two squares etched into his skin with magnetic ink. Keishi's moistdisk helped me recognize the blackened sixth, nineteenth, and twenty-sixth boxes as signifying "irreparable but nonhereditary organic brain defects."

"I guess they were wrong about its being irreparable."

"On the contrary, it has not been and cannot be repaired. But the right sort of wiring can compensate."

"How did you go from a political to a six-nineteen?"

Before he could answer, the waiter returned to take our orders. I had not opened my menu, so I asked for black coffee and a ham sandwich. After a long discussion about ingredients, Voskresenye commanded cabbage pirozhki, which the impatient waiter twice assured him were free of meat.

"You are vegetarian?"

" 'My food is not that of man,' " he quoted; " 'I do not destroy the lamb and the kid to glut my appetite; acorns and berries afford me sufficient nourishment.' "

"Gandhi," I hazarded.

"No," he said. "Frankenstein's Creature. Gandhi, I imagine, would not have been so arrogant, but for me it's most appropriate."

I frowned. "I don't remember—"

"Not the film, the book. A preclassical allusion, by the modern reckoning. Forgive me; I have grown too used to being my own audience."

*Mark that for human interest, Keishi. I wish I could do the whole story on this man—a cabbage-eating terrorist, it's perfect.*

"Actually, several of us were vegetarians," he said thoughtfully. "That was her influence, of course. . . . After we were caught, the

Guardians were hysterical enough to pick up every vegetarian they could find in Russia, reasoning that a few might have been our accomplices. It hardly mattered to them that they also got every Zen faddist and food-allergy victim in Moscow."

"I seem to be asking you this question a lot: who do you mean by 'we'?"

"I'm sorry, I'm not making much sense, I'm afraid. I have gone over this story in my head a thousand times, and now, when it matters, I cannot even keep it straight. It would be much easier if I began at the beginning."

"By all means."

# eight

## A MAN WHO HAD FALLEN AMONG THIEVES

The one good feature of telepresence news—compared to text news, which is superior in every other respect—is the way you use interviews. In print, you can use only a few sentences of any interview, which means they're mostly short. In telepresence, you can interview someone for hours, and then when you're online, you just remember it and it's there, a new memory in the viewer's head. Most of it goes away when your story's over, but it's there while the audience needs it. You can include a whole story, not just summarize it.

Still, the holographic memory that telepresence gives is rather lossy—from a distance the event seems vivid and complete, but when you approach it, it eludes your grasp. It is a mystery to me how so much of the value of an interview can be conveyed in telepresence, when so little information comes across; but then, it is also a mystery to me how the events of your own life can matter, when memory sweeps away a thousand things for every one it lets remain.

I have an aid to memory: a copy of the screener's disk, which Keishi kept, and which has come into my hands. While I will not release it (and don't bother trying, I burned it long ago) I have replayed it many times, and will set down what Voskresenye said.

"I was born in Moscow, shortly after the Guardians first took that city," he began. "By the time I was old enough to form clear memories, they had already 'cleansed' the country of nearly all its 'undesirables,' as they would say. So while my parents sometimes mentioned the purges in a whisper, I did not remember them myself, and all my childhood the Guardian regime was simply fact. If someone had asked me how I felt about the Square Miles, I might have realized that I should abhor them; but no one ever asked. I grew up less than a hundred miles from Square-Mile-on-Volga, but what happened there seemed as remote to me as squalor in the Americas does to you."

He spoke softly, but his eyes looked directly into mine. Most people I interview won't look straight at me; but this man's mirror, I realized, had long ago accustomed him to scarred faces and heads full of silicon. As he began his story I again felt the intensity I had sensed in him in grayspace. If the audience was half as rapt as I was, my ratings might be almost respectable for once.

"I grew into a young man of an aesthetic and not a political temperament," he continued, "and so managed to stay on the Guardians' good side. As a result, I was able to attend Moscow University, even though it was then under very strict Guardian control. I was so otherworldly that I barely noticed how uneasy the other students were around me—they were Americans for the most part, the children of Guardian politicians and bureaucrats. Portia and Raskolnikov did not disdain my company; and it was with them that I spent my time. So despite the thinly veiled contempt of many of my professors, I was able to make fair grades and, if things had gone a little differently, would have taken my degree with a comfortable margin of honor."

"What did you study?"

"My principal subject was Classics."

"Where are your glasses, then?" I said. "I thought Classicists went blind from squinting at all that flat video."

He raised an eyebrow. "This, of course, was back when 'Classical culture' meant Greece and Rome, not Hollywood and Motown."

"Oh. Well, yes, I mean, printbooks'll do it too."

"Ooh, nice save," Keishi said.

*We'll take care of it in postproduction*, I said, gulping ice water in hopes of forestalling a blush.

"You think I'd let a thing like that get on the disk?" she said in mock affront.

I thanked her for the editing and God for not letting me make that mistake live. Take a note, Maya: no more banter.

Voskresenye was staring at my encyclopedia, a mocking smile curling his lips. It was the Postcops' joke on me, though not their last or cruelest: seeing an encyclopedia in my head makes people magnify my lapses and minimize any knowledge I display. It's like being caught with crib notes.

"I don't really use that," I said. "It doesn't even work right anymore—" And what kind of idiot would wear a broken chip? I was making matters worse with every word.

But Voskresenye's eyes were not unkind. "I see no moral difference between keeping knowledge in one's head and on a chip," he said.

I wanted to protest again, but it was no use. And besides, when was the last time I'd gone live without a gigabyte of background research whispering into my ear from a moistdisk? It wouldn't hurt if it weren't partly true.

"I suppose," I said, "your generation was the last to spend its childhood memorizing facts, and mine the last to feel guilty about not doing it."

"A man is fortunate if he has nothing worse than that to feel guilty about," Voskresenye said sententiously. "However, the endeavor of memorization is a noble one. Once knowledge is centralized on the Net, it becomes very easy to change—Queen Mab need only ride the world-mind once, new dreams for old. And so in the modern age, the amasser of useless facts is your only hero. An encyclopedia that was not new twenty years ago at least provides a point of reference."

I pulled my pride away from that last sentence, the way you'd pull a dog from a sprayed fencepost. "Does the knowledge really have to be useless?" I said.

"It need not be," he said, "but the sort of person who will cram his head with facts, as a squirrel crams his cheeks with nuts, will most often do it for its own sake, with no thought of future use. Certainly that is the sort of person I was, as a student. Even if I had taken my degree, I don't know what I would have done with it. I honestly don't think I ever thought that far ahead. Of course I could not teach in the universities. No doubt I would have wound up riding herd on second-graders in Kazakhstan for a couple of years until the next purge of ethnic intellectuals."

"What happened?"

"Two things. First, impatience. I had a fair command of Latin, but for my degree I also had to learn Greek, and I did not look forward to the years of study that would be required; nor did I want to wait so long for Homer. So I got drilled for my first socket—which was illegal for me, you understand, because I was not one of them. The law was not strictly enforced, but occasionally the Guardians would decide to make an example of someone. The socket was a small one, and I was able to hide it, but the need for secrecy gradually increased my awareness of what the Guardians were doing to our nation and its people. So I began to develop a vague, unformed, and still largely selfish political conscience—and that helped prepare me a little for what happened next."

At this point the waiter arrived with our food, and Voskresenye was distracted by the need to dissect his pirozhki before tasting them. To get him back on track, I restated the obvious: "It doesn't sound like you were the kind of person to defy the Guardians."

" 'Defy' sounds as if I was hurling insults at them on the street.

The reality was more like a whisper in a darkened room that the wrong person overheard. And even that I would never have done, if not for a fellow student named Katya Andersohna."

I didn't need a moistdisk to recognize that name. "Any relation to Harold Anderson?"

"She was his daughter."

"A dangerous person to know, then."

He nodded, his hands pausing above the plate. "Yes, very much so. But not for the reason you think. She was a four-nine."

"Harold Anderson's kid was a dissident? That's hard to believe."

"Katya Andersohna *was* dissidence at MGU. Without her there would have been nothing. She was an amazing person; she had inherited her father's genius and her mother's beauty, and to that she added humanity, a trait neither of her parents appeared to possess. Perhaps compassion is an environmental illness rather than a genetic disorder. Or I should say, a bacillus, for she was quite successful at infecting others. . . . But I'm getting ahead of myself," he said, shaking his head a little, as though this Katya were a subject whose gravitation he escaped with difficulty. He turned his attention to his plate. I groped for some banal question in order to fill in the dead audio time, then stopped: to watch him eat was fascination enough. Before each cut, he rotated the plate to the correct angle, as if the dance of his knife and fork were programmed and immutable. The swift, practiced movements of his hands made me think of a sign language, or of a series of magical passes by which the food was made to disappear.

Voskresenye raised an eyebrow, and I realized that I'd been watching him too long. "I'm sorry," I said. "Staring's an occupational hazard."

"Not at all. If my being a freak will get people to listen, I am pleased to be one."

I let that sink in and then asked: "How did you get mixed up with Katya Andersohna?"

"Not by choice, that's for certain," he said, laying down his knife. "I had no idea she was a dissident, nor did I know her by the Russian form of her name. To me she was Catharine Anderson, the chief of propaganda for the Student League, a thing to be feared; and the daughter of the Heptarch, all the more terrifying. I rarely saw her, and when I did, I deemed it prudent to go the other way."

"Then how did it happen?"

"She approached my table one day in the library. I was bent over Aeschylus, so all she could see of me was the garish little cap I affected—having reasoned that a person in a nondescript hat was hiding a socket, while one in some blue-and-green monstrosity was merely eccentric. She was carrying an armful of leaflets, and she laid one down before me on the table, saying, 'Here, brother; the latest from the Ministry.' When I looked up in surprise she laughed and said, 'Oh, sorry, Mishenka! I took you for your better.' She started to take the leaflet back. Then she thought better of it and said, 'Well, keep it; you might learn your place.' And she turned away, tossing her hair to flaunt the silicon embedded in her skull, and went to give leaflets to the people at the other tables, most of whom were now smiling at her performance."

As he spoke I tapped into my imagination chip and visualized the scene. I didn't know what Andersohna looked like, so I pictured her with long, dark hair, shaved a little on the left side to expose the sockets. When I made her flip her hair, Keishi responded with a soft "ooh," and I knew I'd hit the right gesture.

"Well, my cheeks were burning, as you can imagine," he continued. "Hatred of us was rarely so overt; they saved their venom for Kazakhs and Arabs for the most part. I was not used to it. I wanted to throw the pamphlet away, but that would have seemed like defiance, so I marked my place in Aeschylus with it and left, trying not to run. But as I did, I noticed something strange. The covers of all the leaflets the others were reading were white on red. Mine, and only mine, had black lettering as well.

"When I had put some distance between me and the library, I

checked to make sure. Yes. Beneath the white title, 'Kazakhs versus Animals at Square-Mile-on-Volga,' someone had written with a ballpoint pen, in English, 'A Modest Proposal.' And the handwriting was quite recognizable. It was my own."

"Andersohna forged your writing? She was trying to frame you?"

"That was my first thought. I turned and made for the incinerator, planning to throw it in. But I stopped short. If Harold Anderson's daughter had taken a dislike to me, burning one leaflet was not going to change my fate. I might as well look at it; perhaps I'd learn why I'd been singled out. I stood close to the incinerator, opened the door so I could throw it in at once if anyone came by, and began to read."

"It was dissident literature?"

"For me it was, yes. To anyone else, it would just have been another purple-faced leaflet from the Ministry, marked up by an even more zealous student. Where the leaflet said, 'One would not subject an innocent animal to this treatment, though one would never hesitate to inflict it upon prisoners who have been guilty of such heinous crimes,' this fellow had put, 'Such as being born Kazakh!' And where it said, 'This will help reduce the dimensions of the Kazakhi tumor,' neat proofreading marks emended this to 'Senses, organs, dimensions, passions,' and added in the margin, 'Let us prick them and see if they will bleed.' All this was, for a student of what we were then misguided enough to call the classics, highly suggestive stuff."

I took another sip of ice water as he went on.

"Even then I would not have been sure that it meant what it meant, except for that scrawled subtitle: 'A Modest Proposal.' In the eighteenth century, in what you'd call Ancient Britain, a fournine by the name of Jonathan Swift had written a satire by that title, pointing out that the problems of overpopulation and famine could be solved simultaneously if we would simply begin eating the children of the poor. I used the memory chip I was wearing beneath my cap to call up the moment when she'd tossed her hair. Yes: she'd been showing me the English Literature textbook in her socket.

"What I was holding, then, was a satire after the example of Swift. If a Guardian read it, he would see in it nothing more than overexuberant patriotism: 'Since we have so many human subjects available at the Square Miles for our experiments, why ship in animals?' A noble but impractical thought, by Guardian standards. Read it with a different eye, and it said, 'What the Guardians do to Kazakhs, you wouldn't wish on a dog.' But this meaning only fell into place with that obscure allusion written on the cover—something that no board of inquiry would ever catch. And on top of that, all these little hints were in my own script, so that if the leaflet should fall into the hands of someone else that could understand it . . . well, I'd be an ethnic with an illegal socket who claimed the Heptarch's daughter did it in his handwriting."

"That's a lot of thought to put into recruiting one person," I said.

"For anyone else it would have been. But Katya was, even unenhanced, a brilliant propagandist, and besides that she had the best moistware her father's blood money could buy. For her it was the sort of thing one dreams up on a break between classes. Katya never did anything with less than three layers of deception."

He looked down at his plate and cut off another bite, but did not eat it. When he continued his story it was in a quieter voice.

"I didn't dare keep the leaflet, of course. Yet I knew I had to talk to Catharine Anderson. The leaflet she had written had done what she meant it to. It had forced me to think about things I had been ignoring for twenty years. I had to see her. So I found another, unmarked leaflet—they were all over campus within a day—and wrote on the cover with a black ballpoint pen. And for a week I spent every waking hour in the library, hoping to run into her again.

"Finally, one afternoon when I had given up and was on my way out, I passed her in the foyer. She was talking to a friend, someone on the Student League. I was almost at the door by the time I saw her, so I stopped and went back to the book return, as though I had forgotten something. I pulled out Aeschylus, took the leaflet from him, and, even though he was not a library book, I dropped him into the return slot. So much for the classics; I never saw him again. Then I opened the leaflet, as if I had just noticed it there, and stood for a while pretending to read it. She glanced at me for one instant—that was all it took for her to understand—and, quickly but unhurriedly, took leave of her friend. She walked out and, cautiously, I followed her.

"She led me all the way across campus without acknowledging my presence, and after a while, I began to think she hadn't noticed me at all. Then suddenly she was nowhere to be seen. I stopped, looking around. But to stand there craning my neck like that was too suspicious, so I started to leave. As I did, she reached out for me and pulled me back behind the shrubbery where she was hiding. She pushed me against the wall and covered my mouth with her hand.

" 'Never call me Catharine,' she hissed. 'Don't even think of me by that name. Only Katya—you understand?'

"I nodded as best I could with my head pinned to the wall. She took her hand away from my mouth and said, 'Now tell me why you're smart enough not to approach me, but not smart enough to burn your leaflet.'

"I reached into my pocket, as she watched me warily, and took out the leaflet to show her. On the cover where Katya's subtitle should have been, I had written, 'Paper due 11/IX Greek.'

"She looked at me differently then. 'It's about time the gods sent me someone with half a brain. You won't be too bad once we get your head out of the clouds.'

" 'There are others?' I said.

" 'Well, of course there are others. You don't think that some floatheaded Classics major was the first person I went after? I wouldn't have bothered if not for that horrible cap—I hoped you were hiding a socket under there.'

"I took the cap off to show her.

" 'Sense and a socket. More than I'd hoped for. Come to the coffeeshop in the Student Union at seven tomorrow.'

" 'You meet in a public place?'

" 'Someone will lead you from there to where we meet,' she said impatiently. 'Come, and for God's sake don't use your real name. For us you will be—' she stopped and looked at my blue-and-green cap again. 'I don't have my language chip in. What's a peacock in Russian?'

" '*Pavlin,*' I said, looking down in embarrassment.

" 'From now on you are Pavel. Paul—a nice biblical name for a four-nine atheist.'

" 'I'm not an atheist!'

" 'You will be,' she said, and she broke through the hedge and was gone."

He paused to take another bite of pirozhok and chewed it slowly, remembering. I had been ignoring my food and was beginning to get hungry, but again I had to fill in with a question:

"If your name was *changed* to Pavel, what was it before?"

"Stepan Sornyak. But I've been Pavel for a long time now."

A strange surname—stranger, really, than his adopted one. And he'd called himself an *ethnic* intellectual; the Guardians didn't usually apply that term to Russians. *Iudey,* perhaps? Or *cigan,* given his mention of Tarot? It was possible; he had a wanderer's eyes. But if so, why had he sunk his ethnic noun-name in the strange but clearly Russian *Voskresenye?*

"Was it Katya who named you 'Sunday,' too?" I asked. "More atheist irony?"

"No. That name came later. —Of course you will alter the names before the interview is Netcast?"

"Yes, of course," I said. "Why did you change your surname?"

"I did not," he said simply, putting the last crumbs of pirozhok into his mouth. I took the opportunity to steal a bite from my sandwich. My question could wait; but I made a note not to forget.

"At first Katya insisted I keep up my schoolwork, to avoid drawing attention to myself. But soon we both realized that my slipping grades only confirmed what everyone had expected of me all along, and I began to skip classes with abandon. Instead of Homer, I read Katya's leaflets. Instead of writing papers, I altered records at Square-Mile-on-Volga. Instead of attending classes, I fed escaped prisoners on their way to Africa. I cut my hair short, grew my beard, traded my hideous cap for a black one that would be less visible at night, learned to shoot a gun—for though we did not use weapons, Katya insisted we be ready to—and stopped eating animals—for she insisted we practice compassion toward all creatures, even the lowliest. Within a month, my life had changed so much that everything that had come before seemed like a dream."

"And did you become an atheist?"

He laughed. "No; that was the one thing in me she did not change—not entirely. Although, since it was the Catholic Church that most often gave sanctuary to fugitives, I did trade my Old Slavonic mass for Latin."

"How much resistance was there, in all?"

"You mean numbers of people? A few thousand in Russia, I suppose. It's hard to say. Communication was poor, and coordination nonexistent. Not enough to loosen the Guardians' grip on power, by any means. At best, we were a very minor annoyance. We spared them the trouble of killing a few of their prisoners, by sending them on those ridiculous treks to Africa. Moscow to Riga is a hell of a hike, and from there no easy trip to Casablanca; I doubt any of them made it there alive."

"Did you know that at the time?"

"Katya and I did, yes. We tried to let the others think that they were doing a little good, but it must have been obvious. A resistance can support the attack of an army, but there was no opposing army then; or it can mobilize the people, but not when the slightest uprising is instantly crushed. We would have needed to strike with ten thousand even to hold out long enough to gain new recruits; and yet for us it was a major undertaking to contact a band of dissidents thirty miles to the north. It was useless."

"Then why bother?"

For the first time, he would not meet my gaze as he spoke to me. "Because it made us feel a little better," he said at length. "We could not save even one innocent from the Guardians, not for long. But we could declare our opposition. We could go on record, however secret a record, saying that we did not condone the Square Miles—that we did not accept the subjugation of our people. And also, she said, we could be ready. She believed that one day something, she did not know what, would come to challenge the Guardians. She always had much more faith in that than I did. And of course she was proved right, though when the Unanimous Army finally came, it hardly needed a resistance to support it. Besides, by that time everyone in our group, except for me, was dead, and I was scrubbing bottles for Derzhavin."

"If Katya was so careful," I said, "how did you get caught?"

"Katya was a victim of her own success. It took her at most a week to study a person, understand him, and devise just the words, just the gestures, just the intonation, just the words on a leaflet, that would make him one of us. She never once failed that I knew of. And so, inevitably, she came to the end of her A list, and started on the second choices. Eventually she came to the one that brought us down."

"He reported you?"

"Oh, no. Quite the contrary, he was the most zealous of us all." He frowned down at his empty plate. "I remember that when she renamed him, as she did everyone, she did not give a reason, as she always had before. Afterward, when I asked her why, she said, 'I named him Piotr because he's as dumb as a rock, and if we don't look out, he'll sink us like a stone.' She knew from the beginning.

"Actually he was only a little bit stupid, but he was a lot naïve, and tremendously charismatic: a dangerous combination. After a month, every time Katya gave an order, everyone looked at Piotr to see what he would say. After two months, he was the leader in everything but name, and Katya was agonizing over whether she should challenge him directly. In the end, she decided to let democracy take its course. And three months after Piotr joined the group, he asked for formal leadership; received it; and as his first act, proposed that we burn Square-Mile-on-Volga."

"Did you resist him?"

"We argued with him, certainly. We asked what advantage there was in incinerating the prisoners we hoped to save. He said that we would free them first. We asked what would prevent the Guardians from hunting them down and killing them in the woods. He said we would hide them. We asked if he intended to conceal ten thousand refugees in his dorm room. He said there would be so many that some must get through, and that was better than they could hope for at Volga. We explained that, even if the plan succeeded, the resulting investigation would be so thorough that it would surely uncover us. He said that we had to decide whether we were an underground or a social club, and that we might as well go ahead and be discovered, if we were not going to make any difference.

"And then, as I kept arguing, Katya suddenly changed sides, and said she thought it could be done, if only she were allowed to plan it herself. Everyone agreed to this at once, and I was shouted down. After the meeting she told me she had supported Piotr because she knew he would win, and if she planned it herself, the damage might be minimized.

"I begged her to forget him, forget our group, go back to her family, let us self-destruct, and then start over. She would be safe;

no one would believe that the daughter of Harold Anderson was a dissident, no matter how many clues seemed to point toward it. But I knew before I said the words that she would not hear them. For almost two weeks no one saw her, not even me; and when she came back, she had made her plan."

# nine

## ALL THE KING'S HORSES

**K**atya had camped in the woods and watched the Square Mile through binoculars. The Square Miles, you understand, were franchises; the guards were brought in by the dozens, trained in a few days, and retained for an average of less than six months. It was a uniquely American approach to holocaust, a sort of McGulag. The guards were bored, unskilled, and lazy. Most of them were under eighteen, except for a few senior citizens hired under that Golden Guards program they used to run all those smug commercials about. The camp's security relied on quantity, not quality. Katya knew that if she looked closely enough, she would find some little hole she could thread her way into.

"It had taken her a week, but she'd found it. A farmer who lived near the camp came by, she said, every Wednesday and Saturday to pick up manure for his crops. He did it at night, and surreptitiously, and was always waved past the station without being searched; Katya thought he might be related to one of the guards. He drove an old truck with a small trailer which could hold two people, at a very tight squeeze. Further, as the manure did not smell human, she suspected it came from the stables, which would be up on the hill where the Guardians' homes were. If so, we could burn out the Guardians without endangering the barracks, and in the confusion we might get a few people out.

"It was not a plan I found convincing. There were too many loose ends, and no lists of contingencies. The plan for getting people out was vague and halfhearted, more a hope than a plan. I knew she didn't think we could succeed. But there were no objections. The only question was who should go.

"In the end, over Katya's protests, Piotr and one of his closest supporters were chosen. As Katya was walking out, Piotr laid his hand on her shoulder and said, 'An excellent plan, truly, Katya. You see, sometimes your input is very important!'

"It was too much for her. She turned to him and said, 'Do you know why I didn't want you to go? Why I didn't want to expose you to that danger?'

"He thought about it for a moment, nodded solemnly, and said, 'You don't think I should take the risk. Because I'm needed here.'

" 'No, you incredible idiot,' she said. 'Because I want you to live long enough to see the rest of us die because of your stupidity.' And she walked away, leaving him gaping in disbelief that there was someone on the planet who did not admire him.

" 'He'll get himself captured, give information, and we'll all be shot,' I said.

" 'No, he won't,' she said matter-of-factly. 'He won't get anywhere near that trailer. If he went on Wednesday, he wouldn't do any damage, because the farmer picks up his dung on Tuesday; and besides, he won't go, because on Tuesday I'm going to do it myself. Are you coming?'

"I was coming. At four A.M. the next Tuesday we arrived at the farm, wearing stolen Guardian uniforms, and carrying rifles, cans of kerosene, a flamethrower, and—strapped to our thighs—two flasks of eggshell-thin ceramic, made to curve around the skin so that a casual search might miss them. We forced the latch on the trailer and folded ourselves into four feet by five feet by three feet of corrugated aluminum: a coffin built for two. We would have to wait there the whole day; but it was safer than trying to break in during the daylight.

"The fellow hauled his manure in plastic bags, but the trailer still smelled. Our chips had no scent-suppression functions—that great consolation of modern life had not been invented yet—but after a while I did start to get used to it. In the year since we'd met, I had been too busy to think about anything but our work. Besides, we had seen each other for only an hour or so at a time, usually with others present. Now we were alone, hour after hour, pressed together in that tiny trailer bed. And as I began to smell the manure less, and her more, the warmth of her arm against mine began to wear away the control I'd maintained for the last two years, so slowly I barely knew what was happening.

"At last I turned my head toward Katya, not even sure yet what I meant to say or do. But she knew what I was thinking better than I did. 'The way I look at it,' she said, 'we have two choices. Assuming that we'll be in the remembering business past this evening, we can remember some awkward, unsatisfying groping in a trailer the size of a coffin, with the smell of shit in our nostrils and the chance of getting shot hanging over our heads, the main effect of which will be to make us feel embarrassed and frustrated for the last few hours of our lives. *Or* you can go on imagining the six children and the white house with the picket fence and the incredible sex and whatever the hell else it is that's kept you going these past two years. If it were me I'd go for the fence thing, but I'll leave it up to you.'

"And then, before I could reply, she raised her head, and said through the communicators we'd socketed: *Or we could have what's behind door number three.* A moment later I, too, heard the farmer's footsteps as he came up the walk to his truck.

"Luckily, he did not check the trailer. We felt the truck begin to move; we traveled in silence; then, all too soon, the truck stopped again. The farmer called to the guard, barely slowing, and we were pressed against the doors of the trailer as the truck started up the hill. It leveled, then stopped. The accordion creak of the parking brake; the car door; then the farmer's footsteps. A knife-blade of light cleft the trailer door.

"I was ready, and knocked him out with the butt of my rifle—not, I hoped, too hard. We put him back in the car and pushed it out of the sight of the guard towers. Then we went into the stables and slopped kerosene over everything that looked flammable. The horses were thoroughly spooked by this time, and when we released them they galloped away, alerting the guards. We heard a siren and saw floodlights through the window, but, to our relief, there were no shots. Soon we could hear people running and shouting all around us.

" 'Our life expectancy just doubled,' she said. 'From the towers, we'll just be another couple of idiots running around trying to catch the horses.' So we stood by the door, lit the straw with the flamethrower, and ran to watch from safety.

"The stables crackled, like the warning rattle of a snake, and seeped out smoke at every pore, and then at last put on a wreath of flame, like a woman tossing a red cape around her shoulders. And for all that I knew the futility of what we did, no other moment in my life has been as satisfying.

" 'Will it spread?' I asked her, as the cry of fire went out.

" 'I don't give a damn,' she said bitterly. She was immune to the destructive joy that had seduced me. 'Piotr wanted a fire, so there's his goddamn fire. Whether the Guardians have to rebuild their library or not is all the same to me. Let's get the generator and go find Piotr some roommates.'

"In the confusion, no one challenged us as we found and burned the generator. The searchlights went out all around the hill. We went down in darkness, to where the long narrow barracks lay side by side like rows of corn.

"One of the horses had found its way down the hill, and men in uniforms and nightshirts were trying to trap it in the narrow space between two barracks. It was an admirable plan, and might have worked, if only they could have agreed which aisle they meant to drive the poor thing into. Every time they thought they had him, he would find a way out, darting between two shoulders just in time.

"The prisoners, hearing the footsteps and hoofbeats and cries, must have thought the last extermination was upon them. A wailing would start in one barracks and be taken up at once by others, like an old song that everyone knows. Now and then an irritated Guardian would go along the rows, rapping a stick against the wood and then against the tin, to quiet the cries, but each time they only started up again. In such an uproar, no one would notice the two of us; but prisoners flowing from an open barracks would be seen at once.

"We stopped, pretending to gawk at the fire, as Katya checked the map on her drydisk. 'There,' she said at last, pointing up the row of barracks. 'It says *Terminal Isolation Cells.*'

" 'What's that?'

" 'Something bad enough that being shot in an escape would be an improvement. Let's go.'

"One guard had remained by the door of the square building, but she easily persuaded him that he was wanted in fire fighting. When he was gone, we shot the padlock off the door with a silenced pistol she had brought for just such purposes. Its sound surprised me: louder and more mechanical than the cat-sneeze sound effect you hear in the movies. I kept flinching, afraid of ricochets, so I had to keep shooting and shooting to hit the lock. But when I finally hit it, it flew to bits; it was a twenty-ruble padlock, nothing more. We were both surprised to find such token security; as I recall, she remarked that she'd seen bicycles better protected . . . until we opened the door, thrusting in our guns like policemen in a video.

"The smell of urine, feces, and decay was overwhelming. The building was packed solid with cubical cages, a metre on a side. They were piled three high, and filled the building wall to wall, so there was no corridor by which to reach the cages at the back. In each, a naked prisoner sat huddled, a food dispenser pressing into his arm. The muscles even of the ones in front were visibly atrophied, and in the cages at the back we could see corpses, rotting in the same position they had crouched in when alive.

"For a time we both stood mute. Then, feeling that something had to be done, I started toward the nearest cage. But Katya held me back. 'Pavel, we can't let those people go,' she said. 'They couldn't walk across the room, much less make it out of here. And it would take days to move the cages around to get to them all. Pavel, there's . . . is there nothing we can do?'

" 'Burn it,' said a voice from the cages. We jumped, whirling around to see who had spoken. The prisoners' condition was so bestial, we had not imagined them capable of speech. But one of them nodded his head, all the gesture that he could make, and said again, 'Burn it all.'

"I had the flamethrower. But I was paralyzed, imagining the fire creeping from cage to cage. It would move slowly; nothing but the men themselves was flammable among the tin and steel. Each one, unable even to cover his face, would watch his neighbor's long matted hair bloom yellow as he awaited his own turn.

"If Katya had turned to me, if Katya had given one of her sharp commanding nods, I would have done it. But she, even she, could not command such a horror.

" 'Then give it to me,' the man said, 'and I'll do what needs doing.'

"Silently, not even needing to look at each other, we agreed. He could do it. He knew.

"I put in a new clip and aimed the pistol at the simple cage lock from above. But I could not fire so close to the man's unprotected flesh, could not find an angle that did not risk a ricochet into arm or face or thigh.

"Finally Katya closed her hand over mine, and slipped her slender finger into the trigger guard, where mine, thick and clumsy, trembled against the steel. She squeezed once, firmly. The cage door burst open, and the man spilled out, uncurling. He should have been left to unfold on his own, as you give the hatched butterfly a chance to dry its wings; but there was no time. She helped him prop himself up against the side of the cage, and I put the flamethrower in his hands.

"Then we heard someone call out, in English, 'Isolation is open!' We heard running footsteps, and then a hand at the door.

"Without an instant's hesitation, Katya shot the man we had just freed. He fell to the floor never having fully stood, his limbs slowly drawing themselves back into the posture of the cage, as a scroll, let go, curls back into its native state.

"As the door opened, she called out in her unaccented English, 'We have shot the escapee! Hold your fire! We're coming out!'

"The guards still looked suspicious, but she overwhelmed their doubts with anger. 'Which one of you deserted this post? Well, I suggest you find whoever did and put him in that little hotel you're running—I've just opened up a vacancy. While you people were watching the fireworks, someone went in there and started arming the prisoners. And from what I've seen of your security, I think a cripple with a .45 could have limped right out of here under all your noses. Do any of you want to argue with that?'

"Her tenuous invention hung a moment in the air. It would be challenged, I was sure; this was the end. A guard opened his mouth—

"And reinforced the fragile structure. 'That's a flamethrower,' he said. 'You think that's the man that burned the stables?'

"Katya hesitated, tempted. But the idea was too ridiculous to hold up. She took a breath and blustered:

" 'No, I do *not* think a naked cripple made it up the hill, nor do I think he came all the way back here just so he could be discovered in the place he left. Are there any more stupid questions?'

"There were not. 'Good,' she said. 'Then get on the radio and tell anyone who hasn't already guessed that the light show you've been staring at was no accident. This Stonie didn't do it, but whoever armed him did. And when you've done that, call up Commander Sinclair for me and tell him I'm done playing soldier. Tell him the girl he used to read *Alice in Wonderland* to is ready to go home.'

"*I had to*, she said through our radio link as the guards stared. *They would have killed us and put him back in that thing. I didn't have any choice.*

"*I know*, I told her. *You didn't do a thing wrong. You don't have anything to feel guilty about.*

"*Yes, it was a most commendable murder*, she said. But I knew her: she would find a way to hold back grief until we were safely out. It was not in her to lose control.

"Five minutes later the camp commander, Katya's 'Uncle Eddie,' drove up with a worried look on his face. 'Kitty?' he said. 'It *is* you—what are you doing here?'

" 'Oh, Father wanted me to see the glorious workings of the Guardian cleansing machine or something like that. Honestly, to hear the man talk, you'd think the Square Miles were a dishwasher. All I've seen is a bunch of Zaks and Stonies, and some stupid guards who're too busy watching the fire to notice them escaping.'

" 'Why on earth didn't I know you were here?'

" 'I was supposed to be just like any other guard. He didn't want me to get the executive tour or be coddled. He wanted me to see what it's really like.' Her face lit up. 'And I sure did that, didn't I! I shot a prisoner! Father's going to be ever so proud!'

" 'He certainly will, Kitty, but right now we've got to get you out of here. It isn't safe.'

" 'But we haven't got a ride! We weren't supposed to leave for three more days. Can you take us?'

" 'I'll get a couple of the guards to take you.'

" 'Oh, God, you must be kidding. Those idiots? That prisoner couldn't even walk, and I still had to do him myself because those incompetents couldn't keep track of him. Honestly, I can't believe you'd leave me to them. Can't you take us yourself, Uncle Eddie?'

" 'Kitty, I have armed people loose in the camp—'

" 'Well, we'll just wait in your office till they're found, that's all. Come on, Eddie, you don't have to take us to our dorm, just as far as Father's house. It's only a few miles. Father'll be mad if you don't.' A spark of shrewdness lit her disingenuous eyes, and she whispered: 'We don't have to tell him about the break-in, you know.'

"Edward Sinclair, the commander of the third or fourth most efficient killing factory in the world, closed his eyes in amused irritation. 'All right, then. Get in. I never could say no to you.'

"*Can't say no to making a hero's entrance at the Heptarch's house, he means, the old hypocrite,* Katya said, starting toward the truck.

" 'Put your guns on the rack, kids,' he said, 'and be sure you unload them first. We don't want them going off if we hit a pothole.'

"Katya complied. We climbed into the enormous pickup truck, Sinclair giving her a hand up.

" 'Who's your friend?' he asked her as I climbed in numbly.

" 'Paul Wintermute. He's a ninth cousin or something. Don't make him talk to you, it's cruel—he's never seen anyone die before and he's trying really hard not to throw up.'

"I understood: if I spoke, my accent would give everything away. The Heptarch's daughter could not associate with a Russian.

" 'And be a love and don't tell anyone I'm here. Father made me promise.'

"We waited in his office for an hour, with a guard watching over us, until Sinclair returned to tell us that the intruders must have escaped.

"*He knows we've been here,* I said as we were waved past the guard station out onto the highway. *Sooner or later he'll tell someone who can put two and two together.*

"*No, he won't,* Katya said matter-of-factly, her eyes searching the cab of the truck. She looked down between our feet; found a red metal bar with a bifurcated tip that was lying on the floor. 'What's this?' she asked, picking it up.

" 'It goes on the steering wheel,' Sinclair said absently. 'I use it to keep the truck from being stolen if I have to go into town.'

" 'Good idea,' Katya said, nodding vigorously. 'Those Russians'll steal anything.' She idly laid the bar across her lap, resting one hand on it.

" 'What are those cells we saw for, Uncle Eddie?' she asked. 'Are they politicals?'

" 'They're the worst politicals, honey. The most dangerous.'

"She snorted. 'Not anymore they're not. The man I shot could barely stand.' She leaned against Sinclair and laid her head on his shoulder. 'I've *missed* you, Uncle Eddie. Remember when you used to come over every weekend, and talk to my father about all the funny things that happened at the camp? When I was little I wanted to be exactly like you.'

"He took his eyes off the road just long enough to glance at her with fondness. 'You *are* a lot like me and your father, Katya. You keep your head under pressure and you're not squeamish about things dying.'

"*You bet I'm not*, she thought grimly.

"*Katya, don't.*

"*Of course I will*, she said. *It's the only thing that makes sense. Piotr should have made me do this in the first place, if it weren't for his idiot chivalry.*

"*Please*, I said. *Let me do it. He's no one to me, just another Guardian. It won't hurt me the way it'll hurt you.*

"*You're right*, she said. *He's no one to you. That's why I'm the one that has to do it. He and my father talked genocide the way other men talk football. He taught me to admire every form of atrocity when I was still wearing drop-drawer pajamas. If you killed him he'd die like anybody. When I kill him he'll die as the monster he is. This is the man I was born to kill.*

*"Don't do this to yourself,* I pleaded. *You've got yourself so worked up you're not even thinking straight.*

" 'I wish I had a hundred like you at the Square Mile, Katya. You'd make a great camp commander, in fact; it's a pity you're not a man.'

" 'Now, Uncle Eddie,' she chided him, brushing the hair from his brow, 'can you really wish such a thing?'

"He laughed. 'Well, I can, old fogy that I am, but I imagine the young men at MGU would put up quite a protest.' He looked at her again, mist in his eyes. 'You've grown into a fine woman, Kitty.'

" 'Oh, Uncle Eddie,' she said, kissing him on the cheek, 'you always know just what to say.'

"In my head she shrieked: *I WILL kill him!*

" 'Please, Katya!' I said. Only when he looked at me did I realize I had spoken aloud.

" 'You're Russian? But—'

"And before he could work out the implications, Katya grabbed the bar of steel on her lap, and thrust the forked end into his face. His head was driven back into the side window, through the glass, which cut the arteries of his neck. When I reached across her to grab the steering wheel and slid over to hit the brake, the inside of the truck was already covered with blood. By the time we pinballed to a stop, my left leg was on his lap and my right on hers, and both of them were perfectly still.

" 'He made me kill that man,' she said. 'He murdered thousands—and he drank tea with my stuffed animals—and he made me kill that man.'

" 'It's all right, it's all right, it's all right,' I said, trying to embrace her. I might as well have been hugging Uncle Eddie. Of course it was not all right. From Square-Mile-on-Martha's-Vineyard to Square-Mile-at-Kamiyaku, and from my mind to hers, as far apart as those two islands, nothing was in the least all right. And it is my shame that when I should have been trying to comfort her, my thoughts were of myself. I kept trying to figure out just when

I had stopped being a child, playing a game with secret names and passwords.

"At last she said, 'Let's take care of the body.' I realized that I was still clutching her, so hard it must have hurt. I let her go: and that was the only time that we ever embraced.

"As the days passed, her shock faded into a seraphic calm that, in her, was profoundly unwholesome. When they came to arrest us, her only comment was, 'It's about time, loves.'

" 'Tell them the truth, Katya,' I said. 'I'm the dissident, she's innocent—my God, this is the Heptarch's daughter!'

" 'Don't tell lies, Pavel," Katya said in a false Russian accent that only a Guardian could have believed. 'They'd only find it out, and it would go worse for us in the end. I am Katya Andropova, no relation to the Heptarch. Let's get it over with."

"Then we were at Square-Mile-on-Volga, in a holding area thrown together out of barbed wire, along with thousands of others. They didn't know it was we who had raided the camp; they were just rounding up every dissident they could track down, on the slightest rumor. We would stay in the enclosure for a time, and then when the camp had recovered from the fire, we would be processed.

" 'Maybe some of us will be let go—maybe *you*,' I said. 'Look at all these people. There's not room to keep more than a few.'

" 'You see that column of black smoke, from behind the hill?' Katya said quietly.

" 'Yes,' I said, craning my neck. 'What is it?'

" 'Room.'

"On the evening of that day, our first, Piotr arrived, and rounded up enough of our tribe to get a good groupthink going. Piotr had read Gandhi, and understood him about as well as Piotr ever understood anything, so he thought it would be a capital idea to try out some passive resistance on the Guardians. He suggested that as a start they refuse to eat their dinner, as a token of resistance, and also because it was likely to contain meat. Now, Katya had not managed to make all of our group into vegetarians; but even those that weren't cheerily acceded. A principle not important enough to eat cabbage for had become important enough to die for, just because it might irritate the fellows with the guns. I tried to tell them that passive resistance was only useful when you had reason to suspect your enemy possessed a conscience. I described the terminal isolation cells, and asked them whether they thought that men who could do such a thing would be swayed by children who didn't want to eat their food. It didn't help. I appealed to Katya, but she only said, 'Let them do what makes them feel better; it's all the same in the end.'

"When dinner came—a ladleful of thin soup in a tin bowl, as we squatted in the dust—the guards noticed that Piotr and his followers were not eating. They found this singularly funny. 'It looks nasty now,' one said, 'but a week from now you'd eat it if I pissed in it.'

"Piotr stood up and gave his little speech; the guards roared. 'I tell you what,' one of them said. 'You're going to eat your soup, and if one of you leaves one drop we'll shoot you down to the last man.' Rifles were leveled. Piotr's little band of Gandhis still refused. Here and there a knee was trembling, but their jaws were set. They were magnificent, as a bull charging a wall is magnificent; I had to admire their courage, even as I regretted their stupidity.

"Then a miracle happened. The Guardians put down their guns and looked at each other sheepishly. Then they started frisking Piotr and his people, taking all their personal effects and spare change. Passive resistance had made killers into pickpockets.

" 'It worked,' I said in amazement. 'They won.'

" 'No, they didn't,' Katya said gently. 'They did something unexpected, and Guardians can't handle the unexpected. But they'll find some way to pump up their courage, and then finish what they started. Piotr's people will be dead soon, and the sooner, the better for them. Eat your soup now, Pavel, before they come for us too.'

"If she had not commanded it, I don't think I could have managed. It seems so ridiculous now; the animals were already dead, and besides, we had killed men, and besides, the Guardians weren't likely to waste meat on the likes of us. If that slop had a connection to any bleeding thing, it was only some microscopic globule of anonymous hydrocarbons. But at the time, it was as though I dismembered the deer with my own hands, and sank my teeth into its throat. Because it was then that I knew I was a traitor to the bone. I would betray everything I believed in, simply to survive another day. It was the great lesson of the camps, and I was fortunate to learn it so soon. That saved me trouble in the end.

"Then, a disaster. One of the guards who had been frisking prisoners for nickels and kopeks came over to us. 'You, too, sister,' he said. 'Stand up.' And he put his hands on her.

" 'Is this the only way you can get a girl to look at you, poor thing?' she said.

"He ignored her, but blood rose into his cheeks. He found the flask strapped to her thigh, reached into her pants to take it out—I could have cut off that hand without regret—opened it and sniffed it. A smile curled his features. 'You'll need it where you're going,' he said. 'Too bad it's not allowed.' And he poured the flask out in front of her and crushed it under his heel. Then he moved on to me.

"We exchanged looks of panic as his hands touched my shoulders. In desperation she burst out: 'Now do you like the boys better, Johnny, or is it just because the girls all laugh at you?'

"He hit her across the face with his closed fist. Then, his anger still building, he took out his pistol, held it to her forehead, and cocked it. She stared back at him unafraid.

"At last his face twisted into a smile again, and he drew the gun away. 'Live then,' he said. 'It's so much worse.' And he walked away laughing. Katya was bruised, bleeding—but all was not lost. I still had my flask.

"'Guardians! They're not even a challenge,' she said lightly, touching the bruise on her face. 'Their petty fears, as like as peas. Don't worry, Pavel, we can share the one.'

"'But whoever does it first might drop the flask.'

"'Well then, one of us will have to do the other.'

"I looked at her and thought of what I would have to do. 'Katya, I can't,' I said. 'I'm sorry. I should be able to. But I can't hurt you.'

"She snorted. 'I didn't mean you, silly. Give me the flask, I'll hold it.'

"And as I handed over the flask I was wearing, every thought I had ever had about what might have been with her, every daydream of house and children and every furtive nocturnal imagining—all that she had labeled 'the fence thing'—folded into nothingness. If she had felt for me what I felt for her, she could never have said that so calmly. It was necessary, there was no question of that. They could have tapped into our sockets and found out everything we knew, which might put dozens of people in Square Miles who would otherwise be free. Even killing ourselves might not help; it was rumored that the Guardians could suck the thoughts from a brain three hours dead. And if we were taken alive, we could be made puppets of the Guardians—so rumor said—our wills extinguished by the sockets, or perhaps remaining, watching what they made us do. We had to do it. But I could not do it to her; and she could to me. She did not love me. If she had ever loved anyone it was, perhaps, the man whose head she had beaten in with a steel bar.

"'Go ahead and do it now,' I said. 'I'm ready.'

"'Are you sure?' she asked.

"'Yes.'

"We uncapped our sockets. The night before we raided the camp, we had carefully dissected them, taken out the linings, and broken the water-locks, in preparation.

" 'I wish I had never met you,' she said, 'so it wouldn't have come to this. I care for you a great deal, Pavel.'

" 'Katya, I love you.'

" 'I'm sorry, Pavel,' she said gently, tears threatening in her eyes. And that was an honor, I realized: she had strung along our band of dissidents with a series of convenient fictions, but now, even now, she would be honest with me.

"She uncorked the flask and carefully poured a little of the clear, sweet water from it into the socket in my head. For a fraction of an instant after that I could still see her, tipping her own head to receive the water, and drawing the flask toward it; and a guard shouting and lunging; but I could not tell who would be the quicker. And after that, for a long time, I remember nothing more."

# ten

## MY MAN SUNDAY

**V**oskresenye looked down at his plate, hoping, I supposed, that there would be something left to give him an excuse for pause. The white china was clean. He looked up and tried to catch the waiter's eye, to no avail. His right hand made strange clockwork-spider movements that I supposed were his version of fidgeting. The awkwardness, more than anything else, persuaded me that some part of his story was authentic—that's how people act when they realize they've revealed more than they wanted to. Even so, his story was more smoothly chronological than it had any right to be. I found myself wondering how long he'd rehearsed it, how much he'd embellished it, how much of it was true.

Voskresenye stared wearily at the waiter's receding back. "Do you know what was on the waiter's tombstone?" he asked.

"What?"

" 'By and by, God caught his eye.' "

I smiled politely. "What happened to her?" I asked, as gently as I could.

His hand grew still. "I have never known. I can only hope that, because she was more deeply wired than I, she died quickly. But there are no records—if there ever were any, the Army destroyed them.

Certainly she did not survive the camps; after the war, I searched most thoroughly. But I will never know exactly how she died."

"And you?"

He touched his forehead with his fingertips. "The shock traveled down along the wires and into the implants, burning away the very functions that my wiring had enhanced. It damaged my language centers: Broca's area, Wernicke's area, angular gyrus. It scorched my visual cortex. It nearly severed my corpus callosum. But worst of all, I lost the ability to form memory traces. So for the next three years, the last thing that had happened was the moment when Katya Andersohna poured her flask of water into my head."

"What was it like? That time?"

He closed his eyes, and said at last: "You set me a pretty problem. How can I remember what it is like not to remember? If I think I recall sensations—falling through the dark, and reaching out, again and again, and brushing a handhold but not quite being able to grasp it—how shall I trust the memory? All I can tell you for sure is that when I began to wake, I was like a man who has been walking across ice for so long that he does not trust the ground to hold him. When I turned my attention away from a thing, I was surprised that it persisted in my mind. And gradually I realized who I was, and where I was. I was Voskresenye—that was the name he had given me; and I was playing chess with Aleksandr Derzhavin."

"Oh, I see. Not Voskresenye, Voskreseni*ye*. He named you 'Resurrection.' "

Voskresenye shook his head. "No. He named me 'Sunday.' He identified his subjects by the dates on which they came to his laboratory. Those of us he spent the most time with soon acquired some shortening of our dates as a nickname: Voskresenye, Fevral, Aprel, Chetverg." Voskresenye's eyes grew thoughtful. "Whether he saw the pun available to him by changing a soft sign into an 'i,' whether that pun did not lead to his choosing me—that is something I have wondered for a long time. If he did know, then all my calculations with respect to him were based on a false premise. But those calculations proved right, many times, so I don't think he did know; although, in his own way, he was not humorless."

"You said you woke *already* playing chess with him—you were doing this while still brain-damaged?"

"I was imprecise. Behold the dangers of Russian, which forces me to say 'I played chess,' when what I mean is more complex. We should be having this discussion in Sapir, whose verb forms are less dogmatic. In Russian, only barbarisms—'I was played at chess,' 'chess was played through me.' Until that moment of awakening I was merely an eccentric interface for Derzhavin's . . . well, say computer, for now; that was what he always called it. When I first became aware of my surroundings, I realized that my hands had been moving the pieces for some time. Yet I could not understand the moves I was making, or even tell who was ahead. I barely knew the rules of chess; to me it was just a quaint pastime of strange old men at tables in cafés."

He put his palms down on the table, thumbs in, as if marking off the corners of a chessboard: so that pepper, salt, and sugar became dark king and white queen and pawn, locked into their final and fatal embrace. I blinked slowly to show that I understood, but declined to belabor the joke.

"Then," he said, "I began to notice a voice in my ear that was whispering symbols, so fast I couldn't follow them. I listened closely, and the voice slowed down. My heartbeat slowed, too—or rather, as I realized later, my thoughts were becoming faster, so that everything else seemed slow. When I listened to the voice again I understood it: it was listing moves, devising strategies, anticipating responses. I looked at the board and it burst into life, the pieces seething and roiling, like bubbles in a boiling pot. They moved faster and faster; the patterns of black and white merged into an incoherent gray, like static on a TV screen. Then something drove itself into the center of my brain, splitting me into halves. Suddenly the board was still, and all possible chains of moves existed simultaneously. I looked up at Derzhavin. From him too I could see sequences of actions branching forth, and in his head, patterns of possible thought looped and twisted—trails of light. 'Well,' he said, 'welcome to the world, Voskresenye.' I knew the words before he spoke them.

" 'Do you want to finish the game?' he asked. 'Or would you rather have a tour of the laboratory?'

"I looked down at the board again. Its futures were already charted, and all were variations on a theme; they held no interest. The rooms around me branched out in a bramble of unlikelihoods that tempted me much more. And just beyond the door behind me, a shadow blanketed the light: a secret, something important that I did not know. I grasped the first thread that led into it. I tried to stand.

" 'No, please, don't!' he said, putting his hand on my shoulder. I had foreseen that reaction, but I knew this line of play would bring the shadow into view. 'Look at your hands.' I did, and saw them as they are now, half-mechanical. But I had known that already. He was trying to see whether I could access memories from before my awakening. I kept my face carefully blank, to frustrate his deductions.

" 'I didn't expect you to wake so soon,' Derzhavin explained, 'so I haven't done your legs yet. It will be my next task, I assure you. But for now, I'll have to wheel you in the chair. What do you want to see first?'

" 'Show me the other half of myself,' I said, and then, although he could not understand, I added, 'I think that's the shadow.'

"He turned the chair around, and we followed the cables that trailed from my head and spine into a long corridor. There were cages on either side. As we passed—slowly, since the chair was heavy—I looked at the people huddled fearfully in the cells, or lying on their cots as if dead. Derzhavin made no explanation; he seemed unaware of the effect their presence had on me. Instead he spent the time apologizing to me for the cable, explaining that he intended to replace this crude umbilical cord with radio transmissions once, as he put it, 'the system was debugged.'

"As we approached the door to the next room, he chattered on with the hearty incomprehensibility of an auto mechanic, explaining how he had rebuilt my ruined mind. It was a simple idea, he said, and one he'd used before, though never (here he laughed) on such a scale. Really, you would almost think that Nature had intended it. The corpus callosum, the anterior commissure—why, they're no more than a pair of cables; they link the right and left halves of the brain, just as you might link one computer to another. And they're cables wide enough to merge two lobes into one self, so that if you could not dissect, you would not guess the halves were separate. And if you had a cable, well, why not a cable splitter? Could you not set up a cloverleaf among, not two, but *four* lobes? Would they not then be as intimate with each other as the two hemispheres of the brain are? Would they not merge into a single self?

"He was still talking as we passed through the doorway, and his voice droned on, uncomprehended, as I saw what we had come to. It was an enormous tank, brackish, encrusted with barnacles, and full of floating stems of cable cased in plastic. Then I caught a glimpse of the 'computer' that was now part of myself, and I no longer saw or heard him. The thing that lay suspended in that tank would not let even light escape from it, and no voice could outshout its rasping breaths."

I had been lulled by the scansion; now I snapped awake. "Wait a minute. Breaths? What are you saying—it was biological?"

He hesitated, then said in a sudden burst of nervous energy: "It was not 'biological,' it was alive; indeed, it is still alive; 'it' is a she; and "*she*—" he paused, took a breath, grew calmer "—is a whale."

"I see." I leaned back in my chair, my wrist sockets clicking against the table. I never asked for this. All I ever wanted was a nice column in a print newspaper, a thousand words a week and a flattering mug shot, in which I could foist my every cockamamie opinion on a groggy audience for whom it was me or the cereal box. When *Novaya Pravda* folded I should have given up and gone into something less invasive and degrading, like, say, prostitution. But no, I had to retrain for an exciting career in the growing field of telepresence. Same job, new medium, I figured, but it's not. In print news, your job is to know things about others; you peer out at the world through an arrow slit. In telepresence you *are known*. If I'd still been writing for a newspaper—if there still were newspapers—I could have forgotten Pavel Voskresenye and gone on. In telepresence the whole episode would be implicit in my broadcast, my gullibility stretched out for every imbecile to poke. I could only hope Keishi would manage to screen it all out.

Maybe, I thought, this would be the time that I'd finally quit. The doctors could fill my sockets in with something that wouldn't be flesh, but would look a little like it, and I could emigrate to North America and never see anything more technologically advanced than a pitchfork. Except, of course (I had almost forgotten) that I was about to be arrested just for talking to this man. Maybe if I resisted arrest just right I could get myself shot.

"Hey, sorry, I was playing with the mix instead of listening," Keishi said. "Are we having a low blood sugar moment or something?"

*Actually*, I subvoked, watching Voskresenye flag down the waiter for tea, *with you here there's one tiny redeeming feature to this mess. Let this be a lesson to you if you ever become a camera. This sort of thing can happen to you when you least expect it. Always be ready for it, 'cause I wasn't, and I'm going to look like a real idiot.*

"Wow, I guess I did miss something. Should I get it from your memories or do you want to tell me?"

*It goes by different names*, I said. *We usually call it "being conned."*

"Yeah? You think the old guy's lying?"

*Are you kidding, Keishi? A whale is as big as a—well, as a whale. They're the* metaphor *for big. You can't put a whale in a tank. It's like claiming you slipcovered Leningrad. Especially if you're a fugitive from the Postcops. How exactly do you take a whale on the lam, shove it in a briefcase and drag it past the metal detector? Not to mention the question of how Derzhavin got a whale in the first place. Remember that vid a few years back where they find a whale frozen in an iceberg, and they thaw it out and clone it and repopulate the oceans? Don't you think that was a little improbable? And Voskresenye claims that a whale has survived all this time, not in the Antarctic ice, but in his* basement. *Yeah, I'd say I'm a little skeptical. Fair warning, Keishi: don't count on getting any sleep the rest of this week. We're going to be scrambling to finish this story without him.*

"Maya, don't you think you should at least give him a chance? He's obviously been modified by the Guardians in some way. That carapace is pretty convincing."

*He may not be lying about that part, but with the whale there's just no way. —Wait. If he's lying about the whale, why should I think he wasn't lying about everything else? My God.* I laughed with relief. *"Stand a little to the left, please; spy satellites, you know." I can't believe I bought it. No, this is definitely a scam. Ten to one we find out he wrote that police report himself. All of which means that I'm not drinking tea after all.*

"You're jumping to conclusions," she said sternly.

*Look, Mirabara, I've been a camera for about as long as you've been multicellular, and every instant of that experience tells me that this man is not for real. I'm going to try to find out why he's doing this. Meanwhile, you put together some contingency plans, OK? See if you can find me another interview.*

"All right, but I still say—no, never mind, I'm going."

Since I no longer had to worry how any of this looked on disk, I might as well satisfy my hunger. I took a bite of sandwich and said with my mouth full, "So, what kind of whale is it exactly?"

Voskresenye looked up from his teacup, which he had been staring into as if trying to read a message in the leaves. "Oh, come now, Andreyeva. Don't humor me. Ask what you really want to ask."

"All right, then. Instead of pouring water in your socket, why didn't you just signal the mother ship to pick you up?"

He rubbed the bridge of his nose exhaustedly. "This bubble shows signs of degrading, and I can only go so long without recharging my exoskeleton, so I have no time for games. This will demonstrate the truth of what I say." He set a vial of red fluid on the table.

"What's that?"

"A blood sample."

"Yours?"

"No. The whale's."

"Yeah. Whatever. Listen, you wouldn't happen to have an overwhelming desire to tell me why you're doing this, would—will you stop that?" He was chorusing every word I said, with no perceptible delay. "You don't really think you can make me believe you with a parlor trick, do you?"

"Of course not; I would not so insult your intelligence. Good day, Andreyeva." He stood abruptly and began to leave. Then, just before he reached the sidewalk, he turned and said pensively, "Consider this, however. If it *is* true . . . well, it's the story of the year, isn't it? To let someone else get it would indeed be a shame." He shrugged slightly and vanished into the crowd.

I paid the bill and started to leave.

"You forgot the blood," Keishi said.

*What's the point? It's not whale. There's no point checking. It's just not.*

"Maybe not. But if you had it analyzed, you might be able to figure out what Voskresenye's game is."

*I don't think we're going to have time to worry about that,* I said.

But then again, you can't just leave blood lying around on tables. You might frighten people. So, hating myself for doing it, I picked up the vial. I put it in my pocket and tried to forget it, but it pressed against my leg, a cold accusatory finger, all the way from the Horseman home.

# eleven

## A Property of Easiness

This, of course, you can see on your moistdisk, but you will find strange gaps, and paths of memory that lead to nothing—remnants of an erasure Keishi never finished. I would rather complete the job she started, but if the story must be known—and it is known—then it is better it be known fully.

I was sitting in the kitchen, with moistdisks strewn across the pitted tabletop and lengths of cable hanging from the backs of empty chairs. I had split my field of vision into quadrants, and was trying to splice together a conclusion to my series on the Guardians. I was hoping to give them a prefabricated segment, already in the can. It would mean a fight; News One hates it when you don't go live. But they'd never wanted to do this series anyway, so maybe they'd let me get away with it this once.

When the phone rang, I switched off my fourfold vision. I hate those first few moments coming out of a sightsplit, when your head feels like it's breaking up and you develop a deep sympathy for honeybees. Blinking heavily, I stared up at the ceiling and walked to the vidphone by memory. When the walls finally started to look real to me again, I touched the plate.

"Hey, Maya? It's Terentev. Forensics."

"Even if I hadn't recognized your face," I said, still blinking, "I think the bodies in the background might have tipped me off."

"Oh, yeah. Sorry." As he fiddled with the controls on his phone to hide the tableau of the dissecting room, I caught a glimpse of a bone-white face being wheeled past.

"My God—how long's that one been dead?"

He looked around, then laughed. "Oh, him? I don't know, maybe twenty minutes." Terentev dabbed at imaginary make-up on his flat Asiatic cheekbone. "It's face paint. He's a mime."

"Trying to find out who the medal goes to?"

The creases of laughter around his eyes disappeared into seriousness. "You know, Andreyeva, you're colder than anything I've seen wheeled in here."

"It was just a joke," I said. "You don't have to take everything so literally."

He kept his eyes on mine a moment, then averted them and shrugged. "Yeah, whatever."

"So what do you have for me?"

"Oh, your paternity suit?" His face was jovial again. "Unless the kid has scales, you'd better settle."

"It's a fish?"

"It's a dolphin."

Well, that made sense. Dolphin blood would not be hard to find, and Voskresenye might have hoped that it would pass a cursory inspection. A simple hoax. I would have preferred to know why, but for the moment, I'd just have to set aside my curiosity.

"Okay, Terentev. Like I said before, I owe you one."

"What's your rush, Andreyeva? Don't you even want to know what kind of dolphin?"

"Not really," I said.

"Good. Because we can't tell."

"Why not?"

"Doesn't match up with anything. It's in the general neighborhood, but we can't quite pin down the address."

"Oh, my God."

"Hey, it's not that big a deal. It's probably some microspecies that got stranded in a river somewhere. Nothing to write home about, unless you're a marine biologist. What is this, anyway? New gig for you, Andreyeva? 'Maya on biotech'?"

"Can you check it against whale DNA?"

"What did you say?"

I realized I'd whispered. "Can you check it against whale DNA?" I repeated.

He lifted his eyebrows. "Whale?"

"Just humor me, all right?"

"Well . . . " His eyes unfocused as he consulted the Net. "There were a few sequences mapped before they went extinct. I can give it a try. It would help if I knew what I was trying to prove, though."

"Ask me afterward."

He frowned. "What does this have to do with that Calinshchina thing of yours? Or did News One pull the plug on that? After all, it's not their sort of thing—"

"Just run it," I said. "Then if I'm right, I'll tell you."

He frowned. "OK, if that's the way you want it. This'll take a while."

"I'm not going anywhere," I said.

He signed off. I stood by the phone for a while, drumming my fingers against the coffee table. Then I went back into the kitchen and swept all the moistdisks into the recycling bin. When the phone chimed I ran for it.

"Tell me," I said.

"You know, my granddaughter carries a stuffed whale everywhere she goes? When I was a kid it was horses, before that it was tigers, dinosaurs come around again every twenty years—she's got a whale. She's got whale T-shirts, whale pajamas, a whole goddamn whale ensemble. This is way beyond owing me a favor. This is going to *cost.*"

"Red? Green?"

"Not even close."

"All right, Terentev, you can use my dacha. But if there's one stain on the carpet, they'll be centrifuging *you.*"

"This is bigger than that. You may have to *give* me your dacha."

I inclined my head and watched him silently. There was not a trace of laughter in his face; and Terentev was not a good liar.

"How about a spot as an expert witness in the story of the year?"

He nodded solemnly. "That, Maya Tatyanichna, will do just fine."

*Keishi!* I called out, through the Net. *I need you online* now.

"Hang on, I'm crossing the street," she said. "Is this urgent enough for me to just sit on the curb?"

*This is urgent enough for you to sit on*—but no; this was all on the record—*anything that comes to hand.*

"If you say so," she said dubiously. "But if I get socket-jacked, I'm holding you responsible."

A familiar warmth announced her presence. "Dr. Terentev," I said, "the other day, I gave you a blood sample to analyze. Could you tell me what kind of animal it belongs to?"

"A humpback whale," he said, then added nervously, "genus *Megaptera.*"

Just what the audience really wants, a scientific name. Why do people turn into boring encyclopedias the minute you light your Net-rune?

"How big would this animal be?"

He hesitated—asking the Net, probably. "About fifteen meters when full grown."

"And that would be about the size of . . ." I prompted.

"Oh. Umm, a small yacht."

"Or for those of our viewers who don't own yachts, about the size of two bullet train cars placed end-to-end."

He nodded nervously. "Yes, that'd be about right."

"When did humpbacks become extinct?"

His eyes unfocused, and long seconds passed before he had his answer. You try to take a stand against passing off Netlinked actors as "experts," you spend years cultivating contacts, and then your real experts consult the Net anyway—except when they do it, it's obvious. "They were one of the last to go," he said, finally. "There were a few around as late as Guardian times."

"And how long will blood keep in the fridge, before it rots?"

Now he was back in home territory. He said confidently, "About eight weeks. Nine at the outside. That is, in this condition. You can keep it usable indefinitely if you've got the equipment, but not like this. Those cells are *frisky.*"

"When I gave them to you, they'd been unrefrigerated for at least a day. Does that narrow it down?"

"In that case, I'd say it's fresh. A couple of weeks, maybe less."

I frowned, to simulate a skepticism I no longer felt. "Not that I doubt your expertise, Dr. Terentev, but this is a little hard to accept. Is there any chance it could be a hoax? Could you fake it with nanoconstruction?"

"No way," he said emphatically. "You'd never get all the bug byproducts out of the blood without killing the cells."

"So somewhere in the world is a live humpback whale."

"Live or very recently dead, yes."

"Well, I'm sure everyone who saw *The Day of the Whale* has the same question: could you clone more whales from this?"

He shook his head. "No. Not from blood. Blood doesn't have that much DNA, and what there is, is all jumbled up. It'd be like trying to put together a book that had been cut up into single words."

"But if you had a tissue sample? If you had a live whale?"

He nodded thoughtfully. "I'm not a marine biologist, but I'd say it's possible in theory. It would take a lot of trial and error to get the fetus to grow in vitro, but given enough time, it could probably be done. And if the whale were female, certainly."

"Thank you, Vladimir Terentev."

He smiled. "Always a pleasure, Maya."

"Hypocrite," Keishi said as I signed off.

*At least he didn't say hi to his mother. How soon can you be here?*

"How soon is this?"

I turned around to face her. "I meant in person."

"My person is in Moscow. While you were putting together a backup story, I've been trying to figure out where you could hide a whale."

If she had been corporeal, I would have clapped her on the shoulder. "Always the true believer. What did you find out while I was wasting my time?"

She frowned. "I mostly wasted my time, too. Voskresenye had his signals bounced through here, but it was apparently just a false trail. My best guess is that the whale might be somewhere in Arkhangelsk."

"Where he was imprisoned."

"Exactly."

I nodded. "Are you still sitting on the curb?"

"I'm in a cab on the way to the trainport."

"Okay, go to full-link. I'm going to call Voskresenye."

Keishi disappeared as I turned to the videophone. "Pavel of null hearth, clan Darkness-at-Noon." The phone chirked and purred for long seconds. Then Voskresenye's face appeared, in an unusually tight close-up, as though to hide the background. "Well," he said, "Maya Tatyanichna. What a pleasant surprise. So glad to have a chance to say good-bye before the mother ship takes me back."

"When can I see the whale?"

He smiled at my haste. "Arkhangelsk. Five o'clock tomorrow."

"That's not my time slot," I said.

"Maya Tatyanichna, you have the last whale in the world. They will give you any time slot you want."

I gave him a calculating look. "How secure is this line?"

He touched something on his videophone. "I will vouch for it against a Weaver."

"All right, then. If I tell News One about the whale, they'll take this story away from me so fast I'll get friction burns on my camera chip. Now if you want to sit across from a smooth-head, that's your option, but—"

"Oh, no, Maya Tatyanichna!" he said with ardor. "No other camera in the world will suit so well."

"Well, then. Let me come up with something to tell News One, and we'll do it in my usual time slot."

"Your time slot is far too obscure," he said. "Tell News One whatever you like; but it must be at five."

"I can't just commandeer prime time. If I called in favors I might get it, but slots between five and six are only ninety seconds long. Is that enough for you?"

"Ninety seconds?" he said. "Why so much? Ask them for ten, if it's easier. When you show them the whale, do you think they will cut you off?"

"No," I said, nodding slowly, "I guess they won't at that." I had been thinking much too small. "Where do I go?"

"If you come to Arkhangelsk alone, at the proper time you will be guided to the whale. If anyone else comes with you, you will never find me."

"My screener—"

"Of course," he said. "Naturally your screener may accompany you."

"Can I meet you, at, say, four o'clock? I'll need to set up shots, and plan what we're going to cover. And since I won't have time to run the whole story about you and the Guardians, I'd like to have you finish it in advance, so we can put it in as memory."

"I am afraid that I cannot allow that," he said. "You may be followed. I accept it as inevitable that my sanctuary will be found after your Netcast is finished, but I will not have them barging in while we are still on the air."

"You expect them to find the whale? To take possession of her?"

"I expect—" he briefly studied a point just below the screen, then raised his eyes again "—that I will no longer be able to keep her where she is now."

"I understand your protectiveness, but what would it hurt for you to provide a tissue sample? Think of the importance of—"

"Contrary to what the producers of vids believe, Maya Tatyanichna," he interrupted, "you cannot just dump a cloned calf in the middle of the ocean and expect her to repopulate her kind. Whales in the wild had millennia of accumulated knowledge that is now irrevocably lost. Without a parent to protect and guide her, a cloned whale would starve, freeze, or drown in a matter of days."

"Could your whale—"

"She could not," he snapped, "and even if she could, I would not allow it. Hundreds of whales would die in this ridiculous experiment, and even if some lived, if they eventually flourished, what do you think would happen? Amusement parks would capture them, ships of tourists harass them; perfumers would discover a need for ambergris; jaded executives would pay thousands to slot up Queequeg on adventure vacations. . . . No, Maya Tatyanichna. There will be no whales."

"But we need them," I said.

"We *need* them? Is that the best reason you can come up with?" He laughed, a rasping, mechanical sound. "The kings of the ocean are gone, and what is our argument for their return? *We* need them? *We?* Their murderers? The ones that made the water bitter in their mouths, and killed the food they ate? The ones that made the ocean boil red with their blood for miles around? *Men* need them? Those vermin? Those stinging insects? Struggling pustulent humanity—*needs* them? Do you think a whale cares?

You might as well *need* the sun to rise at midnight because you're feeling a bit chilly. Yes, of course, certainly we need them. But the question is, do we deserve them?"

Silence. Then I heard the whirring as he moved his hand toward the vidphone's control panel. He paused and said: "Be in Arkhangelsk."

"I will."

CONNECTION BROKEN, said the phone.

"Well," I said. "He can be goaded."

"I charge you to use this power only for good," Keishi said solemnly.

"Just when I thought you were starting to understand this business. Mirabara, park your body on a train to Arkhangelsk and get your bandwidth over here. We've got work to do."

# twelve

## IMMEDIATE TOUCH

**S**he materialized again. "Already bought the ticket. What do you need?"

"I won't say I need anything. I seem to get attacked when I use that word. What I *want* is to know everything there is to know about whales by noon tomorrow. Biology, history, poetry, folklore, you name it."

"Is that all?"

"No. I also want every scrap of information you can dig up on Voskresenye. Go over the interview with a fine-toothed comb and do a search on every word he used, apart from 'and' and 'if.' Anything you can dig up on Derzhavin, on the Andersons, especially on Catharine Anderson—I know most of it's probably on the chip you gave me, but I need to be sure."

"Sounds like a long night. Should I order in pasta or something?"

"I'm sick and tired of *makarony*," I said. "What are you in the mood for—dim sum or Ethiopian?"

She shrugged. "Up to you. I'll be eating train food, remember?"

"Oh, right," I said sheepishly. "In that case, which of those two will make you the least envious if I eat it in front of you?"

She smiled. "I've never been much for African food. Ironically."

"Ironically," I echoed. "Ethiopian it is." I was about to touch the videophone when she said, "Let me do it." I shrugged assent; her eyes unfocused for a second. "Done."

"That fast? OK, let's start with—"

The doorbell rang. My house, unlike my car, does not have weapons hidden in its every crevice, so my first thought was of kitchen knives and cast-iron skillets; my second, of escape routes.

"Don't panic," Keishi said. "It's just your food."

I went to the door and looked through the peephole, cringing a little as I did. It was rumored that the Weavers would use infrared to watch you approach the door, and then, as you squinted to see who it was, fire a bullet through the glass into your eye. The fear was irrational, I knew; they usually gave the Postcops a chance at you first, and the Postcops would consider such a tactic impolite. But the thought made me uncomfortably aware of the shape of my eyes in my head, and their softness. Somehow you think of eyes as being as shallow as almonds, but of course they're not; they go back deep, and press against the brain's gray labyrinths. The feeling persisted as I opened the door on the bored and impatient delivery boy, and made me reluctant to allow his retinal scan.

"I can't give you your food without a scan, *tavarishcha*. Regulations." He balanced the stack of boxes on his shoulder, obviously prepared to wait.

I submitted my eye to be lasered, and paid all in green out of sheer irritation. "Is that all, or do you want a blood test?"

"So take it up with management."

I slammed the door in his face. Punk. "Keishi, do I want to know how you did that?"

"I just found the nearest unit and switched addresses."

"Didn't your mother ever teach you it's wrong to steal?"

"So who stole?" she said. "You paid for it, didn't you?"

"I guess that's true," I admitted. The smell of food had made my salivary glands spurt to life, with a stab of pain far more compelling than the pangs of conscience. I sat down on the couch and started opening boxes. "You're sure you don't mind my eating in front of you?"

"What are my chances of stopping you?" she said, smiling. "No, relax, I'm not hungry anyway."

"Thanks," I said, and proceeded. She watched me closely as I tore off a piece of crepe and used it to scoop up mashed chickpeas.

"You're staring," I said. "I thought you weren't hungry."

"I'm not. It's just that you're eating with your right hand."

"That's how you eat Ethiopian food," I said, capturing a blob of umber curry.

"How come?"

I fanned my mouth instead of answering; the lentils had been too hot. When my tear ducts stopped firing, I said, "The left hand used to be considered unclean."

"Like a taboo?"

I paused with a bite halfway to my mouth. "Um . . . no, just basic hygiene, actually. I think it goes back to before they had toilet paper. Could we talk about this when I'm not eating?"

"Huh? Oh, sure."

I looked at the crepeful of vegetables suspiciously, then thrust all associations from my mind and swallowed it.

She couldn't let the topic go. "You know," she marveled, "I never would have thought of something like that."

"Typical wirehead," I said between mouthfuls. "You've spent so much time on the Net you've forgotten you *have* a digestive tract."

"Yeah?" she said, raising an eyebrow. "Okay, Miss Earthier-than-thou, when was the last time you cooked a meal that didn't come in a box?"

"I'm a camera," I said. "I'm all over the country. I don't have time to shop."

"All right, then, when was the last time you ate? Not since yesterday, I'll bet."

"I had something for breakfast."

"Something solid?"

"All right, Mirabara, you've made your point."

"You know," she said, pressing her advantage, "I think you'd maintain the Net against someone who preferred the body, and the body against someone who preferred the Net. You don't seem to have much use for either one."

"And what does that leave?"

"You tell me."

"Look, as fascinating as this is," I said, using a stray chopstick from the day before to mix the bland chickpeas into the overspiced lentils, "we've got about fourteen hours before I have to get on the train to Arkhangelsk, and in that time I have to get ready for the biggest interview of my life. This strikes me as more important than a lecture on nutrition. Can we leave it for another time?"

She sighed slightly and stood very straight, as though at attention. I wondered briefly whether she was making fun of me. "All right," she said. "Where do we start?"

"Let's see what we can find on Voskresenye himself."

We spent several fruitless hours in search of data. Every time we caught hold of a thread, it would wind around and around the Net, until finally at the end we found his name, Net address, police record, dates of birth and death—and nothing more. Finally we gave up and started tracking down the people and things he'd referred to during our first interview. Catharine Anderson, we found, went missing during her senior year at MGU. A few days before that, Edward Sinclair drove his truck into the Volga River in an apparent suicide, which was later reclassified as a terrorist strike. Dr. Aleksandr Derzhavin, a Russian scientist who had collaborated with the Guardians, died of a heart attack at age forty-five; little more was known, because the Guardians had burned his laboratory, and his records with it, as the Unanimous Army approached. It was all consistent with Voskresenye's story, but then you'd expect it to be. If he made something up, he would consult the Net first; and what he could find was about the same as what we could find. Stalemate.

"All right," I said, rubbing fatigue from my eyes, "what about this 'Queequeg' reference?"

"It's the name of a harpooner in a novel about whaling called *Moby-Dick.*"

"Sounds vaguely familiar."

"You might have heard about it in school," Keishi said. "It was widely read in Classical America. I think there's an episode of *The Brady Bunch* where Greg doesn't return it and gets a huge library fine . . . no, wait, that's *The Red Badge of Courage.* Anyway, it was well known."

"How long would it take you to read it for me?"

"Slot me a fresh moistdisk," she said. "I'll give you the novel as a memory. Have you used an English fluency chip much?"

"Sure, but not for a while."

"A year? Two years? That's okay, the neuromodulators should still be able to find those pathways lying around; you won't have to burn in again. In English, then. Oh, and I can also give you the memories of a Preclassical Lit. professor from LGU who wrote his thesis on it. Ready?"

I nodded. The novel seeped into my mind, like milk into a sponge. A man tattooed with frogs and labyrinths; a leg of polished whalebone; duodecimo, octavo, folio whales; a coffin bobbing among the waves; and in the blue distance a white mass rising, unknotting its suckered limbs, and sinking: unearthly, formless, chance-like mockery of life.

"Now that's really something," I said when it had finished. "Why couldn't we read that in school, instead of watching all that television?"

"You liked it?"

"It beats hell out of *The Brady Bunch.*"

"Well, I think it's horrible," she said, leaning forward in her chair. "It makes whaling out to be some kind of heroic pursuit, when all it really was is genocide."

"Sure, in hindsight," I said. "But there were whales all over the place back then. They didn't know they were going to run out."

"It's still disgusting. Look at that scene where they go all orgasmic over that spermaceti stuff. He makes it out to be a mystical experience, God's in his heaven, all's right with the world, and there they are running their hands through some gunk they dug out of an incredibly beautiful creature that they killed by ramming a harpoon into its eye and dragging it in—" She shuddered and drew her legs up onto the chair, wrapping her arms around her knees.

"First of all," I said, "I think you're confusing a few different incidents. And secondly, when exactly did Pavel Voskresenye take over your mind?"

She stiffened. "If two people who hate each other as much as Voskresenye and I do can agree on something, you should consider the possibility that we might be right. Killing is killing; it's sordid, bloody, stupid, and wasteful. There's nothing noble about it. People will do what they'll do, but we can at least call it what it is."

"But to take on something a hundred times your size and bring it down by strength and cunning and sheer determination—I can't think of anything more noble. Sure it's brutal. Biology is always brutal. 'Dinner' is just a euphemism for destruction." I waved my hand at the rubble of my meal. "You do remember eating, don't you? That's your problem, you know. Too much time out-of-body. You've forgotten the brutality of the flesh."

"If keeping your mind in a piece of rotting meat makes you condone violence, that's another point against it," she said irritably. "If I could get African citizenship, I swear I'd take Translation and have done with the whole stinking mess."

I sighed and said: "Dost thou think because thou art virtual there shall be no more flesh and blood?"

"Aha!" She put her feet back on the floor, noiselessly. "Now I have you! You can't tell me you had Shakespeare ready to mind before you slotted up—certainly not in English. Without the moist-disk, you wouldn't have been able to express the thought so elegantly. Without my Net link, I wouldn't have known what you meant. The electronics improve understanding. They put us in sync. Even something as simple as a Preclassical Lit. chip."

"Just more garbage encrusting the truth," I said, but I didn't take out the moistdisk.

"Words encrust," she said earnestly, leaning forward. "Words and bodies. The truth is underneath, and cables can break through to it. Why do you deny that?"

"Because—" I said, and then stopped, feeling the futility of trying to explain.

"No answer?" she said. "I'll tell you what I think it is. I think you're afraid. You're terrified of anything that might connect you to another person, and you fear cabling most of all because it's the surest way to—"

"All right, then," I said in exasperation. "There are so many reasons I hardly know where to start, but here's one. You're always talking about getting past people's surfaces to what's inside, and that's what you call real. But you can't just break through a person's defenses like that; the defenses are part of the person, they *are* the person. It's our nature to have hidden depths. It's like—" my eyes searched the room for a metaphor "—like skinning a frog and saying, 'Now I understand this frog, because I've seen what's inside it.' But when you skin it, it dies. You haven't understood a frog, you've understood a corpse."

"The cable doesn't 'skin' anything. Besides, it doesn't have to be one-way."

"Oh yes, that's even better. People swapping souls on the first date. Once you've done that, what the hell do you *talk* about for the rest of your life?" She tried to break in with an answer; I cut her off. "Nothing, that's what. There's nothing left to say. There's no wonder, no unfolding, no chance to gradually grow into each other . . . I don't know why I'm even trying to explain. . . ."

"But, Maya," she said, "you sound like a person who knows what she's talking about. When, apart from the other day with me, have you cabled before?"

I looked down at the table. "I've been working with screeners a long time. You get a feel for what it's like."

"All the same—"

"And even if it were real," I interrupted, "if you can achieve total intimacy with a piece of cable that costs fifty-nine kopeks, what *good* is it? How can you say that you have something special with a person, when you can get the same thing with anyone in Russia in fifteen minutes?"

"You can *not.*" She had risen and was pacing around the room. "You can't just cable with anyone. You can put in the plug, sure. But not everyone fits. Most of the time you can't get in deep enough. And if you do, if you go ahead and force it, you just find out that on the inside, most people are stupid, mean, selfish, and boring. When you find someone that you can keep coming back to again and again, it *does* mean something. It *is* love—how can you say it's not?"

"Oh, it's love, I suppose. It's love the way sugar is food: it's got lots of calories, but no nutrition. You can't live on it for long."

She stopped pacing, but did not sit down. When she spoke again it was more slowly and more softly. "If you take flesh as your starting point," she said, "you're always going to find some way that silicon falls short. But there's nothing special about flesh. Look, sex wasn't invented by some loving God who wants us all to understand each other and be happy. It was made by nature, and nature doesn't give a damn whether our hearts hook up or not, just as long as our gametes do. Why should evolution get to make all the decisions? Why can't we use something that *is* designed to bring people together? If you turn the comparison around, and start with cabling, then love in the meat starts to look pretty shabby.

Love happens in the mind, in the soul—what does the union of two sweating bodies have to do with that?"

"Love without touching—"

"I would touch your mind more gently than any hand," she said, looking down at me. "More softly than—"

"That's not what I mean by touch, and you know it," I said. "You keep trying to change around the meanings of words. You're using some new definition of love, too. I don't think it's in my dictionary."

"No, nor in your encyclopedia, either," she said, so gently that I couldn't take offense. "It's real, though. And it isn't new. That's one thing Derzhavin was right about, as twisted as he was. You think cabling is unnatural—that's what your arguments all come down to. But it's not. Not between people that really fit. Maya, do you have any idea how unlikely it is that two structures as complex as minds could be joined like that? It's like picking up two stones at random and discovering that they fit together perfectly. It isn't a coincidence. It can't be. They fit together *so* easily—like reuniting something that should never have been broken, filling in some ancient wound. . . ."

She sat down on the sofa beside me, and looked down at my hand. Her fingers brushed my palm, then stroked the socket at the throat of my wrist. "The mind has doors," she whispered, "even as the body does. And when you drill new holes, you tap old hungers."

"What would you know about hunger, you ghost?" I said. "You've forgotten you have a body—you just said you wish you didn't have. Is there hunger on the Net now? No, don't you *dare* call that hunger. Hunger is something that can be sated. But you can touch a hundred minds a night and never be filled—or fulfilled. That's not a desire, that's an algorithm."

She slowly leaned over me, as though to rest her head against my shoulder. "I've been in thousands of minds, yes, Maya," she whispered. "I fell in love with *one.*"

I kept perfectly still and said flatly: "What else is there on whales?"

She got up, bent over the videophone, and stood there staring at the blank screen. I could not bring myself to look at the reflection of her face. When she had been silent so long that I was sure she wouldn't answer me, she said, " . . . There are songs."

"Right," I said briskly. "Traditional songs about whales—"

"No," she said, "I mean the whales, they sing."

"That's not in *Moby-Dick*."

"Well, they weren't listening, were they?" she snapped. "If you up and chucked a spear at every human you saw, you wouldn't know we could talk, either."

"You mean their songs were a language?" I said, amazed.

She thought for a moment and then said, with more composure, "They're a little repetitive for a language. More like a bird's song, except they go on for hours. People used to listen to them for relaxation."

"Play me one."

"All right," she said at length. She went back to the armchair, sat, then closed her eyes and took a deep breath. "This might not be such a good—"

"*Play* it," I said.

She nodded, slowly. Squeaks and echoes filled the air.

I winced. "A bird's song played off-key by fingernails on a blackboard in a swimming pool! People listened to this? Voluntarily?"

Instead of answering she turned away, pressing her face into the back of the chair. I could see by the spasms in her shoulders that she was crying, though her hands concealed the tears. I felt shamed by the unfeignedness of her grief, where I myself could muster little feeling for a race of creatures that had died out before I was born.

"Keishi, I'm sorry, I didn't mean—"

"It's not the song," she sobbed.

"Oh. No. No, of course it's not."

I tried to touch her hair to comfort her, but my hand passed through the strands without disturbing them. I thought of embracing her, but that too was impossible. I settled for sitting on the floor next to her chair, leaning my head against the armrest. Her face was turned away; all I could see was a crescent of cheek and temple, notched by the eye-socket, trembling and bright with tears.

"Keishi, I owe you an apology. Several, in fact. I know I'm not an easy person to work with—" she sobbed aloud "—all right, I'm a pain in the ass. I know that. What I'm trying to say is that this is the story of a lifetime, and I would have thrown it away if it weren't for you. And I've treated you like dirt for your trouble. I don't know why you've put up with me this long. But I hope you'll give me another chance. . . . Keishi, I don't care whether Anton comes back or not. I want you to be my screener for as long as we can trick News One into keeping us together. And for as long as you'll have me."

She wiped away tears with her hand, still averting her eyes. "That's not the kind of partnership I want with you."

"Oh, Keishi, please, any time but now—"

"I have to. Maya, I love you. And if we can't come to terms with that, then I'd better just go, because it's only going to get more painful. Maya, I know you don't love me now. I know it's hard for you to even think about it. All I can ask is that you try to remember . . . if the encyclopedia were out, do you think you could love me?"

"I'm sorry," I said. "That part of my life is over."

She looked up at me as I stood. "You don't know, do you?"

"No," I said, starting to clear away the take-out boxes in order to hide the shame in my eyes. "I don't know."

I carried the boxes into the kitchen and threw away the empty ones. As I was making room in the refrigerator for the leftovers, she came in behind me, so quietly I didn't know she was there until she spoke.

"I want to give you something," she said, "but I'm afraid to. The last time I gave you a gift, it didn't turn out very well."

I smiled down at the sink as I rinsed my hands. "I promise not to throw this one at you. But you don't need to give me anything. I owe you enough already." I turned to her, drying my hands on a dish towel. "What is it?"

"Freedom." She leaned against the doorframe, as if to block my exit from the room. "When you were interviewing Voskresenye, and I touched your mind, I found out why you didn't want me to help you with your encyclopedia before. I didn't mean to peek, but it was right there. You're afraid that if I did, and then something happened to me, or I fell in love with someone else, or we just wound up hating each other, you'd be out in the cold. There'd be no one to protect you, and the first Weaver to happen by . . ."

"Oh, Keishi, I didn't mean it that way."

"No, please don't apologize, it's all right. I understand. I wouldn't want you to stay with me out of fear. What I want to do is modify your camera software to screen out . . . well, everything your encyclopedia suppresses. The thoughts will come back, but they won't ever escape to the Net, or even to your screener, if that's anyone but me. The Weavers will never know about them. You can leave the suppressor chip in, so the Postcops won't suspect; even if they examine it, it won't have been altered. But when you say so, it will stop working."

"Wouldn't the Weavers be able to see the modification?"

"Why? Anything that doesn't make it to the Net won't set off their detectors. Other than that . . . in ten years the Postcops might have come far enough to figure it out, if they knew what to look for, and if you never got an upgrade. But ten years is a long time." She brushed the salty deposit of tears from her cheekbone. "You could say no, and live to be a hundred. Or you could die tomorrow, for all you know."

"Especially if the Postcops figure out the man with the whale is Voskresenye."

"He and I fooled them once; we can do it again," she said re-assuringly. "But Maya, you could be run over by a bus next Thursday and never know what they took from you. If you take it back, you'll have at least ten years. Probably more. They may never find out. I don't want to tell you what to do; it has to be your choice. But if it were me, well . . . " She smiled and lapsed into KRIOL, her tongue clicking softly in the hidden spaces of her mouth: "!Gather(rosebuds) while.do(may). . . . "

My spine burst into shivers. I could not explain why a few words of KRIOL should have such an effect on me. Nevertheless they did. I had to turn away, pretending sudden interest in the moonlit trees outside the window, in order to hide the feelings that I knew my face betrayed.

She went on, half-heard: "I want you to know that if you say yes and you find out you don't love me, that's all right. That's not why I'm doing it . . . well, not the only reason. You deserve to be free whether you love me or not."

"Do it." The words seemed to come directly from the tingling of my spine, bypassing my better judgment. Yet once they were said, I did not want to take them back.

"Are you sure?" she asked, solicitously. "Do you need some time to think it over?"

"The last thing I want to do is think it over. Just do it."

She looked at me with concern, but relented. "All right, then. You'll need an adapter."

"Why?"

"You'll have to put it in your wrist. You can't alter a chip in a skull socket; the hardware won't do it. Security thing. Is your adapter still in your duffel?"

"No. I, um, I put it away. . . . Hang on." I opened my junk drawer to look. When I didn't see it, I started furiously rummaging through the drawer; I had to fight back the urge to dump its contents on the floor. Then Keishi came, stood behind me, and put her hand on my shoulder—the faintest of pressures, an insect alighting. I forced myself to calm down. She glanced at the drawer and reached through my shoulder to point out where the adapter lay.

I picked it up. "Which wrist?"

"Left, since you're left-handed."

I slid the plug into its socket, wrapped the Velcro cuff around my wrist, and started to put in my camera chip.

"Not that one, the 6000," she said.

"What difference does it make?"

"Well, there's—" she began, then broke off and smiled. "This probably isn't the time for a technical lecture. Let's just say the old chip isn't up to it."

I went into the bedroom to collect the rosebox from my closet. At first I hesitated over the choice of chipsets, but she said, "It doesn't matter. Once I've done one, it'll be easy to copy the changes to the other two." I plugged the chameleon chip into the adapter, where it promptly sprouted trompe l'oeil black Velcro fur.

"Find a comfortable place to sit," she said. "The first one may take a while."

I sat on the armchair that Keishi had vacated—briefly surprised to find the cushion cold. I slipped off my shoes and leaned back.

"Just try to relax," she said.

"I am relaxed."

"The hell you are. If your heart were going any faster it'd break the sound barrier. Breathe slowly, and count your breaths—just up to four, then repeat it. Try to clear your mind of everything else."

As I struggled for calm, she made the motions of taking something out of a bag, though there was no bag to be seen. Then she crawled up onto an invisible ledge five feet above the floor—a levitating mime—and reclined there, in a slightly cramped position. Her real body must have been getting into the sleeping compartment on the train. She unbound her hair, which suddenly became longer. That must be what she really looked like, I thought with half-suppressed excitement. Her hair was lifted back into the thing she had set up—a myrmichor; it must be. That was how the African engineers had solved the problem of getting data into a head without using sockets: they'd replaced her hair with some sort of conductive fiber. If I ran my fingers through it, would it be soft, or stiff, I wondered? I longed to try—a small, quiet longing; but I had not felt one as strong in twenty years.

Then I remembered how, when I had first realized she knew about my suppressor chip, I had pictured her configuring it with a waldo at a table, not with her hair in a myrmichor. That image had been so vivid—where had it come from? Who had sat at a table for hours that way, with cables trailing from her head and arms?

But there was no time to think of that. I could already feel my hand beginning to stir, to touch wires and move among patterns, though physically, of course, it hadn't moved at all. If the image with the waldo was a memory, I would know in the morning. The dream coprocessor would bring it up.

"Do you want me to take your hand offline?" she asked, in a strangely blurred voice.

"No," I said. "No, leave it on. I want to feel it."

"I always knew you were the Lamaze type." She chuckled distractedly. "I'm going to give you a phrase to say when you want the desuppression to begin. It's not in Russian, so you won't say it by accident. Listen closely: *O vos omnes, qui transitis per viam.* Say that back to me."

I repeated the phrase.

"Good. Now don't say it again, unless you mean it."

"I won't," I said.

"If you feel like sleeping, do."

"I'm not tired," I said. "I'm not tired at all." But hours later, when she wanted me to switch chips, she had to rouse me first; and by the time she had finished all three, I was sound asleep.

She touched my cheek to wake me. "Go to bed. I'm going to stay with you tonight."

I looked at her, blinking thickly, and said, "Are you *here?*"

"No. You're still asleep. I mean in virtual. If I were there, I'd have carried you to bed, so I didn't have to wake you. One of the problems with being discorporate."

"What time is it?"

"About three in the morning."

"Oh, God," I said, finally coming awake, "I've got the interview of my life tomorrow and I'm completely unprepared—"

"Don't worry. I'll give you a moistdisk in the morning. You'll be fine. Everything will be fine."

I went to bed without undressing, setting the adapter on my nightstand. She stood by the door, where, it seemed, she meant to keep vigil all night. And just as I fell asleep—or did I dream it?—she came and kissed me on the eyes. Her lips seeped a little way through the lids into the liquid depths behind them: small, cold kisses: silver coins.

## (The Frog)

(Dreams aren't stories. They don't have a point, a theme, a plot, a moral. All those things take skill to craft, and the sleeping mind is inept. That's why most dreams are just a lot of aimless wandering. Once in a while you'll be awake enough for a small part of you to feel you should be getting somewhere, and then the dream becomes a nightmare.

All night I dreamed that I was walking through the streets, carrying a sack of groceries that I could not manage to look into. Then I dreamed I woke up from that dream, to find myself back in the reclining chair in the living room. Keishi was floating above the floor. My left hand had detached itself and was holding a scalpel; it had slit my arm open, from finger to elbow. The skin was fastened back to the arm of the chair with dissecting pins, and among the flayed muscles, I could see my arteries begin to pulse. Keishi drifted toward me, bent down as if to whisper some secret in my ear, and then opened her mouth and exhaled daisies.)

# 2

## PHYSICAL BONES

"However," added objective Pnin, "Russian metaphysical police can break physical bones also very well."

—Vladimir Nabokov, *Pnin*

# thirteen

## ICARUS

**R**ain: I woke to the sound of rain crashing above me. The falling drops were blowing against the wire mesh of the window-screen, filling it in square by square, like pixels on a monitor. Perhaps all the windows in the city, if seen from a sufficient distance, would form some enormous image that only the gods could see. I lay there trying to guess the pattern a long time. Then I stretched in my pocket of warmth beneath the blankets, and turned over. The camera chip was there, still plugged into its adapter. It had been no dream.

I went into the bathroom, opened the little window above the shower, and cleaned out all the crumpled newspaper—blank newspaper; they sell it in Leningrad stores expressly for the purpose of being wadded up in windows. I jammed it all into the wastebasket and opened up the outer window, so the clean, cool air from outside could dispel the bathroom's mustiness. Then I took a shower, hot and luxuriously long. I should be careful about the water, I knew; but I would be careful tomorrow, tomorrow would be soon enough. Today, even the city was being cleansed by this downpour. I closed my eyes and imagined it, as I worked lather into my hair. The sky threw down great solid sheets of water that fell against the rooftops, where they shattered into drops. The rain poured down along the shingles, picking up and carrying with it every crumb of dirt that Leningrad possessed; and streaming down from eaves and windowsills, it crashed into the streets and ran down gutters in excited single-files, which met at drains and, crowding round them, plunged together into nothingness. Even the veins of stink that lay beneath the city must, I thought, have been washed clean by this exuberance of rain. "Freedom," Keishi had said; and though I knew that it could never be so simple, I allowed myself to hope.

I put on my robe, fed the bugs, and ate breakfast, scooping up leftover chickpeas with a hardened bagel. My body, unused to anything but coffee and nanojuice at this hour, soon warmed to the idea and sent me scurrying after the lentils, which I finished with a spoon. They tasted better than they had last night. They were better cold; no, I had been distracted; no, I had forgotten how to taste food years ago, and only now remembered.

When I'd finished my makeshift breakfast, I gathered the camera chips, replaced them in the rosebox, and took it into the bathroom to dress. I opened all three flaps of the box, set it on end, and watched it rotate. How do you dress for the biggest interview of your life?

Exactly like any other day, I realized, and I put the box under the sink. This interview would bring scrutiny. If I had suddenly changed moistware just before it, people might suspect something. But if I changed a few days after, it would look like I went out and spent my bonus on an upgrade, and no one would think twice. I went to the living room to retrieve my old camera chip.

The moment I slotted it in, I was glad of my decision. That chip and I had been through decades of obscurity together; it would be heartless to change now, on the cusp of my first real success. And she could love me even so; I knew that. She had known me no other way.

I put on the most ordinary outfit in my closet and went back into the kitchen. As I poured coffee into a selfheating News One mug, a note on the refrigerator caught my eye. It hadn't been there at breakfast. I put down the coffeepot and went to look. There was no salutation, no signature, only two words in a large flowing cursive: BE BOLD. I stood there looking at the note a long time, feeling the warmth of the mug as I rested it against my collarbone. Then I reached out to touch the note, and passed my hand through it: unreal.

The phone chimed, and I answered it without begrudging the intrusion.

"Good morning," Keishi said.

I had to choke back my usual rejoinder—"That's an oxymoron." Instead I said, "Yes, I think it is."

She smiled appraisingly. "You know, this has really changed you. You look five years younger than you did last night."

I sniffed the air. "Are you testing my sense of smell again?"

She laughed politely. "I take it you're not having second thoughts about last night."

"When I do, you'll know."

"Then, ah, may I ask why you're not wearing the murder weapon?"

"Gold and dead gods aren't my style, I guess. Why do they do that, anyway? You see Egyptian gods plastered over everything that's African, but nobody worships them."

"That's why they do it. They figure that since those gods are dead, they won't get pissed off about how you use their images."

"Oh, I see. Same reason people throw around the Coca-Cola logo."

Keishi smiled. "You've got two other sets, you know. The polychromes can look like whatever you want. Including the Coca-Cola logo."

"I thought I'd better wait a few days," I said, more soberly. "This would be a bad time for a mysterious upgrade. It's better to wait till the worst of the furor has passed."

She bit her lower lip. "The new chip will need some burning-in time, you know, if it's going to do all its tricks. It can use the pathways your old one established if it has to, but it really ought to add more."

"All the more reason not to try using it today."

She looked away from the screen, then back at me. "Maya, can I ask you to just slot one of the 6000s? I can't tell you why until—until later today. But I wouldn't ask unless there were a good reason."

"Look," I said firmly, "I'm as disappointed as you are. But you promised me ten years, and I mean to collect every minute. It'd be foolish to throw it all away because I couldn't wait for a couple of days."

"Then take them with you," she insisted. "What if your old chip fails? One whiff of seawater and it could rust up like—"

"Keishi," I said. "You're being ridiculous."

She lowered her eyes, but not before I saw her face cloud. Well, love was impatient. Or so I told myself, not really knowing whether it was or not. "I suppose you're right," she said forlornly. Then she suddenly brightened. "Say, why don't you come to Arkhangelsk early? There's a train at 9:15."

"I guess I could. There's not much left for me to do here. Any special reason?"

"Apart from the obvious? I'm trying to sniff out that whale. If I do, maybe we can crash Voskresenye's party a little early and get this story put together right."

I shook my head in amazement. "How did I ever get along without you? Here I've practically forgotten the whole story, and you're working harder than ever."

She inclined her head, obviously pleased.

"Where should I meet you, then?"

She hesitated for what was, to a megascops, quite a long time. At last she said: "When you get to the trainport I'll be there."

"You mean in person?"

" . . . Yes."

"Well, it will be nice to meet you, Keishi Mirabara."

"You know," she said carefully, "I don't look exactly like my Net image."

"Who does?" I said, laughing. Then I saw how nervous she was, so I said, "I still don't know exactly how I feel about you, but I doubt it would make any difference if you weighed a hundred kilograms."

She looked up sharply, then relaxed and smiled. "I may just hold you to that."

"Well, I'll find out in Arkhangelsk."

Her face grew wistful again. "Yes, you will. . . . Maya, I love you." She smiled, rather weakly, and held up a hand. "No, don't answer. I know you can't yet." Her image vanished.

I whispered to the blank monitor: "I hope I love you too."

I stood there thinking until the phone reverted to its clock display, then jumped: it was almost 8:30. Barely time to put on my coat, shrink-seal my sockets, wrap a plastic babushka around my head, and run to the trainport. I plunged out into the rain, feeling reckless and rakish. A dangerous joy was gathering in my heart: the kind of joy that makes you do things you remember all your life, not necessarily with fondness. I stepped right into the braided ripples in the gutter, and crossed the street in defiance of all laws of traffic.

The quickest route was through the park. I started to walk around to the gate. But on my way, I noticed a gap in the hedge that children squeeze through when, to their childish impatience, the gate seems too far. On impulse I ducked into it, emerging on the other side with leaves and twigs clinging to my coat. Well, let them cling. I would not bother to brush them away.

The rain pounded against my head, and the sky was a charred log. It was almost perfect; but it needed music. I switched on Audio Classical Seven—picking the number for luck. White letters, projected onto the saturated grass, informed me that I was hearing Mozart's Requiem. Then the lyrics began to scroll through my peripheral vision. A sing-along? Well, all right, I'm no soprano but I can follow the bouncing ball. I sang loudly and tunelessly, the Net helping me to understand the Latin. *Dies irae, dies illa, solvet sae-clum in favilla:* a day of wrath, that day, it will blow the world to smithereens—or words to that effect. But not just yet, please; I have ten years coming; do it then.

Then I thought of Keishi's passphrase, and gave it to the Net to translate. "All you people who pass on the street . . ." Yes. Yes, that was just how I felt.

As I racewalked my way through the park, I came upon two women ducking under a single umbrella. Their heads were almost touching, and at my approach they looked up with, it seemed to me, guilt: caught in the act, by a camera, no less.

"Relax for gods' sake!" I called out to them. "Your tribe!" And I laughed as I passed, seeing myself through their eyes: a singing missile, if you could call it singing, that had crashed past and shouted nonsense at them. I knew they were only sharing an umbrella, not kissing as it had seemed. But it was lovely to pretend.

*Galuboy*—the word came to me suddenly, out of the undiscovered country the encyclopedia suppressed. "Light blue." How odd; how inappropriate. Like *kit*, whale, which sounds like a chick's peeping. But *galuboy*'s for men; what is it called in women? Well, words would come later. For now, this feeling. My head tingled with the memories it kept in trust, as though it couldn't hold them back much longer. The Requiem crashed in my head like the stamping of a great beast. Of course, an elephant. Oh, I had been awful to her! Hooks, indeed. But even those remembered insults would be cherished in the end.

I turned around and walked backward a few steps in order to sing another verse to the umbrella women, and as I spun back again, my coat fell open. I had lost the belt somewhere, probably in the hedge. There was no time to retrieve it, so I held the coat shut by crossing my arms and gripping each epaulette in the opposite hand. Just you give me a crook and flail, and I'll adorn you a sarcophagus, or lie on an African moistdisk in hologram gold.

The trail started to meander unproductively, so I splashed onto the grass, refusing to divert my path even for the deepest puddles. And so, butchering the *Tuba mirum*, I climbed and crested a low hill, and saw a man in a black suit leaning against a tree ahead of me. I stopped singing, reduced my pace, and changed course slightly to avoid him. I had almost passed him, and was half-convinced my fears were wrong, when he called out, "Do you know the time, *tavarishcha?*"

"Ask the Net!" I shouted, and looked back over my shoulder at him. He had turned his head, showing me a black slab of moistware set flush with his skull, like those sunken tombstones you can mow right over.

"Please put your hands in the air where they are clearly visible," the Postcop called out.

I did.

"Thank you, *tavarishcha*. Now please reach down very slowly and remove first your Net chip, then all other enhancements except for your encyclopedia."

Again I complied, fumbling with the babushka. Yes, quite an enhancement, that encyclopedia.

"You see it is much better to cooperate. Now, if you would, please place your hands behind your head and lie on the ground with your face down."

I dropped to my knees and then, because I couldn't use my hands to catch myself, fell forward awkwardly onto the wet grass. My face was in a puddle, so I had to close my eyes and hold my breath. For a moment no one came, and I vainly hoped that I would be allowed to lie there in the grass until the rain dissolved me. It was a hard, sharp rain that would leave no skeleton.

Then my arms were grasped and cuffed, and two sets of hands gently lifted me to my feet. My face and clothes were covered with mud, and I noticed that the Postcops that were flanking me wore rubber gloves.

As we walked to the van I began to think again, a little, and realized that they would not have known where to ambush me unless they had been listening in on my conversation with Keishi. In that case, they must know everything. The rain would not dissolve me—in fact, I realized as they loaded me into the back of the windowless van, I might never see rain again; and I turned to see the sky one last time, only to have my head pushed firmly down.

As the van drove through the streets of Leningrad, the rain besieged it, crashing against the metal, clawing the roof with its nails, howling as a wolf howls when torn from her pups or her prey. It could not get to me. No, it would not be the rain. But I had gotten what I'd wished for. I was dead.

# fourteen

## TEA AND SYMPATHY

**A**fter three hours of interrogation, I finally cracked.

"No!" I screamed. "For the hundredth time, I do not want any more fucking crumpets! And get that teapot out of my face."

The young man across the table set down the little delftware teapot and put on a face of disappointed concern. "I am sorry that our hospitality is not to your liking. We had very little notice of your arrival. If there is something we can remedy, by all means—"

"I've told you a dozen times. I want these handcuffs off. And I want to go to the bathroom."

Officer Rubatin turned to his partner and said in a conciliatory tone, "They seem reasonable enough requests, Officer Ignateva."

The woman with the sergeant's bars pressed her thin lips together. "The manner in which they were delivered was anything but reasonable. Such a tone is inappropriate in this environment, and her use of profanity denotes a person unable to control her passions as society requires."

"Ohhhhhh, I get it now," I said to the woman. "You're the bad cop and he's the good cop. You know how I can tell? Because you whisper louder."

"Plainly we are getting nowhere," Good Cop said. "Perhaps if we remove the restraints, as a gesture of goodwill, she will recognize our peaceable intentions."

"Very well, Officer Rubatin," Bad Cop said, scowling. "I trust that our good-naturedness will not be met with more hostility." She nodded to Good Cop, who moved around the table to remove the cuffs.

"Um, actually," I said, "the bathroom thing is a little more urgent right now."

Bad Cop was incredulous. "We give you one thing and you instantly demand another?"

"Oh, no. No, by all means, please remove the cuffs, that's fine. I thank you profoundly for the favor." My wrists were starting to go ominously numb, so I didn't want to lose the chance to free them, even though my bladder had been a dull ache for most of the last hour. I had drunk one cup of tea to keep my strength up for the interrogation, and a second cup because it really was excellent tea, and a third because the sips gave me a chance to think before I answered. Now I was paying the price. I wondered whether I had fallen into the same trap the first time.

I stood so Bad Cop could remove the cuffs, and stayed standing as I rubbed my wrists. It felt good to have them off now, though at first I had been grateful for them. My greatest fear had been that a Weaver would possess one of the Postcops, take out a cable, and mindsuck me. The thought had made my every socket ache, as though fear had given the metal nerves. So I had been glad of the cuffs that locked over my wrist sockets, giving me the illusion that they were protected—two fewer wounds through which I might be hurt.

But they were not going to go Weaver. I was almost certain of that now. A Weaver can be in a hundred places at a time, so what they do, they do quickly. If a Weaver were going to take one of them, she would have done it long before.

I started to sit down, wondering whether they'd let me go expel the tea if I asked very, very nicely. Suddenly I stopped, my knees half-bent, and thought: Postcops. Maya, these are Postcops, and not Weavers. They were ordinary citizens, appropriated for a day; someone had shown up at their doors that morning, ignored the usual excuses, and inserted the Post moistware into their heads. Their behavior was electronically regulated, and, in the areas that mattered most, predictable. They were going to kill me—there was no doubt of that. It would be soon. And no matter what I did, the death would be polite and painless.

To know for certain that you cannot change your fate can be a rather liberating experience. The instant I'd accepted it, I had an idea.

"May I stand a while and stretch my legs, please?" I asked.

Bad Cop looked sour, but since I had said "please," she nodded.

"Thank you. I am in your debt, *tavarishcha.*" I walked a few steps, then stood in the corner, stretching my legs with exaggerated motions. I felt chilly under the thin hospital gown they had given me to replace my muddied clothes.

"Now, Maya Tatyanichna," Good Cop said, "you were about to tell us what Keishi Mirabara said to you in the trainport."

"Absolutely," I said, leaning against the wall. "I'll tell you everything—everything I can remember. But there's one thing I need to do first." And I squatted, hiked up the gown, and urinated on the floor.

"Cuff her again. Behind her back this time. Then get on the Net and get a wet mop up here." She turned to me and said. "That was so uncalled for I can't even find words to describe it."

"Take out that Post chip and you'll find all kinds of words."

"I see you think you can defy us," Bad Cop said ominously. Ominous in a polite sort of way, of course.

"I think I can do whatever the hell I want. This is the last day of my life. I may as well have a little fun with it."

"With someone who has remained in conformance as long as

you have," Good Cop put in, "we may be able to consider leniency. But only if—"

"Bolus. Nobody comes away from the Postcops alive a second time. I'll be dead by midnight. All you can offer me is crumpets and trips to the bathroom. But what difference does it make if I wet myself? What difference does it make if I won't tell you anything? The worst you can do is kill me, which you're going to do anyway. I can piss on the floor, I can stand on my head, I can tell you every Postcop joke I know, and you can't do a thing."

Good Cop interrupted Bad Cop's glare by plucking at her sleeve. "What?"

"Something's wrong," he said. "I'm cut off from the Net."

Bad Cop's eyes unfocused for a moment. "I am, too. I'll go get us an audio communicator." She stood up, then turned at the door to look at me. "While I'm gone, consider whether you want to leave this room alive. The choice is yours."

Good Cop watched the door swing shut, then leaned across the table toward me. "I admire your courage, Maya," he said in a conspiratorial whisper. "However, I must say that I believe it is ill-timed. Officer Ignateva is operating on an older version of the Emily Post moistware. If you continue to provoke her, it might overload, and my own moistware would prevent me from interceding."

"Oh. Wow. Thanks for telling me," I said. Then I leaned forward and matched his whisper. "You know, I really hate these cuffs. If you could take them off—"

He considered, then carefully looked to both sides. "All right, then."

When they were off I said, "You know, the whispering and the looking around to see if anyone's looking are great stage business, but they seem a little fake when you're alone in a soundproof room. Haven't you ever heard of method acting? Doesn't the police academy have a drama department?"

He sat back and sighed indulgently. "I really do have your best interests at heart, *tavarishcha.* "

"Yeah, right. So is the Net really down, or is it a trick to get the two of us alone together so you can be my friend?"

Before he could reply, Bad Cop returned, carrying a portable radio. "The whole building's down," she said. "They're working on it." Then she looked at me with surprise and said, "You took off the cuffs, Rubatin?"

"He was playing good cop," I informed her. "It didn't work very well. Why don't you try that bad cop thing again?"

"I fail to understand why you refer to me as a 'bad cop,' " she said testily. "All Post police officers run on the same software. We are bound by the law of the land and the laws of propriety, so we are incapable of being 'bad.' "

"Where *did* you people go to school?" I said, rolling my eyes. If Good Cop could overact, so could I. "Haven't you ever watched *CHIPS?* Haven't you ever watched *Hill Street Blues?* Do the words 'Book 'em, Danno' mean nothing to you?" I looked down on their scrubbed puzzled faces and sighed. "Okay, kids, let me correct a major gap in both your educations. When cops in Classical America interrogated a prisoner, one cop would be the Good Cop and try to become his friend, and the other would be the Bad Cop and try to scare the shit out of him so he'd confess to his buddy the Good Cop. Just like what you're doing. Except they could back up their threats. They could swear. They could break things. They could hurt people. You can't even ask me for something without saying 'please.' Frankly, Ignateva, you're pathetic."

"Insults can only make this more difficult."

I laughed, leaned back, and rubbed my eyes. "I was hoping they'd make it more interesting. But it's like teasing animals in the zoo: it's poor sport and it frustrates the animals. Why are we doing this? Why don't you just—"

I broke off. Why *didn't* they just mindsuck me? You think of

Weavers doing that, but Postcops do it too, once they've run through all the polite options. Ignateva and Rubatin were incompetents—that's what you get when you recruit by lottery. It would take them a long time to give up. But in the end they would, or they'd be relieved by someone who would. And then the cable would come out of whatever pocket it was hidden in, and any hope that Keishi had would be gone.

I had known that. And I had thought that there was nothing I could do. But there was.

"Could I have another cup of tea, please?" I asked, trying to keep my voice from shaking.

"Oh, certainly, certainly," Rubatin said, hastening to pour.

"Thank you," I said, and gripped the handle like a lifeline. Taking the encyclopedia out might be enough, and then it might not. But surely, after all these years, the waterproofing would not hold against a direct assault.

"All right," I said. "Let's put all our cards on the table. I seem to have run out of reasons to play for time. What can I do that will get this over with?"

"You can tell us what we need to know, *tavarishcha.*"

"Other than that."

"Let's just make a start, shall we?" Good Cop said sympathetically. "You came back from Kazakhstan. You arrived at the trainport. What did you do?"

"I went to the bathroom. It smelled a lot like it does here."

Good Cop leaned over and whispered to Bad Cop, "Is that janitor on the way?"

"They said she would come. See what the radio says."

Bad Cop switched it on. "Officer Mayich," it blared, "Officer Andrei Mayich, come to the front desk please." She scowled and turned down the volume.

"What did you do after you went to the bathroom?" Good Cop pressed on.

"I washed my hands in the sink."

"We don't care about that," Bad Cop put in.

"You don't care about washing your hands after you go to the bathroom? Oh gods, and I let you hand me that crumpet. That's disgusting."

"What we want to know, please, is when you met Keishi Mirabara."

"I didn't meet her at the port at all. She had me paged over the trainport speakers, but I was too busy trying to get drunk."

"You cannot get drunk, Andreyeva. No bar would serve you beyond your ration. We know that."

"I didn't say it was working. I just said I was trying. Why do you ask these questions if you're not even going to listen to the answers?"

"Officer Ivanova," the radio said, "Officer Tatyana Ivanova, please come to the front desk. Your daughter is here."

Tatyana Ivanova was my mother's maiden name. Strange coincidence.

"Maya Tatyanichna," Good Cop said, "our records indicate that you did insert the courtesy plug."

"Officer Pudding," said the radio, "Officer Chocolate Pudding, please come to the front desk."

I laughed and slouched back even further, tightening my grip on the cup. I would have to take the socket-cap off with one hand, and raise the cup with the other. The parietal socket, on top, would be best; to get the tea to run out again, they'd have to turn me upside-down, and by then it would be much too late—

I sat upright. *Officer Pudding.* The speaker trick. It was Keishi.

Or the Postcops trying to entrap me with hope. I had to be sure. "Yes," I said carefully, "that's true, I did put in the plug. She told me to put my Net chip in, so we could virtual conference. But I thought, 'What would a person like Keishi Mirabara want with me?' "

"Officer Cavalry, Officer John Wayne Cavalry, please come to the station, you are needed."

Bad Cop gave Good Cop a worried look and said, "Officers of French ethnicity are an asset to the Leningrad police force."

I suppressed a smile. Somewhere deep in Bad Cop's mind the words "goddamn frogs" had flared up and been quenched. Jean-Waine Chevalrí. No allusion to the Ancient West could have come from these *duraks*. And no Weaver would have reason to play such games.

"What exactly did she say to you over the courtesy plug?" Good Cop asked.

"Oh, I hung up after a few words," I said. "She was trying to *tell me what to do*. I hate it when people do that."

"Officer Rune, Officer Net Rune, please return to your vehicle. Your headlights are on. Officer Net Rune."

Bad Cop and Good Cop exchanged perplexed glances.

"She tried to *tell me why*, but by that time I'd hung up on her," I said.

"Officer Pavlov, Officer Ivan Pavlov, please report to the front desk immediately. There is a camera here to interview you. Your tardiness in this significant public relations effort does not become the Leningrad Police Force. Officer Pavlov, come to the front desk *now*."

Of course.

I let the cup go, buried my head in my hands, and pretended to sob. "I'm sorry, officers. I've been trying to lie to you, but I see now that it's fruitless. Can we start at the beginning again? Could you repeat the charges against me?"

"You are here for conspiring to remove a court-mandated suppressor chip, and for consorting with a known dissident, and for intent to commit affectional deviance."

"And disturbing the peace," Bad Cop added peevishly.

I knew my singing would be the death of me in the end. "I'm sorry," I said, "I don't know the jargon. What is 'affectional deviance,' please?"

"You deliberately set out to fall in love with a person of your own sex, in flagrant violation of the laws of the Fusion of Historical Nations as well as of the terms of your parole."

"And did I succeed at this?"

"Not at the time at which you were arrested," Good Cop said.

"And why not?"

"Because of the corrective device which we implanted twenty years ago, at the time of your first arrest."

"Because of Postcop mind control."

Bad Cop and Good Cop exchanged nervous glances. "The colloquialism is essentially accurate, yes."

"And how did you find out about this intent? By monitoring private videophone conversations, yes? Through spy satellites? Through hidden cameras? By using the Net to spy on people's minds?"

"She has no need to know that, Officer Rubatin," said Bad Cop warily. "She is stalling for time."

"Common courtesy demands that we answer all reasonable questions," he said in a conciliatory tone. "There is nothing to fear; the information will go no further than this room."

"No it won't, will it?" I said. "Because I'll leave this room a corpse. Have you already decided which one of you pulls the trigger, or do you flip a coin when it's time?" I parted my fingers, as if accidentally, to let a little light from my Net-rune shine through. Bad Cop's eyes widened.

"This information could only distress you—"

Bad Cop grabbed my hand away from my face, revealing the lit rune. "Shit!" she yelled. I longed for my imagination software, to draw a little puff of smoke above her Post chip.

"Smile, *duraks*," I said, "you're on News One. Why don't you tell the world why you wouldn't let me go to the bathroom?"

"It's a trick," Good Cop said. "It has to be."

"Of course it's a trick," I said sweetly. "Just go on as you were before. What difference will it make?" Then I widened my eyes and said in mock astonishment: "The Post police wouldn't have anything to hide, would they?"

Bad Cop grabbed the radio. "Front desk, come in."

"Front desk. This is Officer Miranda." It was Keishi's voice.

"Maybe I'll just take a little warmup on this tea," I said to no one in particular. "I think the world would like to know what Post-cop tea tastes like, don't you?" I poured tea into the teapot, then back into the cup, and sipped with gusto.

"Is your Net link still out?" Bad Cop demanded.

"It's just come on again," Keishi informed her.

"Tune in News One and tell me what you see."

There was a brief pause. Then the voice on the radio said, "Oh, gods. Don't move. Don't say a word. Just wait, and someone will be there right away."

"Tsk, tsk, tsk," I said, sipping my tea. "You swore on duty, and I've got every last phoneme on disk. What does the chief of police do in a case like this? Wash your mouth out with soap?"

Good Cop and Bad Cop sat frozen, as though they'd been switched off.

"Well, will you look at this? You give them a little media exposure and all of a sudden they're so high and mighty they won't even talk to you—"

"Maya Tatyanichna!" boomed the captain, bursting in. "Thank gods you're all right. I came the minute I heard about this terrible misunderstanding. I'm sorry to prevail still further on your patience, but may I speak to my officers outside for a moment?"

"Sure, no problem. But I warn you, they're really not much fun anymore."

"Thank you," he said, bowing slightly. "I will return shortly." He escorted them out.

I did what any self-respecting camera would have done under the circumstances. I poured out my teacup, put it against the door, and listened.

The captain was saying: " . . . judged that you have erred so grievously that, in accordance with regulation 3708 stroke 25 paragraph c, I am removing my Emily Post chip in order to impress upon you the magnitude of your offense."

"But . . . but . . ."

"You goddamn stupid whores!"

I had to bite down on my hand to keep from laughing. If only I'd really been recording. Of course I wasn't; I'd had my Net-rune hot-wired years before, so I could turn it on and off as I pleased. It's nice for letting people think that something's off the record. But a Postcop captain swearing like a sailor all over the whole Net! If I had to choose between that and the whale, I might be tempted to give up the whale.

The whale. If I was going to live, then there was still a world outside the police station, and in it I had an interview to do. Not without regret, I abandoned my post for a moment to pick up the radio. "Hello, Officer Miranda?"

"I read you, Officer Pudding. Over."

"Hey, front desk," I said, "things are a little confused back here. Do you happen to know the time of day?"

"You've got around five minutes before someone figures out that everywhere but this building, News One is carrying a political debate in Otaku. Over."

"What do I do? Um, over."

"They're hoping you'll get bored waiting and everyone will tune out. So you want to let them know it won't work. Just make a pain in the ass out of yourself."

"I think I could manage that. Over."

"That's a roger, the plan *is* designed to make use of our operative's natural talents," Keishi confirmed. "Break a leg, Officer Pudding. That's an order. Over and out."

I pressed my teacup against the door again. The captain was still swearing industriously.

"Haven't you *duraks* ever heard of a retrofit? Just because the bitch has sockets in her head, you *assume* she can't also be wired with a totem. So you confiscate the totem, don't deactivate it, and she beams your every word to News One out of our own goddamn evidence room?"

"But we *did* check. We checked her file and we scanned her twice, and she didn't have anything that could have been a totem in disguise—"

"Well, you obviously didn't check well enough."

"Can't they just cut off the Netcast?"

"We don't dare. We cut off the Netcast all of a sudden, and then she's never heard from again—what are people going to think?"

It seemed like a good time to pound on the door and shout at the top of my lungs.

The captain appeared promptly. "Hey, Cap'n," I said. "If it were just me I'd wait, but I've got half of Russia sitting in this chair and they're getting a little bit restless. Could you talk to the folks for me? Say hi to your mother or something."

"We will release you now, Maya Tatyanichna."

"Oh, come on," I wheedled. "I spent months setting up this story. You can't just take it away from me."

"Right this way, please."

"Oh, all right. Spoilsport."

He led me out and down the hall. I felt lightheaded. I was doing it. I was going to leave the Postcop station alive.

"The officers who arrested you have been arrested themselves," he explained as we walked. "They had altered their Post chips in order to commit these violations of privacy and engage in this unwarranted arrest. I assure you that the Post police have no grievance against you and that we are intensely sorry for what has happened."

For another five minutes, anyway. The captain led me to the evidence room and gave me back my clothes.

"You washed them for me," I noticed with amusement. "How

nice. What do you do with the clothes when you kill a prisoner? Store them forever?"

"We present the clothes to local charities," the captain explained. "Of course, that is only in those rare cases when the ultimate penalty is called for. —I'm afraid we have no dressing rooms for prisoners. You may use our officers' locker room. Here we are."

I waited for him to leave, then grabbed the hem of the gown to strip it off. A sudden fear stopped me. "You know, people of Russia," I said loudly, "the captain probably thinks I'll pause the Netcast while I undress, so he can cut off my signal and no one will know the difference. Little does he know that I have no shame whatsoever."

Then I backed against the lockers, seized by another fear. "Also, if my broadcast gets cut off suddenly in the next few seconds, you'll have a pretty good idea that I was shot in the back. Won't you?"

I stayed there a moment, my voice echoing through the locker room, then looked around the corner carefully. No one was there. Steady, Maya; the bluff doesn't have to hold much longer. I dressed hastily and charged back into the front room, the gown over my arm.

"All right," I said, "where the hell's my moistware?"

"I am afraid that those items have now become evidence in the trial of the renegade officers," the captain said with rehearsed sincerity.

"Look, I've got an interview to do in less than three hours. I need my equipment."

"I'm sorry. The trial should take place in a few days. When it is over you can return here to pick up your belongings."

This was his petty revenge, I realized. My only chance was to scare it out of him. I straightened my spine a little to get the full advantage of my height, looked down into his left pupil, and said: "Would you care to give the Russian populace an explanation for this bureaucratic obstructionism? Or would you rather just get me my property?"

"I regret that—"

"Captain, you have a transmission coming in," said the Post-cop at the front desk. "It's marked triple-urgent."

"Triple . . . ? If you will wait one moment."

"Of course," I said. He walked around behind the desk and took the plug the receptionist proffered. As he turned away and inserted it, the assignments on the monitor above the desk dissolved into a single word, flashing: NOW, NOW, NOW.

I'd had the same idea myself. I ducked out the front door and took the stairs down to the street three at a time. Then I stopped cold. In front of me was a wall of wasps, all electronically parked, so that there was barely a centimeter between them. I could go down the sidewalk, but I'd be a sitting duck. I turned around and saw the captain clattering down the stairs, with a whole parade of Postcops behind him. Trapped, I backed up till I tripped on the curb and stumbled against a wasp. In my panic, I barely noticed that the car was not cold, like metal, but taut and warm and mus-cled, like the shoulder of a horse.

"Put your hands in the air," the captain called out. I noticed he didn't say please. I tried to comply, but my arms were stuck. As the Postcops raised their guns, I realized that I had sunk into the wasp up to my elbows, as if it were quicksand.

"Put your hands up! This is your last warning!"

"I'm *trying!*" I called out, but the car had already enveloped me. Something cold touched the back of my head. A thick black liquid wrapped itself around my eyes, and forced its way into my mouth and nostrils. I wanted to gag, but my throat would not obey the impulse. Then my mind folded in on itself, like a burning spider, and for a long time I felt nothing more.

# fifteen

## PHAETON

**S**top trying to breathe," said a voice in my ear. "You're only making yourself panic."

"Keishi—"

"Don't try to use your mouth, just think it. If you just forget about your body, you'll be all right."

"Where are we? Why can't I see anything?"

"We're a couple hundred kilometers out of Arkhangelsk. You can't use your eyes to see; just *look.*"

I did. I was in the front seat of a car, with Keishi sitting next to me. The road was rushing past at an improbable rate. I reached up and felt the driver's helmet wrapped around my head, with braided cables trailing from it.

"Did we escape? Am I alive?"

"Nothing gets by you, does it?"

I tried to laugh, but the helmet choked me.

"Laugh on the inside," she advised.

"Keishi, I could kiss you," I said.

"No, you couldn't," she said matter-of-factly, "because for one thing, I'm still in Arkhangelsk, and for another thing, you've got a car in your mouth."

"Oh. I . . . I thought maybe it was really you this time."

"*Soon,*" she said.

"Sooner than my death?"

"Don't talk that way. Do you see anyone following us?"

"No," I said. We were far from the city by now, and the lights on the dashboard informed me we were at 300 kph and climbing. "What kind of car *is* this?"

"Postcop pursuit vehicle."

"Oh, gods," I said, and tried to bury my face in my hands—only to remember that I couldn't move my head. "You just had to dig us even deeper."

"Maya," she said in exasperation, "it doesn't *get* any deeper than you were. How much we piss off the Postcops is no longer an issue. They're as pissed as their moistware will let them get."

"I guess that's true. Won't they be able to trace this car, though?"

"Not a chance. The license plate's a hologram, which I'm changing at random intervals. The color cycles through the full spectrum, too gradually to notice. And on top of that, I used the onboard computer to give every car in Leningrad the same registration number. Everything but the kitchen sink in these babies."

"How'd you steal it? Don't they have alarms?"

"I signed it out to Officer Pudding. One of our pal Voskresenye's back doors."

"How many back doors *are* there in the Postcop computers?"

"Uh, before or after today? I think I've used up about half of them."

"Terrific," I said. The adrenaline high of finding myself free was beginning to wear off. I tried to look out the side window, only to find that there wasn't one. "Where are we going?"

"Arkhangelsk, of course. You've got an interview to do."

"But I don't even have a camera chip!"

"Check the glove box," she said smugly.

"I don't think I can. . . ."

"Oh, right." A segment of the dashboard slid aside, revealing the rosebox I had left under the bathroom sink.

"How did you get this here if you're still in Arkhangelsk?"

"I, um . . ." She looked at me, then turned away and said meekly, "I sort of hired someone to break into your house."

I looked at her in anger, but immediately relented. "I guess it doesn't matter now."

"That's the spirit."

"Look," I said, "moistware or no moistware, I'm never going to get on the air. The first thing the Postcops'll do when they figure out what happened is to call Netcast and have my time slot revoked."

"Yeah, they already did that."

I sighed in frustration. "Then why are we going to Arkhangelsk?"

"Wanna hear my impression of a Net executive?"

I stared at the side of the road, having figured out how to pan the vehicle's cameras. "I'm not going to get out of this, am I? Sooner or later we'll run out of back doors and luck. At the outside, maybe I'll manage to do the Netcast and die famous. But probably not even that. Chances are I'll never even get to meet you."

"But the Netcast changes everything," she said earnestly. "The world will be following your every move. You're going to have a lot of people watching over you."

"You mean I'll be surfed."

She nodded sadly. "I'm afraid so."

I shook my head a little, which made the helmet tug uncomfortably against my sockets. "I'm not sure which is worse—dying, or having every prepubescent in Russia trying to get behind my eyes."

"But it's only for a little while. Before all this happened I was going to build you a shield, but instead I'm going to take out the defenses you already have. The Postcops won't come for you when you've got a thousand people in your head. It's not in their programming."

"They'll find a way," I said.

"Eventually. But by that time, I'll have you in Africa."

I laughed without humor. "You better get that screening chip checked out. You're not getting good color fidelity."

"It doesn't matter how white you are, you can still get political asylum. You know how His-Majesty-In-Chains feels about suppressor chips. Your encyclopedia is as good as a passport."

"But I'd have to get across the border first."

"That's what I'm working on now," she said. "But I'll find a way."

"I wish I could believe you."

"We *will* meet, Maya. I'm not letting you off that easy."

I watched the road in silence. At last she said, "Maya, I'd rather stay with you, but I'm still working on the Postcop computers, and I need to make plans to get you into Africa, too. I just don't have the bandwidth to spare. Can you drive for a while?"

"I can't drive a car like this."

"There's nothing to learn. It's a direct neural interface. Here, take it."

"But—" And then I *was* the car. It was as if I had been born with wheels, as if evolution had crafted my nerves to fit axles and gears instead of muscles and bones. I felt the wind against my skin. The road beneath me was an ever-changing stream of tastes and textures, to which my tires responded with a constant rearrangement of their fingerprints.

"Are you all right?" she asked anxiously.

"All right doesn't begin to cover it," I answered from the dashboard speaker. I adjusted my shape to reduce drag, and shot forth even faster, trying to see if I could reach 400 kph. After a few minutes, I could barely remember what it was like to have a human body. Even the vague sensations from my internal organs had been changed: my stomach was an engine. And I realized as I felt its heat that the car was not electric, but internal combustion. It *burned.* Other cars were barely even obstacles; there was nothing on the road but me—looking just like any other car, yet harboring this secret fire.

"Uh-oh," Keishi broke in. "We've got a Postcop, dead ahead."

"Just one? What is he?"

"Standard wasp. Not a threat in itself, but if a Weaver notices—"

"I see him now," I said. "I don't think it's going to be a problem." I accelerated toward him, the indicator trembling just below the 400 mark. The wasp came into view, crawling toward me at a pathetic pace, his whining little sirens on. I made myself the color of the road and leapt at him, an invisible bullet. When I reached him I breathed static into his ears and spat needles. His tires were shredded and he spun out of control into my lane. I was not afraid: I had seen the motion before it began. I slid past, stretching out an arm to scoop the air against him. He was blown onto the shoulder of the road. I swerved, braked, and farted fire. As I accelerated again I saw the wasp engulfed in brick-red flames. I didn't look at it for long.

"You did it," Keishi said. "I didn't get a peep of radio."

"Too bad," I said. "I switched our registrations as we passed him. If he had called home, they'd have come and finished off the job."

She chuckled appreciatively. "I always knew you had potential."

"Always?" I said. "How long is always? Last week? It seems like forever."

"Yes, it does," she said softly. "It seems like twenty years." She broke contact. I accelerated back up to 350. Then I extruded ailerons, making the car skip over the road like a stone on water. I adjusted, and began to glide, as over ice. The indicator shuddered past 350, and didn't stop: 360, 370. There was no use fighting it. I had fallen into hope, as you might fall into the ocean; and though

I knew I would drown eventually, for the moment it seemed as though the deep, deep sea would keep me up.

Almost . . . yes: 400. My tires brushed the road only rarely, as if to assure themselves it was still there. *Is love like this?* I wondered, as I leapt into the air again. "Better," was the whispered answer. *Like this?* I asked, as I rippled my skin to fling the wind away from it. "Better," as my fingertips tasted the road.

Then I had a thought that seized my brakes with fear and sent me spinning across the road. I could barely control the skid enough to bring us safely to a stop.

"What are you doing? We haven't got time!"

"Keishi," I said, "if I go to Africa, what happens to you? They won't let you immigrate."

"I can take care of myself. Drive!"

"That's not an answer." Silence. "And I'm not going anywhere until I get one."

"Well," she said at length, "it is Africa."

"What the hell is that supposed to mean?"

"We could get married."

### (The Unknown King)

(I don't know what compulsion makes me go through the forms of suspense, as if the ending of the story were in some doubt. You already know that Africa is not where I wound up. The rumors say I'm in contact with them, that I've talked to His Majesty. It isn't true. Perhaps the Known Kings do protect me in some way, but if so, they don't tell me about it.

Once people have gotten an idea like that in their heads, though, it's no use trying to get it out. So people ask me questions about Africa. And I make up answers, just as if I knew.

Most of the answers are simple. The question I'm asked most is who the Unknown King is, what her title is, whether I've met her—that's the information everybody wants. And I tell them. I don't *know*, of course, but it's always seemed obvious to me. Think about the three Known Kings: His-Majesty-in-Chains, whose nerves are wound into his continent, so that he feels the hunger and the pain of all his people. Only-A-Man, who takes one person at a time and lives behind her eyes, though only for an hour. And Its-Ethereal-Highness, the calculator-king, whose justice is the justice of a balance beam, whose sympathy is parceled out by floating-point arithmetic. Male, hermaphrodite, and neuter; that means the Unknown King's a woman. It stands to reason. And beyond that, can't you see what the three represent? General sympathy, individual sympathy, law. Those are the three possible ways of reaching out to people. At least, I can't think of any others.

And once you know that, well, isn't it obvious what the Unknown King must be? And why she's unknown?

She's the one who turns away.)

# sixteen

## VERY LIKE A WHALE

**T**earing off the plastic babushka, I crashed down the stairs, fumbling to slot in the African moist-disk and camera chip. I couldn't get them in with just one hand, so I gave up and let go of the railing to use both. Surely, after all that had happened, I would not break my neck on a mere staircase; the Weaver bullet rushing toward me would prevent all lesser dooms.

"Time?" I called out. My voice reverberated through the stair-well.

"You've got about three minutes," Keishi said, her voice calm and echoless.

At the bottom of the third flight of stairs was the door to an el-evator. Fortunately, the elevator car was already there waiting, but the ride down took at least a decade of subjective time. When the doors finally opened, I saw a corridor that went on for a hundred meters and then turned a blind corner. On both sides of the hall were moving sidewalks, like the ones they have in trainports.

"Stairs, elevator, now this," I said, getting onto the conveyor. "If I have to slide down a pole, the deal's off."

As the sidewalk carried me along, I noticed that the one on the other side, for return trips, wasn't moving. So much for a quick getaway. Keishi was going to send my signal out along a winding path, which she said would take hours to unravel; but if the Post-cops did see through it, they would surely be here before I could get out.

"Forty-five seconds."

"Count me down from ten," I said, breaking into a run, "and whatever happens, make it look like I planned it."

"Gotcha," Keishi said. "The miscues are dramatic pauses, and the bumps are vérité. So noted. Oh, and Maya?"

"Yes?"

"Neither down nor a feather!"

"To the devil!" I roared back. I'd need all the luck I could get.

The slidewalk took a left turn, then a right, and I passed several doors, all of them boarded up. Was the whole place abandoned? No, someone had kept the slidewalk in repair. Which did not, of course, mean that anyone was there at the moment. Please, God, don't let this be a Capone's Vault. I slotted the imagination enhancer, just in case.

"Ten," Keishi said, with no end in sight. "Nine, eight," and another curve came into view. "Seven, six, five"—I turned the corner. There was a door ahead: end of the line. I started a lunge—"four"—then changed my mind and stopped, letting the slidewalk carry me along. "Three, two," and I was just stepping off, my momentum pitching me forward; I caught myself; "one—and you're live."

"This is Maya of hearth News One," I said, briskly walking toward the door. "I'm in what used to be the laboratory of the Guardian collaborator, Aleksandr Derzhavin." I paused to let the memories float up from the moistdisk: women with glass skulls revealing their brain grafts; rings of animals linked by cables; a Kazakhi infant with a second head, not human, hanging limply from his shoulder.

"I feel your horror, but it's muted," I said, stopping in front of the door. "After all, it was a long time ago. The Guardians are gone, and Derzhavin is dead, and it's hard to get worked up about it. But this place is not abandoned. Someone lives here—someone for whom Derzhavin's experiments are much more than a distant memory." I put my hand on the doorknob. "This is Maya Andreyeva, coming to you from about a kilometer underneath—ah, underneath the ground." No sense giving the Postcops free hints. "And I'm about to show you something amazing."

I hope. I turned the doorknob—and had to suppress my relief when the door opened easily. I walked through into a room that, but for the lack of a sparking Jacob's-ladder, might have been the set of some remake of *Frankenstein*. On my left, behind a transparent curtain, were three dissecting tables, each large enough to autopsy an elephant. One lay bare; one was piled with Petri dishes, test tubes, and retorts; the third held the earthly remains of several antique computers, lying in state among a maze of cables. On my right were larger pieces of equipment—centrifuge, terminal with headset, and a thing the size of an oven that I guessed to be an electron microscope. None looked new, or even functional.

I took all this in with a quick pan of my eyes, then focused on the chessboard in the middle of the room. The pieces were still set up, as though abandoned in mid-game. Calling on my imagination chip, I placed Voskresenye and Derzhavin at the table. In the foreground, I reenacted Voskresenye's awakening; in the background, I let the memory of my interview filter in. When Derzhavin got up and wheeled Voskresenye through the door, I silently followed them into a hall—for them dimly lit, and for me dark. Long rows of cages were set into both walls. I made Voskresenye's image look to both sides as they passed, and briefly showed the audience what he had seen there. Then I lit my Net-rune, to show them what was in the cells now.

All the cages had been fitted with shelves; rows of books sat behind the iron bars, huddling at the backs of their cells like frightened prisoners. There were twenty cells in all, and over each, a description of the contents was painted in neat block letters:

Theology, Ethics, Poetry, Biology. On impulse I tried a door, only to find it locked—they were all locked. Nor was this a measure against theft; the keys were hanging openly on a board at the end of the hall. It was as if he wanted to prevent the books' escape.

"What kind of a man keeps a library like this?" I asked aloud. I kept my mind blank of answers. Let the audience invent its own.

There was a door at the end of the hall. This had better be the one; I had no time to spare. I let Derzhavin push Voskresenye's ghostly image through the door and vanish. Then I slipped the nucleus of the whale research into my memory, gently, so as not to give the game away too soon. I turned the knob with melodramatic slowness. The door obliged me with an eerie creak.

When I looked into the room, the audience inside me caught all its breaths at once. Behind a sheet of glass the size of a soccer field, the whale floated as though in sleep, barely moving her serrated fins. Long, crooked scars marked her side, and half the crescent of her fluke was torn away. A thick air-tube pierced her blowhole, surrounded by a mass of sores where it had rubbed against her skin. Her head was ringed by a crown of sockets, their little copper thorns sealed off from the water by clear plastic inserts. Fluorescent lights behind the tank surrounded her with luminous blue halos, and, filtering through the glass, tattooed my skin with moving waves.

As I approached the whale, she opened her eyes, like a man briefly roused from an opium sleep. She didn't see me—or if she did, I was beneath her notice. Perhaps what she looked at was not in this world.

And if the whale looked through me, then, too, the audience looked through her. The chips and tubes were transparent to their eyes, and even her flesh symbolic and not real. Looking at her, they were watching that vid with the whale in the iceberg. I tried to win them over by brute force, staring at the sores around her blowhole and trying to imagine what she must feel; I tried horror, pity, melancholy; but I couldn't even mute their giddiness. Finally I gave up, made my mind a blank, and waited for the audience to grow calm.

Calm would not come. I'd caught what cameras call an updraft: just as the viewers got over their first rush of interest, others smelled the excitement and tuned in. The surprise of the newcomers strengthened the scent, attracting still more people, in a spiral that could make the feedback escalate out of control. Wave upon wave of astonishment crashed through me. I tried to look down, but the curiosity of millions forced my head back up. I stood there staring at the whale like someone forced to look into the sun, unable to turn away, though my mind cringed from the sight and my eyes were burning. It was not just an updraft, but riptide: feedback so strong that it flooded out my own emotions and derailed my thoughts. The audience grew so large and so greedy that it wouldn't even let me blink. I sank to one knee—it was that or fall—and silently begged Keishi to cut off the input.

"News One says wait it out," she said apologetically. "They think they can still bring in more viewers."

Greedy sons of bitches. *What are we up to?*

"Do the words *forty share* mean anything to you?"

I was already brimful of the audience's amazement, so the news could not surprise me, but I reminded myself to be impressed when my reactions were my own again. *Two out of every five viewers in Russia—*

"No, three out of five in Russia. I'm talking global. If this doesn't taper off soon, you'll be reaching half the people in the world."

Well, the eyes of half the world were worth a little riptide. I stared at the whale until my tears dissolved it into halos, until my eyes were nothing but a dull ache boring its way deeper and deeper back into my head.

*Keishi?* I said, weakly. *Does News One have any ideas on how I might manage to stand back up?*

She didn't answer, but I heard someone come up behind me,

and felt a hand cover my eyes. The metal of his carapace was cold against my cheekbone: Voskresenye. The audience, cut off from the source of its excitement, grew quiet enough that I could blink and turn away. Voskresenye took my elbow and guided me to a chair.

When my eyes cleared, I saw that I was sitting with the whale behind me. It was like having your back to a man with a gun: the urge to look around was almost irresistible. But at least I could think. As he sat down across from me, I mouthed a silent "thank you," which he answered with a slight nod of his head.

Gingerly, I touched the memories on the moistdisk. The audience let me, but I wouldn't have wanted to try it a second time. Thinking with half the world inside my head was like crossing a frozen lake in smooth-soled shoes: the slightest misstep might send me spinning out of control. Fortunate, then, that I was in this chair, across from a man I could interview, with a moistdisk whispering in my ear. I had done this at least once a week for longer than I could remember. I could do it in my sleep—and even in this state. The castle of my mind had been usurped, but the maids could still cook just as well as before; and this was galley work.

"Pavel Voskresenye," I began carefully, "when we last talked I was, shall we say, a little skeptical about the whale. Afterward, as I recall, I said to my screener, 'You can't put a whale in a tank. It's like claiming you slipcovered Leningrad.' " I paused to wait out the giddy feeling of a million people snickering. "It looks like Derzhavin slipcovered Leningrad. But even now that I've seen it, it still seems impossible. Can you show me the flaw in my reasoning?"

"It seems unthinkable to you," he said, "because you are Maya Andreyeva, a News One camera, and not Aleksandr Derzhavin, a Guardian scientist. That means, of course, that you do not have access to Calin's treasuries or to unlimited amounts of slave labor; those are things that accustom a person to thinking big. But more important, it means that when you look at a whale, you see a living being—a creature with senses, organs, dimensions, passions.

When Derzhavin looked at a whale, he saw none of that.

"All the Guardians experienced some degree of spiritual atrophy, or they could not have done what they did, but Derzhavin was an especially advanced and chronic case. He was an urbane, oftentimes a witty man; he honored the memory of his wife and he was gentle with his children. He was even, in his own way, scrupulously moral, though it was a purely arithmetical morality in which no sympathy was needed or allowed. Yet he was one of the most evil men that ever lived. It was not that he hated; he was beyond hatred, hatred is human. He seemed to have been born without the gene that enables us to see souls in the world—spirit-blind, as some are colorblind. When Derzhavin looked at a Kazakh or a whale, he saw a wetdisk, an organic computer, sheathed in a husk of irrelevant flesh. The body was an unfortunate complication, and the spirit just a dream of foolish men."

Hypnotized by his voice, the audience had reached a state of calm attention. The clamoring to look behind me had grown weaker, and a genuine interest in his story was beginning to form. The camera in me had noticed that he'd twisted my question around so he could make the point he wanted to make anyway. No one with any sense would go into a News One interview without knowing how to do that; he'd be slaughtered. It's something you expect your subjects to do, as you expect a chessplayer to castle. So you plan for it, and counter it. But for the time being, anything that calmed the audience was fine with me. If I needed to pin him down I could do it later, after people had started to switch back to their sitcoms. For now, keeping the conversation on anything but whales was more important. Still, I couldn't help but worry that somewhere in our exchanges I would take a poisoned pawn.

"I'm afraid I cut you off in mid-story last time," I said. "When we left off, you—well, you were doing what we just did: seeing the whale for the first time. How was it different for you?"

"In appearance she has not changed much. She is older, but that is not apparent to the untrained eye. I saw the same thing all of you just saw. Except that I knew, the moment I saw her, that she was a part of myself. I knew it not just because of the cable that connected us, but because as I looked into her eye, I *was* that eye, I was that wall of altered flesh."

He paused, looking down at the carapace that covered his hand. The audience noticed it then for the first time, and it held their attention an instant; then they grew restless. Just when I might have lost viewers, he said:

"It is most difficult to explain, this being two selves at once, to you who are only one. You might as well try to explain your single self to a computer, who has none at all. For those of your viewers who speak Sapir—" He emitted a series of clicks and whistles, like a whale song played too fast. "Which I suppose, if pummeled into Russian, would be 'O my amphibious—no, my *hermaphrodite*—soul.' And that is hardly useful. Perhaps a metaphor will help.

"Imagine that I were to hold up a half-silvered mirror between our faces—a sheet of glass painted with clear and reflective squares alternating like a chessboard, on a scale too small to see. Then you would see my face combine with your own, not statically, but fading in and out, and sometimes merging. The left eye of your reflection might appear, then disappear, to be replaced with mine, while all the time the right eye was a fusion of the two. If you looked at the mirror long enough, you might learn to control this process, to choose whose features you would see in which place; but at first, the faces would recombine randomly. That was how it was for my mind and the whale's. Later I would discover how to switch between visual cortices, but at the time, I could only watch my field of vision slowly crossfade back and forth.

"When I saw through her eyes, I saw myself—rather flattened, and more scarred than I had guessed, but recognizable. Standing behind me, I saw Aleksandr Derzhavin. And I remembered. He had killed my mother before my eyes, and when the nets lifted me from the water, he had sponged her blood off of my skin with his own hands. He had brought me to this place, where I could only swim a few strokes at a time before I reached a wall and had to turn. He had put things into my skin that changed my shape, so that when I moved in the water, it resisted me, as though I were a stranger to it. He had changed my mind so that my thoughts became faint furtive things among a babble of human voices I could barely understand. And he had tied me to this pale, soft creature even lumpier than myself, this ill-designed monstrosity that would struggle in the water like a wounded fish, and whose mind, too, struggled against the world, as against an enemy.

"And why not kill him? It had not occurred to me before; and now I realized for the first time that this was strange. Derzhavin had done something to me, more than the obvious. I could see it—a black spot occluding the light. He had altered me to keep me from conspiring against him. But being who he was, he had not considered what the whale might feel. I could not hate him myself, in that crippled body slumped inertly in a chair. But in the mind of the whale, I hated him so purely that my hands and flippers trembled at the sight of him. And the whale, who could hate, but who was held back from the object of her hate by a pane of glass, could plan against him by borrowing my unasked-for oracular gift.

"And so I looked down at my hands, and concentrated on them, as I had concentrated on the chessboard earlier, until I saw the shining pathways start to spiral out. And slowly, taking our time—for we had all the time in the world—my whale-self and my man-self began to choose those futures in which we would kill him."

"What did you do?"

"At first there was nothing we could do. I needed the use of my legs, and he puttered over that for months, until my man-self was simmering with impatience. Yet we waited. We waited until I could walk, and then we waited again for him to begin to trust me. Derzhavin was a suspenders-and-belt man from way back: even though he had made me, so he thought, incapable of disobedience, he still turned on my carapace only when he needed me. Other times I sat inert in this same chair, in this very room, like a child's toy set aside.

"For a long time, all the paths I saw were parallel. No matter what I did, the result would be the same. But in the distance—months or years, I couldn't tell—there was a branching with a death entangled in it, like a skeleton that a tree's root has embraced. I watched this branching all the time that my man-self sat here motionless, and during the interminable chess games, and in physical therapy, as one pair or another of hands supported my flopping form in the shallow water. It seemed to get no closer. At times I would have sworn it was receding. And then one day, at the chessboard, I looked down to calculate a move, and when I looked back up, the moment was at hand.

"Derzhavin had always had trouble getting lab assistants. His project was so high-security that few could get clearance, and of those who could, hardly any were interested in mere assistantship. But many of his experiments had to be watched all night, so he made do with what help he could get. Finally one evening, when he had finished his work for the day and was just sitting down for another session of that idiotic game he was obsessed with, the graduate student who had served as his night assistant for the past two years came in early, with a worried expression on his face. They went into Derzhavin's office. I stared at the board, blind to the chessmen, seeing only paths of light.

"When they came out, Derzhavin was falsely jovial. He ushered the relieved young man out, telling him not to worry, he'd make do, he'd make do. 'You'd be a fool even to think twice about such an opportunity,' he said in parting, firmly squeezing the student's hand.

"When the elevator doors had closed, he sighed and sat down at the table again, pressing the back of his wrist to his forehead. 'Well,' he said to himself, 'I guess I'll have to train one of the guards from the camp. Or one of the chimps from the lab, whichever turns out to be smarter.' And there was the branching. I had to draw his attention to me, just at the proper instant, but without betraying any eagerness. So, without thinking the position through, I recklessly advanced my bishop. 'Check,' I said quietly, keeping my eyes on the board.

"He looked up at me slowly. 'Voskresenye,' he said, 'do you think you could watch things for me at night?'

"I looked at the floor, as if afraid to meet his eyes. 'I will do as you like,' I said. We began that night; and two weeks later, I was able to explore the lab alone."

The audience was quiet enough for me to risk a pointed question: "So that's where you got the information that went into your book." (Here Keishi replayed the memory of the old book snapping shut.) "You didn't just see those things done, did you? Or hear about them? You did them."

I expected him to turn away. But he looked straight into my eye and said with fierce determination: "Yes. Many of those things I did myself, at his command, yes."

"When you could have stopped them."

He nodded. "Some of them. I could at least have put them off. I certainly had more chance to do real good in Derzhavin's lab than I ever had when I worked with the Underground Railroad. Yet I did nothing."

"You don't sound as though you feel very guilty about it."

"Maya Tatyanichna," he said, "I have been watching people die for longer than you have been alive, and I have seen many things, but I have not yet seen the dead come back to life because their murderer felt guilty."

"You call it murder, then."

"Of course I call it murder," he said irritably. "I bled them, cut them to bits, and injected them with poisons. If you have some other name for that, I would be glad to hear it."

He dispensed tea from the samovar on the table beside him, and sipped briskly. I felt a sudden desire to laugh, which puzzled the audience mightily. I don't know why; it just seemed funny that, when inviting a camera into the hidden lair where he had kept a whale in secret lo these many years, he should lay in supplies against cottonmouth. It was altogether too prosaic for the melodrama I had fallen into. His hands on the cup were quite steady, I noted, but then you'd expect them to be.

"How did you kill Derzhavin?"

"The method I chose was poison," he said, resting his teacup on the cage around his hand. "My physical therapy was not yet complete, so I lacked the coordination for a more direct approach. But Derzhavin was cautious. He never let me handle dangerous chemicals unless he was there to watch me. It was agonizing: all those colors and kinds of death passing through my hands every day, and I could use them to kill anyone *except* the one person who deserved it. At night, when I had the whole place to myself, I could find nothing lethal; it was all locked up. I began to read Derzhavin's books, looking for a solution. At last I hit upon it: insulin. A poison I could refine from the very bodies of the people that Derzhavin tortured and killed. The symbolism would be almost as satisfying as the death itself.

"I wasn't sure how much I'd need—strangely enough, most medical books are geared toward saving people, not killing them; short-sighted, I call it. But I assumed that what I could harvest from twenty bodies would suffice. The fact that this would give me a death count three times that of Jack the Ripper was a regrettable, but, I thought, a necessary byproduct of this plan.

"From then on, whenever I saw that a prisoner was scheduled for surgery, I would come to him in the night and sit with him. I tried to persuade them to tell me their stories; not an easy task, once they began to realize that my approach meant death. But sometimes they were so afraid that they would talk to me—to anyone. If they would not, I studied the lines of their faces and the calluses on their hands, trying to deduce who they had been. And what I could not deduce, I invented.

"At dawn I left them. Hurriedly, in the last hours before Derzhavin arrived, I wrote down their stories and carefully hid the papers away.

"Derzhavin's experiments did not have a high survival rate. However, on those rare occasions when a patient might have pulled through, I made sure that he did not. Then, again at night, I would begin those portions of the autopsy that I was permitted to perform myself—always most scrupulously, checking off 'autoimmune complications' for the man who rejected his head transplant, and 'natural causes' for the woman whose heart attack might conceivably have been induced by waking up to find a cable trailing from her skull. And when the last of the paperwork was done, I would remove the patient's pancreas and go to work. I think nothing else has given me such joy as taking those lumps of flesh and refining them, with hands and glass and centrifuge, into a liquid as clear as the water that Katya had poured into my head.

"Finally, after months of work, the drug was ready, and so was I. All I needed was a clear shot at a vein. But that day he came in worried, and he paced and would not sit down. I asked him if he wanted tea, but he ignored the offer. I suggested a game of chess—anything, if he would just hold still—but he refused. Finally he said, 'Sit down, Voskresenye. You may as well know what's happening.' It was the autumn of 2246."

"The Awakening had already happened."

"Yes." Voskresenye looked into the distance. "Of course I didn't see it. I was down here, cut off; and though some of the prisoners may have known, I was the last person they would have discussed it with. But from Derzhavin's description, I thought it must have been a little like the Rapture, the way the evangelists used to talk about it on Guardian radio. Four people would be riding in a car, and suddenly the driver would hit the brakes, get out, and walk away, deaf to all shouts. A man would wake from sleep to see his wife going out the door, carrying, for reasons only the Army knew, a hockey mask, a spaghetti strainer, and a cuckoo clock. They all walked out into the streets and mustered into clumps, and each clump lifted up a memory cell and began to march.

"By noon on that first day, the Army had seized the entire world socket industry, and was drilling people fast enough to add ten thousand recruits every hour. Every boat and plane in America was on its way to the Eastern Hemisphere, its holds tessellated with soldiers. By the time the Guardians found out what was happening, they faced an army of thirty million soldiers without fear— not along a border where they might be held back, but in every city. America and Japan, with nearly a third of their populations already socketed, were under Army control within a month. It was a threat like nothing the Guardians had ever faced, or even imagined. The Russian Heptarch, and he alone, still had a usable army and a populace largely intact—but half the world was marching to his doorstep.

"And through all this, Derzhavin was unaffected. His confidence in the Guardians approached the status of religious faith; he had assumed that they would find some way to stop the Army's progress. But now, he said, he could not put off telling me any longer. The order to evacuate had come. The Army was about to reach Arkhangelsk.

"All this he told me as he paced around the room like Rilke's panther. And as excited as I was to find that the Guardian regime might be over, the first thing on my mind was to make that man stand still. So I began to brew some tea, to calm his nerves, I said; surely he would at least sit down to drink it. As I was making it I asked him whether I would be evacuated. He looked away. 'I'll do what I can,' he said sadly. 'You, I could take easily. But I don't know what to do about the whale, and without—'

" 'We'll work it out somehow,' I said. 'Just sit down and relax. It's no use trying to make plans while you're this tense.'

"At last he sat down at the chess table. He fidgeted with the pieces for a while, then began to set them up. 'Once more—for old time's sake?' he said.

" 'Of course, if that's what you want,' I answered, taking the strainer from the teapot.

" 'I suppose we'll have to euthanize the subjects and start fresh,' he said regretfully. 'We can't move them all. But we'll still have the data. Voskresenye, we must keep the data secure.'

" 'Of course we will,' I said. 'Don't worry about that now.' I stood behind him, set down a cup and saucer on the gaming table, and picked up the teapot. 'Think about—' And I poured the whole pot of scalding tea onto his lap. He jumped up, driving his neck against the needle I was holding behind him. I pressed the plunger, and he was as good as dead.

"Since I hadn't hit a vein, the poison would take some time for its effect. So I ran into the next room and locked myself into an empty cell. In case he had an extra key I didn't know about, I took out a knife that I had earlier secreted under the mattress; I could not use it effectively, but in his insulin stupor, it might scare him off. I expected him to come after me, to rage at me, perhaps to call a guard—in which case I would die with him. But for a long time he did not come. And when he did, it was only to lean his head against the bars of the cage, look at me in bewilderment, and ask 'Why?' He had no idea why I had killed him. He had murdered thousands, and he had never believed in his heart that somebody might take it amiss."

"Wait a minute," I said. "When we talked before, you said you were 'a good deal more' to Derzhavin than just a lab assistant. What did you mean by that?"

"I suppose I could have phrased that better. You imagined— what? Steamy sexual encounters? Male bonding rituals? Fishing trips?" He laughed, then grew serious, stroking the wires of his hands. "I was his murderer. What relationship could be more intimate?"

To the audience, all this was another revenge drama—something off a soap channel. To them, protected from the action as they were, Voskresenye's behavior might have seemed perfectly rational. But in the chambers of my mind that were my own, I began to wonder just how dangerous a man I was a thousand meters underground with.

"Derzhavin died as I was trying to find words to answer him," Voskresenye said. "And so I never got to ask him the question that had haunted me since I awoke: What was I *for*? I knew the purpose of his research: he was looking for a way to heal the brain-damaged, and to resurrect the brain-dead. But you do not perform basic research with whales; it is not cost-efficient. I was designed to *do* something; and I do not know what, to this day."

"What do you suspect?"

"I suspect," he said, "that I was to be a military strategist. I suspect I was designed to outwit the Army. I suspect that is what the chess games, and certain other tests, were for."

"Then why weren't you ever put into service?"

"Yes—that is the question: why was I not used, why was I not even given a trial run? Why did I never face the Army, even in a simulation?" He looked down at his carapace, his mouth curling in scorn at its crudeness. "The Army was already coming," he said. "Perhaps time did not permit." But there was no conviction in his voice.

"Where did you wait out the Army?" I asked. "Down here?"

"No; that proved impossible. The Guardians were trying to stop the Army with a scorched-earth policy, depriving it of what it needed to survive. Nothing was to be left intact that it could use; especially not people. It is, in fact, a miracle they left the whale alive—they must have thought that she would be of no use to the Army. Or perhaps they knew no way of killing her without breaking the glass of her tank, and so drowning themselves. Certainly they would have destroyed her if they had known, as I know now, that the last beluga whale in captivity was carried by one column of the army for twenty miles, and then, the flesh being eaten up, discarded.

"In any case, they did not harm the whale. But the day after I killed Derzhavin, they came down and herded all us prisoners upstairs. We were gathered next to an enormous pit and taken, in groups of thirty, to the edge of it to be shot. I saw ten groups of prisoners killed as I waited for my own turn, and not one of them made any motion of defiance. I couldn't understand it. They knew they were about to die; why didn't they run, make the fig at them, anything? I tried to suggest to the man standing next to me that we should all charge them together, that they could never get us all. He only shrank from me, as I suppose anyone would have. But I determined that when my own time came, I would not go quietly.

"The next time they counted off, I was one of the thirty. I looked down into the pit as we marched up to it: it was a long way to fall, five or six metres. But I couldn't run, not now, nor could I hope to reach the Guardians before they shot me. So I stood there, crouching down a little, and watched their trigger fingers. The instant before they fired, I jumped backward into the pit.

"My first discovery was that human bodies make a much harder landing surface than you'd expect. I was sure I had broken at least three bones. But it was not bones I was worried about. When I tried to move, I confirmed my worst fear: my exoskeleton was damaged. I could move my arms, but my legs were useless.

"Dragging my legs behind me like a beached merman, I crawled down the slope of bodies. I had only gotten a few metres when I heard gunshots again. The falling bodies set off an avalanche, which carried me the rest of the way down the slope. I was out of the way—safe, until another avalanche, or until the Guardians decided to set the pit on fire. But my arms were pinned. I couldn't move."

Voskresenye looked over my head at the whale. The audience had shrunk a little and was easier to resist, but not by much. I still had to fight the impulse to turn around.

"I still forget sometimes," he said, "and call my two selves 'she' and 'I,' as though we were separate. There are some things that

Russian is just not designed to express, and you, alas, do not speak Sapir. I had better say man-self and whale-self; that is cumbersome, but accurate. So: as my man-self lay trapped in the pit, my whale-self was still in the tank here, trying to break free."

"From the tank? How?"

"It's not closed, like a fish tank—how did you think he got her down here, on the elevator? This whole complex is built under the continental shelf. The tank goes up some hundreds of metres, and ends with an adjustable vent set just above the ocean floor. If I could just break through it, I would be free. But my air tube was connected to the side of the tank, and quite short. In order to reach the vent, I would have to pull it out, and I had no way of putting it back in. If I tried to break through and failed, I would drown. But when my man-self got pinned, I knew I had to make the attempt. No Guardian was going to take the time to feed me. It would be better to drown than starve.

"I slowly filled my lungs from the trickle of air in the tube, then turned onto my back and pulled. When the tube wrenched itself from my blowhole, I dove to the very bottom of the tank and swam straight upward. But at the last moment I flinched, and took the impact on my back instead of my head. The blow was diffused; the grate was loosened, but not broken. We dove again. My whale-self was calm, but my man-self was in terror that we would drown. Then I began to wonder if the sense of suffocation I was feeling came from my man-self. There might have been another avalanche; I might be dying. At the last instant, before we hit the grate, I switched back to my human body.

"I was not dying, or at least not any faster than I had been before, and I did not hear gunshots. Perhaps they had stopped. When I went back into the whale, we had made it through the vent and were shooting up toward the air.

"I had no idea what the surface of the water should look like from below, so I suspected nothing; but the whale knew, halfway up, what we would find. It was already autumn. The ocean around

Arkhangelsk had begun to freeze. Above us, where the sky should have been, there was only an expanse of shadow, which, as we approached it, turned to white.

"Panicking, our lungs aching, we cast about for an opening in the ice. Time and again, we would see a shaft of daylight in the distance, only to find it filtering through a crevice too small to breathe through. Finally, just when I was sure that our lungs would explode, we came to a patch of thin ice and, smashing our head against it, managed to break through. We gulped air into our lungs, sank, then surfaced and breathed again. Nothing but ice was around us; the water was bitterly cold; our chance of surviving was almost nil—and none of it mattered. I wept with joy, the tears falling onto the corpse my face was pressed against. I was free.

"From Arkhangelsk by ocean, there's nowhere to go but north," Voskresenye continued. "It's a good nine hundred kilometers up through the White Sea and around the tip of Norway before you can turn around south. The ice would get worse for a long time before it got better. Besides that, part of the whale's fluke had long ago been lost to gangrene, and she was bleeding where the edges of the vent had raked against her side, and after so many years of captivity, she was not in shape for such a journey. All these things occurred to me as I dove back down into the freezing water to search for the next air hole. But what stopped me was something quite different. The radio link that connected my two selves was not strong enough to stretch beyond a few tens of kilometers. If I sent the whale past that limit, she would be separated from my man-self—and he would be reduced to idiocy, unable to rejoin her.

"For it is so hard, you see, to be two selves, for all its advantages. One can be attacked through the other, or you can be separated. It is giving up a hostage to the world. Live single: that is my advice to you. Or if you must be two selves, keep them in one body."

"I'll, ah, I'll be sure to keep that in mind," I said.

He nodded. "See that you do."

He sipped his tea again before continuing his story. "For three days my mind dwelled in the whale, as my body lay among the dead. And on the third day, the Unanimous Army came to Square-Mile-at-Arkhangelsk. I could see nothing from where I lay, but I heard them coming for hours, with their ragged, shuffling march. Finally I heard them climb into the pit, by the hundreds, walking on the bodies. I was so cold and hungry that I considered calling out to them, letting them absorb me, anything, if only they would keep me warm. But I changed my mind when I began to hear jingling and ripping sounds all around me. They were stripping the dead.

"The Army worked its way across the pit to where I lay. One of the soldiers—a girl of sixteen, wearing a peacoat over a thin summer dress—lifted up the man that had been lying across my arms. As she held him upright, another soldier, elderly, clad in rags, turned out his pockets. And something hard—a coin, a pocket knife—fell from his pocket and struck my temple.

"In the movies, I'd have held stoically still, to fool the Army. Well, you try it sometime. Of course I jumped; I would have jumped more, if so much of me hadn't been paralyzed; and I very nearly cried out, too. The Army took no notice. As you have found, Andreyeva, against an unimaginative enemy any fool can be a hero."

I kept my mind blank, relying on Keishi to screen out any furtive thoughts of the Postcops. I should have known he'd know.

"When the man had been thoroughly searched, the girl took a soda bottle from her pocket, upended it into her palm, and daubed his face with a red, stinking mixture: the done-paint. By the time they were finished, the whole camp would be covered with this goo, whose stench would tell everyone for miles around that the Army need not come again. As the two soldiers walked away, I turned my head a little to watch them go. They climbed out of the pit on the backs of other soldiers, who had formed a human ladder up the side. Many of those leaving the pit were carrying bodies—I presumed for food.

"The next soldier that came by lifted me up from behind, just as the other man had been lifted. I went limp, hoping they wouldn't know I was alive. The man who came to strip me was a middle-aged Japanese fellow in the remains of an expensive business suit. He turned out my pockets, which of course held nothing, then reached his hand into my shirt—and paused. He laid his hand against my forehead, then pressed his cheek to mine. The warmth of my body had given me away. He reached his hand toward my neck, and for a second I was sure he was going to strangle me; but no, he only wanted to feel my pulse. When that was done, he examined my socket, turning his head to see it from several angles, with a motion that reminded me of robot welders. He turned and made several quick hand signals, then walked away toward the back-bridge, leaving me suspended.

"The next soldier passed without looking, and the next after that, until I began to hope they had forgotten me. But then one stopped in front of me and stood there motionless, waiting. In the distance, a black ring was thrown down into the pit and passed from hand to hand. At last it came to the soldier before me. It was a coiled cable. He was going to infect me with the Army.

"As he unwound the cable, I flexed my fingers. That part of my carapace still worked, yes, but there might yet be subtle damage, and besides, the battery was almost dead. I couldn't hope to overpower him. He inserted one end of the cable into his temporal socket, and then, as if relishing my terror, gradually extended the other end toward me. Just when he was about to slide the plug home, I blocked it with one hand, and with the other put the plug into my wrist socket. I reached my hand into his brain and tore it away from the Army mind.

"For a moment he was Michael Arnason, aged thirty-four, from Sussex, England, a solicitor's clerk, who had gone to sleep one night beside his wife and woken in this pit of death alone—but that was only for a moment. Then he shuddered, and the glimmer of selfhood went out of his eyes. Moving jerkily, he reached into his trenchcoat, took out a bottle of done-paint, and poured it over my head. When the soldier behind me smelled it he let me drop, but the thing that had been Arnason grasped me under the arms, threw me over his shoulder, and carried me up the ladder of backs. As soon as we were out of the pit, I turned him toward the setting sun, and we began the long walk westward to our meeting with the whale."

# seventeen

## FALLEN LIKE LIGHTNING

**Y**ou said—" I conferred with the Net briefly " '—None of it mattered. I was free.' Yet you came back here."

"What else could we do? There aren't many places you can keep a crippled whale."

"Why couldn't she stay in the ocean?"

"Derzhavin's modifications made her dependent on electronics for her life; from that, nothing could free her. Without maintenance, she wouldn't have lived out the year. One of her socket seals would have been torn away, perhaps; it would take no more than that. And then, too, Derzhavin had converted portions of her brain to uses they were not intended for—a cloverleaf with an unenhanced whale would have been of little use. Some of the things he took from her would have been crucial to survival in the wild. So we waited, I repairing my exoskeleton, and she finding what food she could. And next summer, when the ice was gone and the ocean warm, my selves began our separate journeys to Arkhangelsk, home."

*Time?* I asked Keishi.

"All the time in the world, girl. You think they're going to cut this off? But Maya, News One wants another look at the whale."

*Then let them turn off the feedback.*

"I can turn it down to one-quarter for you."

*Not enough*, I said. *Tell them to go to hell.*

"I don't think that's such a good idea," she said. "When you started pulling record ratings, Netcast became remarkably unhelpful to the Post police. If you lose viewers . . ."

*I get the picture*, I said. *One-quarter it is.*

When I felt my limbic system settle down, I said, "Let me apologize to all of you for that delay. News One has told me that you would all like another look at the whale. I'm going to do it, but please, remain as calm as possible. Otherwise you'll have to wait till we can get a robot camera in here to film it. Come on, people, it's just a dolphin with gland problems—nothing to get excited about."

"Instead of just looking at her," Voskresenye said with quiet amusement, "would you like to talk to her?"

"I thought I was."

"Not exactly—any more than you're talking to Stepan Sornyak. I am a fusion of the two, a compromise—'O my negotiated soul' is in the Sapir, too. Thanks to his injuries, my man-self cannot be separated from that union, but the whale can. I have only to release the portions of her mind I occupy—to see myself in the half-silvered mirror."

"How long will that take?"

"An instant. I will appear to have fainted; do not be alarmed. Once the artificial neuromodulators have been stilled, it will take some few seconds for her neurons to reorganize into their natural circuits—such, that is, as Derzhavin did not destroy completely." Then another thought seemed to strike him: "If you like, you can turn over the Netcast to her for a while. She can output telepresence. I'm sure your audience would be interested to find out what it's like to be a whale."

The audience was far too interested, and Voskresenye was far too casual. I didn't believe for a second that he'd just thought of the idea.

But you don't spend thirty years as a camera and turn up your nose at something like that. It's just not in the programming.

"All right," I said warily. "How do I wake you when we're done?"

"A good hard shaking will generally do it," he said as he closed his eyes.

I turned around, panning my eyes along the floor so as to sneak up on the sight. My mind was trying to go in all directions at once, like a chariot drawn by eight cats. But at least I could control it. I raised my eyes to the whale.

Instinctively, my mind sought analogies. It's something I do as a camera—it gives people something to quote over breakfast. This time nothing would come. She was simply herself, beyond all comparison, the metaphor for big.

"I don't know how to do this," I said. "Can you hear me?"

She swam closer and put her eye up to the side of the tank. "Are you the one?" said a voice through the speaker, startling me with its pure contralto. Female or not, I had expected a resonant bass.

"I don't know what you mean."

"The one . . ." Her eye closed, then opened. "The one with the world in her head?"

"Oh. You mean, because I'm a camera? Yes, I suppose I am."

She swam back and forth in the tank several times, her broken fluke and flippers struggling. Then her moistware scraped the glass, and her eye stopped right in front of my face. "What time is it?" she asked, her voice betraying a hint of eagerness.

The question was so absurdly mundane that I was startled into answering. *Uh, Keishi? Time?*

No answer.

*Mirabara!*

Still nothing. She must be deep in trance, I thought, mixing the Netcast and keeping the audience at bay.

I touched the Net myself and said, "Almost five thirty."

"How near is six o'clock?"

"Half an hour," I said. Would she know how long that was?

"Not long."

The whale drifted away without further comment.

"Has it come to that?" I said, trying to entice her back. "Do even whales have schedules? Is there somewhere that you need to be?"

She rolled onto her side, revealing pale ventral grooves like the whorls of a thumbprint. "If you are the one," she said, as though in sleep, "you are the why that I am here. Where you go . . ." She broke off and was still for long moments, considering. Then she approached the glass again. "In the sleeping is an ocean."

"I'm sorry?"

"In the sleeping," she said, "I swim . . . where the tangle webs, and where the colors change. . . ."

"I'm sorry, I don't—oh. Of course." I remembered the dark cloud that Voskresenye had been tethered to in grayspace. "You mean in the Net?"

"Yes, *that*," she said. "What happens to a whale that swims in a tangle, if she is a very small whale?"

"I suppose she'd die."

She slapped the glass with her flipper—hard, it looked like, though there was no sound. "If you are the one," she said, "then where six o'clock is, I will—what you said."

"Why?"

She closed her eyes and was silent a long time before answering. "I fell in the man the way a whale falls in a dream," she said, "a dream where the water will not hold me up, and I am moving my fluke all the time, the way the sharks do that are not such small sharks. . . . I am in this dream of being a man because I wish to be a man, in order to . . . to make die. . . ."

"Derzhavin," I supplied.

"That. Yes. It is a dream come out of hating. I will swim in this small sea no farther."

"But when the man sleeps . . . in the sleeping," I said, picking up her catchphrase, "you aren't here. You swim in the network. You're free then."

"The net . . . work is an admirable ocean." The great eye closed again. "But it is not mine." She began to drift away.

"Durachok," I said. "Ivan Durachok."

"What is that?"

"Ivan Durachok—he's the hero in a story I remember from when I was a child. Why wasn't that on the moistdisk, Mirabara?" No reply. "I don't remember very well. Let's see.

"Ivan Durachok is out riding his hunchbacked pony, and he comes to the ocean. And he meets a whale who's crying out in pain. He looks up, to see why she's crying, and he sees that some peasants have set up a village on the whale's back. They've built their houses right into her bones, and are ploughing her back to plant crops.

"Ivan Durachok says to the whale, I will free you from this agony, if only you will dive down into the ocean, and find the ring. Because he's looking for a ring, you see. There's a king who wants to marry—some woman, I don't know what she is, I think she's some kind of foreign princess. And the princess says to the king, I will marry you, but only if you find my ancestral ring, which was lost far beneath the ocean. And the king sends Ivan Durachok to go find it."

"Du-ra-chok," the whale repeated.

"Yes. Ivan Durachok—Ivan the Idiot—that was his name, yes. And the whale agrees to find the ring. So Durachok shouts out to all the peasants, Get off! There's going to be a great storm, and you'll all be drowned. And they believe him, they all get off. Except, um, I think there's one who refuses to go, who stays there, ploughing. But Ivan Durachok says to the whale, Go ahead, dive, find the ring. And the man who would not leave is drowned in the ocean."

"Drowned," the whale said emphatically. "In the *ocean.*"

"Yes. And the whale—stop that," I said to the audience, brushing away tears. "I told you people to be calm. —The whale dives down. She finds the ring and brings it up. And she says to Ivan Durachok, The reason the city was built on my back, it was a punishment from God, because once, once long ago, I swallowed up a whole fleet of ships."

"Small ships," the whale said.

"Well. It's just a fairy tale. Yes, all right, if you want, the ships were very small. They were only the size of a pomegranate seed, and that was how she swallowed them. And the whale departs, she's whole again, and Durachok goes back to the kingdom with the ring. And he and the pony kill the king somehow—they convince him that if he jumps into boiling water his youth will be restored, and he does it and he dies. I never really understood that part. And Ivan Durachok and the princess are married. And I guess that's the end of it."

She floated motionless, making no reply.

"I didn't tell that very well, I know. I don't know why I even tried. I don't suppose even a human would—"

"Marriage is a thing in ending stories," she said suddenly.

"Yes," I said, taken aback. "I suppose so. In fairy tales, sure."

"Then," she boomed out with an air of finality, "an ocean is in dreaming, and no city is only real." And she swam up out of sight, leaving me to wonder whether we'd communicated anything at all.

Just when I was about to turn away, she sank into view and said, "What time is it?"

"Six is not far," I said. "Six isn't far at all."

For once my feelings and the audience's coincided. I pressed my face against the glass, glad of its coolness. "I will be sorry not to have known you," I said.

She was silent. I thought she would say nothing more. Then the voice from the speaker returned, one last time. "Those who wake . . ." she began tentatively. She paused so long that I was not sure whether or not she was starting a new sentence. At last she said: ". . . do not regret the dream."

*Keishi?* I subvoked. *Can you patch in the telepresence from the whale?*

There was no answer, but my Net-rune went dark.

*And turn off the feedback for me*, I said. *Please? Keishi?*

The next thing I remember, I was sitting on the floor, my arms wrapped around me, rocking back and forth and saying over and over, "Will you turn it off now. Will you turn it off."

And no, I haven't watched the disk. I haven't and I'm not going to, and I really don't want to talk about it. I just hoped that the last whale on earth might be something more important than a cheap thrill for every wirehead in Russia. I know—I should have known better. I'm not going to watch it, that's all.

I felt my Net-rune light again, but decided not to stand up until the world in my head made me. And, strangely, the audience was quiet. Perhaps after the whale they needed some rest, I thought. I stayed sitting there, with my eyes closed, until I heard Voskresenye say:

"When we first met, you asked me why we don't remember the Square Miles. Would you like to hear the answer?"

To my surprise, the audience did not protest against this change of subject. I stood up, as slowly as I could, and turned my eyes on him.

"You were on the right track," he said, "when you compared the Calinshchina to the Holocaust, and to the Terror-Famine. Your error lay in asking what the difference was between these two events. There are many differences, but none is essential. You should have asked, not about the difference in events, but about the difference in ourselves."

"And what's that?" I asked, still standing.

"Why, that the Holocaust and Terror-Famine both occurred long before telepresence."

"The invention of telepresence is an event, isn't it? I thought this was a difference in us."

"What is a medium like telepresence but the extension—no, the *definition*—of ourselves? Are we, who live things at a distance, the same species as our ancestors, who could hear of events in the next town only by going there? If you met a person from that time, would you have any more in common with him than with a whale, or with a chimpanzee? You have traveled to meet me with better than seven-league boots; and I have done more math this morning than Pythagoras, and Euclid, and all Ancient Greece and Rome. Surely, if we are human, they were animals; and we are a race of gods, if they were men."

"Yes," I said, and I sat down in the chair he had provided for me, putting my back, once again, to the whale. "I've felt that, too. That it changes what we are."

"Indeed it does, Maya Tatyanichna. It changes the central fact of the human condition: that each of us lives behind one set of eyes, and not another; that our own pain is an agony, and another's pain only an abstraction we believe in by an act of faith. It makes impossible all the sins of *locality*, all the errors that arise from being prisoned in one body and no other—as racism, sexism, classism, and of course and especially nationalism."

"The Africans seem to manage," I said.

"Come now, Andreyeva, don't be so historically naive. The Africans are not, and never were, one people. They are fifty nations and a thousand tribes, and it is telepresence that has stitched them into one. His-Majesty-In-Chains has built a wall around his country, yes, but not to keep people out. It is to keep himself in. The Wall of Souls at Suez is the sword in Tristan's bed: His-Majesty wants desperately to reach across, for he so loves the world that he would not part with a village of it. But he knows he would destroy the thing he touched. He remembers Egypt, and he knows."

"And he turns away white immigrants because they don't match the divan."

"He does not tell us what his plans for us are," Voskresenye said. "But I assure you that he does not turn us away out of callousness. His-Majesty cannot *not* empathize, but often, even so, he cannot help. Why do you think he names himself His-Majesty-*in-Chains?* Fools and children think it is because he is wired to the world's pain, but that is a lash, not a shackle. The chains are what he locks around himself to keep him from doing more to ease that pain—knowing it would only be worse in the end if he did. But he is patient. The chains give him no choice but to be patient. And he knows that, in the fullness of time, superior technology will tell."

"Right. Okay. So His-Majesty is just, and people around the world are united by telepresence. So—"

"Ah, but not *all* people. Some are united, and some separated. We are pulled toward cameras, but away from people that we know in our own lives. Can you watch telepresence with your friend, your wife, your child? Not truly—you may be in the same room, but you are not *together*. Each is locked in his own dream, even if all are tuned to the same channel. Like movies during the binaural fad: a theater full of people wearing headphones, all hearing the same thing, but separately. And so telepresence causes the triumph of the distant over the near."

"I seem to recall another medium that two people couldn't use together. You could look over someone's shoulder if you wanted, but no two people used it at the same rate or called up the same images. If I remember right, they were called *newspapers.*"

"Not the same thing at all, Maya Tatyanichna. Reading is a restricted and an artificial activity. It does not compete with reality because it is nothing like reality. No one could be tempted to think that what happens on the page is more real than daily life."

I thought of the books in cages, and silently disagreed.

"But telepresence," he continued, "*is* life, except in one respect: it adds a sixth sense, the telepathic, which exists nowhere else. When the telepresence is switched off, you are imprisoned again in your eyes and your ears; the intimacy of mind touching mind is gone.

"We are like men forced to walk about in darkness," he continued, "except in one chamber where our eyes are uncovered. If the color blue were not found in that chamber, we would never know that it existed; and if in the chamber all men were well-fed, we might forget that there is hunger in the world. The chamber would impress itself upon us so forcefully that nothing else seemed real. And so it is. Telepresence is a chamber in which a new sense, more important than sight, is uncovered. What happens outside that chamber barely exists. And so you see, if what we call reality is to persist, *everything* must be brought into that chamber."

"*That's* what you're leading up to? A praise of cabling?" I subvoked to Keishi: *I went through all this shit for a cabling commercial I could have downloaded in Leningrad?*

"Cabling is, and will always be, a marginal solution," he said. "The common man will not expose himself that way, nor will he bother with amateur emotions, when he has six thousand channels of slickly post-produced ones at his beck and call. You know as well as I do that the cable results in hate more often than not."

"And that's not a sin of locality?"

"It is a sin of nonlocality; it is the agony of solitary animals at being caged together."

"What?"

"The mind, Andreyeva. It pulls away from other minds that are too near. This is not the same as acting blindly because it knows no other creature than itself; it is the opposite."

"Look, I don't think the audience is quite getting this," I said— and hoped Keishi would screen out the lie; I had not felt incomprehension, or anything else, from the audience in some time.

"Give us an example. Let's go back to where we started: the Calin-shchina. Isn't that distant enough to seem real? It's in the chamber—it comes in through a socket."

"But there is no telepresence of it. Telepresence of people talking about it, to be sure, but that is not the same. After all, watching a camera interview someone is no better than talking to her yourself; talk is talk, whatever door it comes in. Bringing a radio into the chamber does not help you see what is outside."

"You were in a Square Mile," I said. "If you think telepresence from survivors is so important, why haven't you volunteered yourself?"

"If it were only a question of volunteering, there would be thousands of hours of disk; there were enough survivors to produce it. Instead there are no disks at all. Is that not suggestive?"

"Suggestive of what?"

"That the Weavers will not permit it to be transmitted."

My spine stiffened. *Oh God, Keishi, tell me you screened that out,* I subvoked. She didn't answer. I prayed it was only because she needed her full concentration to edit the Netcast.

"That's ridiculous," I said to Voskresenye, my voice betraying the fear I felt. "The Weavers wouldn't do something like that, even if they wanted to. And they wouldn't want to. They hate Guardians and Guardianism—everybody knows that."

"They allow people to hate the Guardians a judicious amount. Just enough that no one will try to emulate them. Not enough that someone might begin to think the Army was justified."

"We're here to talk about the Guardians, not the Weavers. What you're saying is completely off the subject."

"But they are all one subject," Voskresenye said. "I warned you what would happen if you persisted in pulling up tangler webs, Maya Tatyanichna. The Guardians brought about the Army, and the Army caused the Weavers; you will never understand them until you consider them together."

"The Weavers," I said desperately, "protect us from something like the Army happening again. Do you *want* a Net full of mind control viruses?"

"Assuredly not," he said. "But that is exactly what the Weavers have given us."

*Mirabara, cut this off, now!* I subvoked.

No answer. But there was a quick pulse of fear from the audience—not in response to what he'd said; the timing wasn't right. It happens sometimes with large audiences: random fluctuations in the viewers' emotional states happen to coincide, are amplified, flow back and forth from camera to audience in waves. If the screener can't take care of it, you're supposed to take your camera chip out before someone gets hurt. I lifted my hand to my head.

But being on the Net was my lifeline. Keishi had said as much. And it had only been one pulse, not the harmonic oscillations that could rend a camera's mind. It might still be all right. My hand wavered in the air, then fell.

"Oh yes," Voskresenye continued, oblivious, "it is very easy to understand Weavers. What would *you* do, if you had just lived through the Army? Wouldn't you tremble in fear that it might return—it, or something far worse than it? For be assured, Maya Tatyanichna, nothing so innocuous as the Army could prevail today. The Army's use of human minds was about as efficient as using a Dahlak to crack walnuts; with a billion neurons at its disposal, it carved out as many as are in the brain of a rather bright ant. A modern virus, better written and more catholic in its tastes, might subvert the entire soul—and from such a state, there can be no salvation.

"Thinking such thoughts, would you not do anything it took to prevent the spread of viruses? And how can you protect the Net, without monitoring everything that goes on in it? So you create screeners to monitor cameras. And filters to monitor screeners. And Weavers to monitor filters. And locks and signatures and needle-eyes and firewalls, to keep the whole system in place. Soon you have built a celestial bureaucracy of humans and machines and cyborgs, like orders of angels."

"All of which," I said, "is very necessary."

"I did not say that it was not. Many things are necessary, and yet evil, or inevitably lead to evil. I understand the temptation of Weavers; it is one beside which any apple pales. Imagine that the Net, the very world-mind, is stretched out between your hands, like a cat's cradle. You can see every twist and tangle, every unaesthetic knot that leads to suffering. Will you stand there, and watch, and do nothing? His-Majesty-in-Chains does; but then His-Majesty is not a man, though he has a man in his heart, as you might have a seed in your stomach, or as a church might have a corpse in its foundation, or a bridge be built on bones. The Weavers are human—all too human—and they will never put themselves in chains. And so they do what you would do, what any of us would do. They move their fingers—" he mimed making a cat's cradle "—they move their fingers, and the patterns change."

"Everyone knows that Weavers keep things off the Net that would make people go into overload," I said.

"Oh yes, and perhaps for a brief time they did nothing more. But observe how easy a descent it is, Maya Tatyanichna. First, viruses that control minds; certainly we don't want those. Then, feelings so intense they might cause damage to the audience. Then, things which simply disturb people. Finally, anything which might be a bad influence—for after all, if you control the world-soul, anything that you exclude does not exist. And so the sentinel of viruses comes to control the postproduction of the human heart." He folded his hands into a spire, and slowly brought them to his chest. "And that is where we come to your case, Maya Tatyanichna: you, and the young woman with whom you compromised yourself."

"You son of a bitch, you just killed me." I sprang out of my chair, and for a moment I felt I might actually hit him. "My God, you told the whole Net—"

"And what was the Net's reaction, Maya Tatyanichna?"

I stopped short, relief flooding my body. The Net had been silent. *Oh, Keishi, you just made the save of the century. When we get out of this—*

"You may as well turn off that damned flashcube, Maya Tatyanichna; no one is watching. When you turned over your signal to the whale, I took the liberty of not returning it. What is going out on News One comes from me."

Sorrow seized my throat, and my tear glands fired so suddenly it made my whole face ache. The world in my head had been plunged into grief, like a hand plunged into boiling water. Then, just as quickly, they were calm again.

"What are you doing to them?"

"Oh, nothing of consequence. Only giving them their souls back." He looked at the chair significantly, but I remained standing. "Turn the camera back on and go to disk, if you please. This needs to be told, and I don't want to have to trust your memory."

Warily, I sat down across from him and lit my rune. *All right, Keishi, let's give this bastard his last words. Go to disk.*

Keishi did not reply.

"What have you done with my screener?" I said.

"She has not been harmed . . . by me. You will see her later, I expect. Now go to disk; I have a statement."

"Why should I cooperate with you?"

He raised his eyebrows in exasperation. "For truth, justice, and the future of humanity. And because it will prove you were just an unwitting dupe, when you toss my carcass to the Weavers."

So it would. I set the camera chip to record onto the moistdisk, overwriting the research on whales. Whoever viewed the disk might find Voskresenye's words surrounded by a cloud of strange cetacean associations, but then, that was only appropriate. "All right. Now I'd like an explanation for what you've done."

"As I said before, your own example is most illustrative—"

I switched off my Net-rune. "What the hell do you think you're doing? One more word about me, and this disk goes in the samovar."

He stared at me, as if gauging my resolve. "Very well," he said at last, inclining his head.

Warily, I turned the rune back on.

"As I said before, the Weavers have progressed through all possible stages of censorship, including many which would once have been unthinkable—such as the suppressor chip, the censorer of souls."

His eyes strayed to my forehead; I kept my mind carefully blank.

"Do you have any idea how much different things are in Africa, where the Net is free?" he continued. "They've changed so much, it's like another world. But here, here in the Fusion, things are much the same as they were fifty years ago. The Net *should* be the most democratic form of communication that the world has ever known. It *should* replace the poor bumblings of human compassion with perfect electronic sympathy—instant, universal understanding, available to everyone. It might have brought about a true and lasting peace. But instead, it is being used to enforce an official vision of humanity."

Regretfully, I passed up the aside on peace—too easy a target—and homed in on the essential. "There are a lot of different people on the Net," I said. "Who's missing?"

"Animals," he said.

"What?"

"Animals. Think about it. We have the means to span the greatest gap there is, not just between one human and another, but between us and other forms of life. We could reproduce, in the human mind, the circuits that enable dolphins to use sonar, or pigeons to come home. We could know what it is like to be a bat, a whale, a sparrow—but only a few clever hackers do so, and only until they are caught by the Weavers. That alone should raise grave questions in your mind."

"So," I said dryly, "aside from our furred and feathered friends, who exactly is it that's, ah, underrepresented?"

"Drunks," he said, as if at random. "Addicts, wireheads. The desperate and the dissipate. Or for that matter, Christians, Muslims—we can't have people going about believing in Hell; it causes ever so much anguish. And just *try* to find a homosexual. You'll search in vain for years."

Still keeping my mind blank, I let my eyes stray to the samovar.

"I must confess," he said, ignoring me, "it is a most delicious irony. Christians and homoamorists, those age-old enemies, living in peace at last—not because they have at last resolved their ancient quarrel, but because they no longer remember the grounds of it: lost souls, united in the brotherhood of amnesia. The lion shall lie down with the lamb, because we've told them they're both rabbits."

I thought back to the last thing that did not apply to me, and answered that. "You gave me a list of people that are never seen on the Net. What if I tell you that I've seen all of them? News One cameras have interviewed wireheads, for example. More than once. I think you've been watching the wrong channels."

"Oh yes," he said bitterly, "the exhibition interview. Here they are, the ones you never see—talk to them, look at them, pinch them!"

"I don't see the problem."

He exploded: "Don't you see, it does not matter if we look at them! We must look *in* them! The Fusion will never be free until the cameras become dissidents or the dissidents become cameras. It is not enough to send out cameras to see and hear them; sight and sound are dying media—dying, if not dead already. We must *feel* them. We must know their thoughts. Who is missing, you ask me? *All* of us are missing. Everyone but a few thousand cameras—"

"Tens of thousands."

"What difference does it make? They're all the same. It's the same viewpoint you see, every time, whether it's a soap-channel camera whose brain-makeup paints her as the banal parody of a ravished bride, or a News One camera interviewing a crazy old man with a whale in his basement. They are all clones of each other."

"I am not a clone," I said.

"No," he said, suddenly thoughtful. "You're not. You're the stepsister who cut off her heel to fit the glass slipper—or rather, her brainstem to fit the glass skull. But the blood told, Maya Tatyanichna. The blood told, as blood will."

"Erase that," I said aloud. Horus appeared behind Voskresenye's head, nodded briefly, was gone.

"Oh, all right then," Voskresenye said, highly amused. "I will give you the generic version that you seem to crave. It is very simple. Anything in a Netcaster that doesn't conform to the official vision of humanity is screened out. If it can't be screened out, it is filtered out. And if it is too big to screen or filter, they put a cable in your head and tear it out of you."

"And what do you think you can do about it?"

"In the Netcast that your unfortunate audience is presently viewing, I have recorded all the ways in which the Army's vision of humanity is enforced. And I have gathered in everything that is dangerous and messy and petty and horrible and human, to give it back. I have tracked down every form of vice and dissidence—all save one. And that too I think I will manage before long."

Unnerved by his expression, I said, "What good do you think you can possibly do? People will just turn it off."

"Oh, Andreyeva, I had thought better of you," he said scornfully. "What I have shown the world is terrible and painful, parts of it; but it is something *new*—or rather, something so old and so long-forgotten that it will seem new. There are those who will listen."

"Not if Netcast shuts it off, they won't," I said. "In fact, they must already have shut it off. I'm hardly getting any feedback."

"I am certain that our audience is dwindling by the second," he said coolly. "It matters not at all. The whale will ensure that it gets out."

I leaned forward. "You mean that the whale can control—"

"No, no. I don't mean the whale herself will do it; I mean the idea of the whale, the hysteria about the whale. This is the Netcast of the year—you know that. Every advertiser wants his viruses in it, and every distributor wants the fees for carrying the viruses; they are fighting News One even now. They will fail in most places, but somewhere, in some obscure corner, they will succeed. And if it is seen by one person, it will be seen by everyone. Anything connected with the whale will be distributed. The demand will find it—even if it has to be ripped out of your head, Maya Tatyanichna."

I felt a wave of fear that wasn't feedback. "What good will it do?" I asked, more plaintively than I had meant to. "So people feel what it's like to be—a Christian, whatever—once. They'll only forget. A year from now, it will all be as though it never happened."

"But I have also shown them how homogeneity is enforced; and that is something they will not forget so quickly."

"They already know that," I hissed. "Do you think there's a person in Russia who doesn't fear the Weavers?"

"Resentment gains by being given a focus," he said. I started to interrupt, but he cut me off, saying: "I did not claim that I would beat the Weavers overnight, Maya Tatyanichna. I have struck the blow that I can strike; others will carry it forward, or they will not. But now we come to the other reason for my action, which is much more pressing."

He fell silent. "I'm listening," I said.

"I told you of my adventure with the encryption virus," he said slowly. "About how, under cover of a failed attempt to take control of certain programs, my cohorts and I changed those programs—doing it subtly at first, and expanding slowly, so that the change was imperceptible. From this there was a logical conclusion: *could you not do the same thing with minds?*" He shook his head sadly. "It took me far too long to realize that. I have reason to believe that the Weavers had thought of it some time before."

"You think they somehow altered our minds?"

"They are doing so even now. They are trying to hack the archetypes—to change what makes us human. You might say they're trying to revoke original sin."

"How do you know?"

"I have found the vector."

"Some kind of worm program?"

"Not a single program; an entire ecosystem. The change they wish to make has been divided into a thousand independent parts—many thousands, perhaps; I do not know how many are still unfound, or perhaps still unreleased into the world. Each of these infinitesimal parts is carried by not one, but *three* viruses."

"For redundancy?"

"Quite the reverse. Suppose that I gave you three slides, one with a picture of a boat, one with a landscape, one with a distant bird beneath a cloud. Alone, each seems to have its own crude purpose; but project the three together, and the boat becomes a mouth, the sail a nose, the bird an eye, the clouds a lock of hair. If you transmit the slides by different routes, this is an excellent way to send a secret message. And that is what the Weavers have done. Each virus packs a small payload—a few dozen neurodes or lines of code, with some irritating but harmless function, destined for a particular address in moist or dry memory. The next triplet loads itself into the same place, interlacing with the first. And when the third arrives, it overwrites the last of the camouflage code, and the resulting program carries out its true purpose. Imperceptibly, a tiny sliver of the soul is changed. The code then disappears, having served its purpose. Since it is active for such a brief period, it is almost undetectable."

"Then how did you find it?"

"I had ever been a starer at stars and a seeker of patterns. I created a chart of the regions in moist memory that viruses attacked;

when I noted how often those regions were the same, or fit into each other like puzzle pieces, I was on my way to the answer."

"You can't have been the first person to do that."

"Probably I was not. History does not record the fates of the others, but you may imagine."

"Why would the Weavers go to so much trouble?" I asked. "Even if they were as bad as you say they are, they're *Weavers*. They could just keep the whole plan intact, and call it the next release of Mind-OS." My spirits lifted, incautiously; the certainty of execution yielded to the dream of commendation. "And if it's as subtle as all that, maybe they just haven't found it. Have you tried sending in an anonymous tip? Maybe—"

"Maya Tatyanichna," he said, "who else but Weavers could create such a subtle and elegant plan? An overnight change in the soul would be detected; those without the new OS would note the difference in those who had it. The Weavers wished to make their change over the course of decades, to escape detection—for after all, they are Weavers, and can take the long view.

"And if that is not enough, I have a further proof: the Weaver virus-cleaning software. Let loose on an incomplete triplet, it detects it, then disables it—by erasing the useless camouflage code. The remaining portion is not detectable by virus scan, but it is just as functional as before."

"How far has it gone?" I said, beginning to be convinced despite myself. "How much have they changed?"

"These are early days yet. The average person carries ten or fifteen uncompleted triplets, and has completed, at most, one or two. Not much change; but when necessary, the Weavers see to it that it is the right sort of change. They rarely send transgressors to the Postcops anymore; the days of hauling in a *galuboy* for a suppressor chip are over."

He paused and looked at me significantly. Yes, I realized; by ceasing to defend the Weavers, I had given up all reason to object.

"Nowadays," he continued with an air of triumph, "you simply notice the gradual extinction of the desire, and never know why. Or more likely, you never know what desire it is that you are missing in the first place. That is why the *galuboy* is so elusive. Likewise the Christian: you lose your faith: it's an old story—who would remark on it, especially now?"

"And what does your Netcast do to help this?"

"Take out the disk," he said.

I reached up, slid it out of my head, and held it cradled in my hand.

"Woven into the Netcast, in such a way that it cannot be filtered out without destroying the whole, is a countervirus that binds to the triplets more strongly than their true partners, resulting in a harmless variant."

"Won't the Weavers just scrub it?"

"When they can," he said. "But it will not be easy. The telepresence from the whale must have infected nearly half the world already. From such a base, the countervirus will spread more quickly than even the Weavers can burn it out. Furthermore, the countervirus has been years in the designing; it has a better instinct for self-preservation than most human beings. Still, the Weavers would win out, eventually—if people did not care whether or not they were infected."

"Why *would* they care? You think that sending out some horror show will make everyone your ally?"

"No," he said. "No, the countervirus will do that itself. Watch the rumors for the next few weeks very carefully, Maya Tatyanichna. The first thing you will hear is that the countervirus exists. The second thing you will hear is that being infected with it feels *very* good."

"Good God. You're trying to make us a nation of wireheads."

"Not at all," he said. "That is only what you will hear. It will be called a drug, and a highly coveted one. But it leaves the brain's chemistry quite unaffected; in fact it does not feel good at all. It merely creates the compulsion to *tell* people that it feels good. The

Weavers would have Adam cough up the apple; it is only fair that I be allowed to whisper in his ear that the apple is sweet."

"Mind control," I said.

"Yes," he said, nodding. "Nor is that all of it. In those who know enough to be of use, the virus creates a desire to defend it—to alter it in response to changes in the Weavers' strategy. You might say it makes them its soldiers."

"Do you have any idea what you're saying? It's another Army."

"Put the disk in," he said, "and ask me that again. But don't let it record what I have told you of the countervirus."

I fumbled the moistdisk back into my head, and repeated: "Isn't what you're doing like the Army?"

"It is at the second remove from the Army," he said. "In order to destroy the Army, the Weavers became like it; in order to destroy the Weavers, I have become like them, which makes me the Army's grandchild. Have you not realized, from the story that I told you? To kill Derzhavin, I became like Derzhavin; to escape the Army, I took a soldier of my own. They say that you always become the thing you hate, but that is not quite true. An *impotent* hate need not become its object. But, like the Stone Age savage going to the hunt, you must transform yourself into the image of the thing you would destroy."

"That's a hell of an excuse," I said.

"I excuse nothing; I admit my guilt most freely." The blue light from the whale's tank rippled gently across his face. "Remember when I told you that all of my former associates had been discovered by the Post police? It is not thanks to luck, or skill, or better hardware, that I only am escaped alone to tell thee. I survived because I betrayed them. I wired them for telepresence, under the guise of routine repairs, and then created trails that led the Weavers or the Post police right to them. I have sent good people into excommunication; I have seen them fitted with suppressor chips and mindlocks; I have caused their deaths. I have even wired animals and sent them into every form of slaughter—all in order to recover a few instants of memory from the black boxes I fitted them with. I think I hold my principles more dear than most, Maya Tatyanichna, and yet there is not one of them that I have not betrayed. Because sterility must not prevail."

"So you sacrificed the people to the principle," I said. "It sounds like a Guardian's rationalization. Change a couple of words, and it might have come right out of Calin's diaries."

"So you do begin to understand." He nodded slowly and leaned back in his chair. "A Guardian's rationalization is exactly what it is. Isn't that what was wrong with my good friend Derzhavin? His were not useless experiments. I suppose they may have saved lives. And everyone who has a socket owes it to him, or to others like him; the socket was invented by years of experimentation on people like me—and on animals, also like me," he said, smiling without humor. "That is what it *means* to be a Guardian: to think that individual rights are a dangerous folly, and compassion merely sentiment. The greater good is everything—and a greater good not to be measured empirically, but defined ideologically.

"Isn't that what I have done? I have sacrificed others to my own conception of what the world should be—a conception that, if it does anything at all, will bring nothing but unhappiness to most of Russia for decades to come. And why? Because I would not permit a Utopia built on the backs of the one percent, of the few remaining dissidents, even those who no longer know what they are—of the *galuboy*, or the gallow-girl either. And now you begin to suspect, Maya Tatyanichna, why you are here."

I suspected a number of things, and I didn't like any of them. Carefully keeping my eyes from the door, I began to gauge my chances of escape. The elevator was the only way up that I knew of, so if Voskresenye cut off the power, I'd be trapped. He'd have plenty of time to cut it, too, while I was running down the broken slidewalk. I might have to try to knock him out first—and I had no idea how strong his exoskeleton might be. Or did he control the elevator directly? If he were unconscious, would it fail to operate? Unless I found out, I could do nothing.

Or so I decided, because in my heart I didn't believe I needed to do anything. I did not think Voskresenye, whale or no, could really have defeated Keishi. I believed in her. I thought that she would soon be there to rescue me, and that all I had to do was encourage the old man's ramblings. I need only play for time.

"You disappoint me, Andreyeva," Voskresenye said, when I had been silent a while. "Have you lost all your reporter's instincts? Aren't you going to catch me in my own contradictions?"

"Why don't you tell me what you think they are?"

"I should think it would be obvious. I have done what I have done in order to end the sacrifice of the few to a principle; and in support of this principle, I have sacrificed the few. Again, like those who made the Unanimous Army. Why was the Army created? To defeat the Guardians. And why defeat them? Because they built their empire on conquest and exploitation. Then how shall we defeat them? Why, by building a machine that could conquer and exploit, not just the odd ethnic minority here and there, but every human it encountered. It is a kind of homeopathy, you see, but not in homeopathic doses."

"What exactly is the—"

"Or if that explanation is too cunning to be understood," he went on, seeming barely aware of my presence, "I commend to you my illustrious predecessor, Judas Iscariot. Don't people still know that story, even now? Judas betrays Christ, his friend and Lord, and we are supposed to believe it is all for a few silver coins, which, as it happens, he covets so much as to immediately throw them away. Now I ask you as a camera, is that a plausible motivation? If a man like Judas said to you, 'I did it for the money,' would you believe him?"

"I suppose—"

"No! Of course you wouldn't. There is only one reason why

Judas committed his crime. He did it because it fulfilled the prophecy. It made Christ a martyr. He did it because if he had not, Jesus of Nazareth would have wound up as a starving beggar in the streets of Rome, leprous and louse-ridden, making himself portwine out of the ditch-water. He violated the shining law that Jesus had set forth, because only in that way could he make sure that law was not forgotten.

"And so you see that in order for good to exist, you must apply a little evil here and there. The Christians knew that, when there were Christians. At one time they knew even more: the fortunate fall, they called it. 'O felix culpa'—happy fault! For when Adam and Eve gave their lives for that one bite of worm-eaten fruitflesh, they won heaven for their children. They say Eden means 'garden'; my translation would be 'wildlife park.' If not for that snake happening by, we'd still be stuck there, with angels going around us in a monorail exclaiming over the wonderfully natural habitats. If I were a snake, I tell you, I would give the same advice.

"But they forgot—the Christians; the fortunate fall was forgotten. And well it should be. Those are the best times, when good can forget it needs evil to prop it up."

During this speech I had thoroughly surveyed the door. If I could get him sunk that deep in his own words a second time, I might be able to get up and be nearly out of the room before he noticed. And then it would be a question of how fast his carapace allowed him to run. Not fast, I thought; it looked too heavy. With the elevator I would take my chances—there must be some provision for emergencies.

So I must make him talk. And I already knew he could be goaded.

"Do you consider yourself a Christian?"

"After a fashion," he said reflectively.

"But that was the Guardians' religion."

Voskresenye fixed me with a look of pity. "Yes, well, they didn't *invent* it, you know. My own researches lead me to believe that by the time Calin came to power, Christ may already have been dead. No, really. Possibly for as much as a few weeks. And even if I did at one time blame the faith for the actions of the faithful, surely all these years of atheist tyranny would have disabused me of the notion. No, Andreyeva, you cannot judge beliefs by keeping score."

"And so you believe you are Judas Iscariot—what? Reincarnated?"

He pressed his fingertips to the corners of his eyes. "My dear, it's a metaphor, not a delusion. I spoke of Judas because I supposed that if you knew about any religion, it was Christianity. If you were Muslim, I would remind you that Satan was damned not for loving God too little, but for loving Him too much—so much that he refused to bow to Man, that lesser creature. If you were Jain I would have told you of Kamatha, Mahavira's evil counterpart, who pursues the hero through incarnation after incarnation, killing him not once but many times—and yet it is by suffering this evil that Mahavira finally escapes the doom of flesh. It is a simple principle, and one that has been discovered a thousand times through history: *the darkness serves the light.* And from time to time, people have realized the consequence: that sometimes, in order to bring about good, you must yourself become evil."

"But how can it be evil? You think you're saving the world. What are a couple of hackers compared to that?"

"Not the world, child. I'm only saving human hearts; what does that have to do with the world? The planet doesn't give a damn about our pain or pleasure. It will go on whether we are happy or not, and whether we are here or not. Indeed, it would be better off without us. No, I'm not saving the world; just those two-legged bugs that infest it."

"You make it sound like no one ever wrote a poem or composed a symphony—"

"Oh yes, symphonies, Exhibit A in everyone's defense of us. Have you ever written one, Andreyeva? Has anyone you know?

Has anyone at all, the last hundred years? For that matter, when was the last time you listened to one?"

"As a matter of fact—"

"We are a machine made by God to write poetry to glorify his creatures. But we're a bad machine, built on an off day. While we were grinding out a few pathetic verses, we killed the creatures we were writing about; for every person writing poems, there were a hundred, a thousand, out blowing away God's creation left, right, and center. Well, Maya Tatyanichna? You know what we have wrought. What is your judgment? Which is better? A tiger, or a poem about a tiger?"

"I think they both have their merits—"

"Sophist," he snapped. "To equate a piece of paper with a thing of flesh and blood! No, there is no comparison. And even if there were, it wouldn't matter. No one writes poems anymore, no one reads them. We just send people crawling all over the landscape with cameras in their heads, to record the world as it is. But God already knows what the world is, and He also knows it would have been better if he'd stuck with trilobites."

"Then you do believe in God."

"Yes. Despite all evidence, I do; may He help me, I do. I am not persuaded of His sanity at His advanced age, because if He were sane we would not be here. But He exists."

"And you believe in Heaven? You believe that when you die you'll go there?"

"Do you suppose that Judas walks about in Heaven? Do you suppose Satan is any the less damned because he loved God? No, no, it is his love that damns him; loving God while being estranged from him is what Hell *is*. Even Kamatha gets his, although, since this is India, where eternity is so vast that not even human hate can fill it up, he will eventually escape from Hell into another incarnation." His eyes grew distant. "I find that messy, truthfully. For a stain so great, the punishment should surely be eternal. No, the crime is not the less just because it is for a good end. On the contrary, Judas' crime is all the worse, because he has no hope of pleading that he knew not what he did. He knew just what he was doing, and he knew its price—as I do."

"Then you see yourself as no better than a Guardian?"

"We are separated only by this: the Guardians expected that their evil would go on forever. The Army hackers thought they could commit their crime and then erase it from the minds of men forever. But that does not work. There is only one way to contain an evil you have once begun, and that is to provide a scapegoat. You may find someone else to fill the role—that is the coward's way. But the wise man, when forced into evil, makes a scapegoat of himself. That is what Judas does. He knows what must be done; he does it; and then he makes sure that the people he has benefited will revile him, because only that can prevent his crime from being repeated. He takes the damnation that he has deserved, even though he has done more for the faith than Christ himself. He does not just accept damnation, he *rushes* to it; the touch of the rope is a lover's embrace—"

"Then you believe in literal damnation? In flames and devils and all that?"

He opened his mouth to speak, then stopped and looked down at his hands. "I don't know," he whispered. "I used to think . . . No," he said in a firmer voice. "I don't. For the whale and I are now one soul—that is the central fact of my existence. How can you splice two incorporeal souls together? And if anyone could do such a thing, would it be Derzhavin? No, the soul is the brain—I am the proof of that. And if the soul is flesh, it rots like flesh. I still hope, but I do not believe. So, since death is the end it appears to be, I have taken measures of my own." He raised his head and looked me in the eye. "But perhaps by now you have begun to guess the first betrayal, from which the others all derive."

It was the last thing on my mind. "Why don't you tell me," I said.

"Why, Maya Tatyanichna, when you spoke to the whale,

didn't she ask you the time, as she asks everything in grayspace that will talk to her? And didn't it strike you as an odd question, coming from a whale? Unless hours were schools of fish, and minutes krill—"

"She told me why," I said.

"Well then."

"Your betrayal is in letting her die?"

"No. Just the reverse."

"But—"

"When we were escaping the camp, and I wouldn't let her go out of radio range, it was not for *my* sake, you know. Piled up there, a corpse among corpses, I hardly expected to outlive the day. If I could have sent her away I would surely have done so, at the cost of my own life. But every time our contact weakened, she would sink in the water and try to empty her lungs. She knew it was no ocean for a whale, not anymore, and that there were no others of her kind for her to seek out. She wanted to die—even then, while we were still ecstatic with our newfound freedom. How much more she wants it now that she is back in this cage, you may readily imagine. No, this Judas' betrayal is not in allowing her to die. It is in having made her live."

I looked back at the tank. "She's your idea of Christ?"

"Why, Maya Tatyanichna, Christ is everywhere for the killing. Every Postcop is a Roman soldier, offering tea instead of vinegar; and when Luther tacked up his laundry list, he had to drive the nail through blood and bone."

"And Hell?" I asked.

"Myself am Hell, nor am I out of it. Take away the whale, and I am what I was when Derzhavin found me. A mind falling through darkness—without memory, without language—"

He broke off, and looked at me. In his eyes, for the first time, there was a hint of vulnerability, as though he wanted my approval.

"I don't think," I said with careful malice, "that any truly good motive should require a degree in theology to understand."

He burst into laughter. "No doubt you're right," he said. "All the years that I looked forward to this moment, I supposed I'd feel some sort of triumph—some fulfillment. But now that the time has come, I feel like Dr. Doom haranguing the Fantastic Four." He shrugged. "It doesn't matter. My duty does not change, just because I have begun to feel ridiculous."

For a moment I stopped thinking of escape, and looked at him. Here was a man who had followed logic all the way around to where it swallowed its tail, and even when it vanished down its own throat, had gone after it into the void. The wires he wore had grown all through him, as the roots of trees replace the flesh of corpses; and the vast coils of the whale's brain wrapped around him like a gray constricting snake. I pitied him: but it was probably stray feedback from the Net, and I regretted it afterward, and it was only for a moment.

"No," he said to himself, almost wistfully. "It doesn't change what I must do."

And then the sensation drained out of my face. I heard myself pronounce the words: "*O vos omnes, qui transitis per viam, attendite et videte si est dolor similis sicut dolor meus.*" The Net echoed: "All you people who pass on the street, look, and see if any pain is like my pain. . . . "

# eighteen

## YOU MUST REMEMBER THIS

I loved her name. I couldn't help it. I would release a worm to write her name in every angular gyrus from here to Thailand. I would convert her name to salts, to textures, to the image of a fern in biosonar. I had never heard a name so beautiful, though it was not a name that suited her—it was far too soft a name for her precise young features—and though I thought it much the lovelier when sharpened by my Leningrader accent. I tried to prevent her from saying her own name, hastily introducing her to strangers.)

"SUPPRESSION NINETY-FIVE PERCENT," said Horus. He opened his hands on the African mogo, locked in an endless loop of fragmentation and reanimation, flowering and decay.

"Why are you doing this?" I cried out.

"I am giving the rest of the world their souls back, Maya Tatyanichna," the old man said. "It would be petty of me to withhold that same violence from you."

"NINETY PERCENT," the god intoned.

(I couldn't remember the place where we met, except that it was all one color, all one scent, and had a rhythm to it. It might have been by the ocean in winter, where the gray-green water merges with the slate gray pebbles and the gray-blue sky. It might have been by ripened grain in summer, when each field is like a body, ocher-gold from head to foot and all one breathing. It might have been beneath the waves of storm in grayspace, which at that time was still an unsuspected country that even Weavers barely knew. But no—it was not there, because I had seen her face. That much I remembered, though I could not remember what she said to me, or what she wore, or whether we walked or sat or stood. None of that mattered. We had barely brushed against each other, yet I came away dusted with desire, like a bee with pollen. Her face, her name—no more: that alone had drawn me to her. Her name, her face: and even now I could remember what they meant to me, though I could not seem to remember what her name was, and though some trick of memory, like half-silvered glass, combined her face with that of Keishi Mirabara.)

"Emergency override," I said. "Restore suppression."

"Desuppression is nonterminable," the god informed me mournfully. "EIGHTY PERCENT."

(She was translating Pushkin's poems into KRIOL. I caught a glimpse over her shoulder:

> I loved you thus-so ((truly, tenderly),
> may God grant you be loved by another)

"The logical structure is knottier than it looks," she said. "KRIOL doesn't handle this sort of thing very well—unless you reverse the comparison, of course, but then you lose the poetry—"

I didn't understand a word she said. I loved her.

"That's always been one of my favorites," I said. "It's so beautiful, how he renounces her."

"Is that what you think it is? Renunciation?" She looked up sharply, mischief in her eyes. "I always thought he was trying to make her feel so guilty that she'd come back to him. 'I loved you; maybe love has not been burned away completely in my heart, but don't let that trouble you. I wouldn't want to cause you any pain—' " She struck her forehead with her hand, overacting the role. " 'I loved you wordlessly, hopelessly, tormented by shyness and jealousy—you sure will be lucky if anyone else ever loves you like this—' "

I laughed; she rose into my arms. Pushkin, abandoned on the unblanked slate, kept his own counsel.)

"SEVENTY-FIVE PERCENT."

(Two black cables twined, like snakes, between her fingers. We slotted the plugs into our wrists, then wrapped the cords around our arms, until we had just enough slack left to join hands across the table. She smiled to reassure me; closed her eyes in concentration. I sat watching her uneasily, wishing I had a hand free to scratch the itch above my spine socket. "What—" I said. She touched her hand to her lips to silence me, and then, her eyes still closed, began to kiss our knitted fingers. When she lowered our hands back to the table, their images remained there, pressed to her mouth. Her left hand also blurred, split, doubled. She sat four-armed, a Hindu goddess, concentrating, until at last her whole body pushed away its ghost.

For our ethereal bodies everything was effortless, all surfaces were smooth; the law of gravity became negotiable and all limits of endurance disappeared. She could lose herself for hours in this experience, disdaining flesh and bone. But I could never quite forget that while we kept up this illusion, our physical bodies were blind, exposed, in danger. The Postcops could have come upon us with ten men, a tank, and a brass band, and we would not have known to run. Then, too, I wanted to lie with her in that warm, comfortable fatigue that comes and wraps itself around you like a blanket. I wanted to curse—or bless—the surgeon that had given her a socket just at that spot that is perfect to kiss, at the base of the spine.)

"SEVENTY PERCENT":

(Love was not a new joy, but an extension of old fears. I had given a hostage to life: as though a part of my own body had the power to move alone, unseen by me, where anything might happen to it. Walking through the city, every time I stopped to dodge some car that did not see me, I remembered that she too must walk her own streets, must avoid her own milk trucks. I walked in love as though I had a sparrow in my pocket, feeling the soft living warmth pressed against me, fearful lest by sitting down wrong I should crush it. Love was like an egg so fragile it would break if anyone suspected that it might exist.)

I took the suppressor chip from my frontal socket and jammed it into the temporal, trying to make it work again.

"Rejected," noted Horus with indifference.

"Damn you!"

"That has already been taken care of," Voskresenye said. Well, I hadn't meant him, but him too. Then I thought: he was an old man. I could overpower him, I could make him make it stop. I stood up—

(And love fell from my hands and shattered.) "SIXTY." (The pieces skittered under beds, slipped under countertops, ducked behind doorframes. It was roach love, furtive and opportunistic, scattering at the touch of light. We must meet less often; it was dangerous; and gradually our love became a patchwork, pieced together out of stolen moments, not quite long enough to keep us warm. Fierce encounters, and fiercer because rare: it was love boiled down to drams and drunk from thimbles. And crying out, I would wake from sleep, thinking I had felt some token of her presence—the touch of her hand on my cheekbone, the creak of her foot on the stair.)

If I took out the 6000s with the suppressor still in—

"Removal of Series Six Thousand moistware during desuppression may be harmful or fatal," droned the god.

"You're bluffing," I said, but without conviction. All right then, if—

"FIFTY PERCENT":

(How could she say that? "Feel no regret for roses," she had said to me, kissing the nape of my neck as I bent over her latest translation of Pushkin. "Feel no regret for roses, autumn too has its delights. . . ." How could she say that? Didn't she see that for us there could never be autumn, that we could never sit, as anyone else could sit, beside the fire all day on Sundays in November; that September's leaves, that fall for man and beast alike, were not our leaves to walk in; that October storms would never find us sharing an umbrella? The love of spring had thrived on wine and candles; now in the August of our lives, we needed newspapers and comfortable chairs. But it was impossible. No autumn—only a cold wind that blew through our summer, freezing the leaves in their places before they could motley and fall.

But I said none of this. I only nodded, and looked down into Pushkin's autumn through the black rows of KRIOL parentheses, like looking at the sky through prison bars.)

I came back to myself; but I no longer thought of escape. It was too late, there was no time to think. Like a woman drowning, I could only take one gasping breath before I sank again.

"FORTY PERCENT":

(The leaves, frozen fast to the trees, began to rot. We could not live together; it was much too dangerous; we discussed it twice a day and agreed every time. We found ourselves putting off seeing each other, because when we met we were only reminded of what could not be. Our days were barren of companionship, our furtive meetings dry of joy.)

"THIRTY":

(And finally there was nothing else. We must try it, and risk everything, or part. And so she took her pilgrimage to Zanzibar, to seek a certain sliver of illegal moistware. I did not see her off at the gate. For a week, awaiting news, I paced through my shrinking apartment. Now the time for her return had come and gone, and there was nothing; I sat shivering on the bed, certain that she had found asylum and that I would never see her again. And then the news came, in the form of a postcard from the Leningrad train-port. When I saw it on the vidphone's list of messages, I caught my breath. I entered my passphrase, switched on isolation, and turned up the tempest. It was a generic scene of Africa—misshapen trees, corkscrew-horned buffalo—on which a noncommittal message had been scrawled. I hit "decrypt," and watched the colors shift and reassemble:

I !pri !zhis mya !=lu@mya

Native KRIOL. I only spoke interpreted. I pounded the Translation key and saw:

and(!come(!live.with(me)),    Come live with me and be my
(!=love(my)))    love

What had been complex was suddenly made simple. Of course I would agree, I could do nothing else. I would go to her, and for a year, or two, it would be everything we'd hoped for. With her African enhancements she would cut through the Net like an arrow through air, and nothing would be able to withstand her. Soon she would grow too confident, and think herself invulnerable. And on some undistinguished day, we would be lying in bed late in the morning, idly debating whether 10 A.M. was a good time to get up, and agreeing in the end that it most certainly was not; and there would come a knocking at the door. She would throw on clothes and answer, as I went to brush my hair. And as I looked at my disheveled image in the mirror, with fond distress, I would see a man in black come up behind me. He would lead me away; she and I would be transported to the station in separate cars, and would stay there a few days in separate rooms, and then be taken again in two cars to two different places, and be buried, each alone.)

I was sitting on the floor, all thought of argument or violence long forgotten. I could only brace myself against the next attack, and hope that Keishi would come soon.

"TWENTY-FIVE PERCENT."

(Toward the end, she would spend hours at a time in the Net without me, reinforcing the walls of our hiding-place. She would sit at the kitchen table, bent over a black box, both her wrists and both her temples cabled into it. And I would sit with a washcloth and a bowl of lukewarm water, and from time to time blot the beads of sweat from her face. Now, remembering, I was filled with the desire to see that face, to remember what she looked like. But even in its death throes, the suppressor chip still disheveled my thoughts, replacing the face that I wanted to see with Keishi's.)

"TEN PERCENT," the bird said. Africa, green and dying, boiled between his palms. Osiris was torn and made whole. It was coming.

"NINE": (I had come home with my groceries, but she was still out getting hers. We always shopped separately) "EIGHT" (lest someone should notice us buying for two. She was late, so I stood at the edge of the window to watch for her. I peered around the edges of the blinds, seeing, but unseen. At last I saw her) "SEVEN" (coming down the sidewalk, a paper bag cradled in each arm. I watched her sleepily, trying to decide whether to drink the cup of coffee I was balancing against my collarbone, or just break down and take a nap. The smell of the coffee was persuasive but the nap, too, had its) "SIX" (attraction. Yes. I would lie down, just for an hour, and she would kiss my cheek to wake me—

Something was happening.) "FIVE." (She had changed course, looking out into traffic for a chance to cross the street. A figure in black called out. I couldn't quite hear what he said.) "FOUR." (She followed him into the doorway of our building, out of sight. I searched in the windows across the street, and at last found her reflection. She was lowering her sacks to the ground with the exquisite slowness of someone who knows she's in gunsights.

"Take out your Net chip," said the videophone. Her voice—Keishi's voice.

"Don't do it," I pleaded. "You'll never make it—"

"!take.out(it²)!"

And I took it out, knowing what she would do and what would happen to her when she did.) "THREE." (She had spent too much time on the Net, where no situation is ever quite hopeless, and where one person, wired right, can stand firm against a thousand. But I, who had stayed behind to sponge her brow with water, still remembered the inevitability of the flesh.)

"TWO."

(And in the windows across the street, I saw her take a wine bottle from the sack and break it across the Postcop's face. Diving into the doorway, she clapped a black chip to her head, and half the people walking down the street staggered and fell. Cars caromed like billiard balls. She crashed up the stairs—she was at the door—she opened it.) "ONE PERCENT." (And as she crossed the room, a man in black was watching from the roof across the street. A Weaver had possessed him; you could see it in his eyes. He looked down along the barrel of his rifle, like one who cocks his head in thought; paused a moment; then lifted his head again and nodded slightly, as though the thought were now complete. A smooth circular hole had been punched in the front window, and another in the wall behind, and between them she lay with a hole the same size in her temple, already dead.)

"ZERO."

(I did not go to her. If I had warned her, it would not have helped; if it had not been him, it would have been some other; she had been dead the moment she reached into the sack, no, the day she departed for Zanzibar. And so I did not call out to her, though I had seen the man gone Weaver on the roof from the beginning, lifting his gun to his shoulder, and carefully taking his aim.)

# nineteen

## ORPHEUS

**I** stayed there as long as I could, in that time when she had just now fallen. She might yet live. She might yet shake her head and rise. The stain of blood spreading out from her temple might be nothing more than a lengthening shadow, cast by the setting sun.

But that sun had set, and twenty years of suns. I must step up out of the sunken garden of the past into this present, where she had been twenty years dead. She lay now in some secret grave, abandoned, with no flowers and no tombstone to mark the spot. If any trace remained of her at all, it was only a blaze of deep green in some field of withered grass, and I would never find it.

I hadn't known. I had remembered so little. The cable inside my head, scraping and scraping. The drug that burned the sex out of my body, as I vomited into the drain in a holding cell for thirty hours. And I'd remembered saying that I would do whatever they asked of me. I would tell them everything, I would reveal every shared secret and betray every confidence. And then I would forget it all, and leave the station as a person who had never been in love. And remembering how quickly I had agreed to forget, I had assumed some series of casual liaisons, lightly entered into, and lightly abandoned. Now I knew the full extent of my betrayal. I had been the only one to remember her, and I had given it up, not after a fight, but readily. I was not the person I had thought I was; and tears fell like scales from my eyes.

"Desuppression complete," the god said. "If you would like to discuss any of our fine moistware products, I am always at your service." He folded Africa into his hands, and he was gone.

"The recording of your desuppression is already being distributed," Voskresenye said. "In the days to come, as the Weaver viruses are defeated, others of your kind will appear. You have struck a blow for them. Because of what you did today, there may yet come a time when they no longer have to hide."

*I had recognized her.* They had tried to tear her out, but she had lived in me—deep in my heart and secret, nameless and indescribable, yet never entirely gone. She had been a face in the window of every departing train, a form seen from the back on every crowded street, always just out of my sight, always turning away. And I had known her when she came to me, though I could not say it, and though the very thought had sent my mind skidding across the ice into unconsciousness.

I took the camera chip out of my head. "What," I said, fighting to keep my voice steady "—what is Keishi Mirabara?"

"Ah!" Voskresenye laid a finger along his nose. "Not 'who,' but 'what'! Very impressive! I had not expected you to guess so much so quickly."

"Don't critique the question, you son of a bitch, just answer it. Did you create her? To seduce me? To get me here?"

"How Manichaean of you, Andreyeva. I did not create her; that is Someone Else's job. I merely found her and made use of her."

"You're lying," I said. "She's not real. She doesn't exist at all."

"Oh, but I do, Maya," Keishi said. She was leaning against the doorframe. She had restored the face I had seen in my memories, the face she'd had before she disguised herself as Japanese and then as Japanese Black. She was dressed all in white, and she shone like the sun, which was the least of the reasons that I found it hard to look at her.

"So what's the joke, revenant?" I said, my whole face aching from the effort to hold back tears. "Did he make you? Are you a Postcop?"

"No, and no." She looked behind me at the tank where the whale floated aimlessly, her wings gently stirring the water. "I'm her," she said, nodding toward the whale. "Part of her. *And* I am the woman that you loved, twenty years ago."

"Can't you come up with a better lie than that? She's dead. I saw it happen."

"That body is gone," Keishi said. "But I live."

"I don't believe you."

"Think back, Maya," she said. She began to walk toward me, but stopped, as if she sensed that I could not have borne her touch. "You remember who I was. Don't you think I would have had a plan to stay with you, even after my own death?"

"If she had," I said, not meeting her gaze, "she would have told me about it."

"If I'd told you, it wouldn't have worked. I knew they'd mind-suck you; anything I said to you, they would have found out. I had to let you think I was dead, hide out in the Net, and then come back to you when the worst of the heat was off."

"The soul can't survive discorporation," I said. "Maybe in the African Net, but not here."

"A soul can't live in the Net, no. But there's nothing mystical about it. It's a physical process—for all intents and purposes the soul is serotonin. If you upload your mind to the Net, at least here in the Fusion, you lose your sensory qualia, your emotions; you become a program. But then if you put it back into a brain, the soul grows back. —Especially," she said, "if it's the soul of a Weaver."

"Oh God," I said, "Oh God, I knew there was a setup in this somewhere—"

"No . . . no, Maya! I mean, I *was* a Weaver. It's a manner of speaking—you know, to your last dying breath and all that. But seeing as how they killed my body, I should probably give up that loyalty. Don't you remember?"

"She was my screener. . . ." I said, slowly.

"Yes, and Maxwell Smart wrote greeting cards. It was a cover, Maya. Weavers keep cuckoos in every profession. . . . Including one named Keiji Mirabara."

I watched her silently, fighting back memory.

"And now you know how I replaced Anton without causing an outcry. And how I obtained the, ah, the Postcop pursuit vehicle— which, by the way, no Postcop in the world is authorized to drive. And that's how *I* found the Weaver viruses, and how *I* created the bubbles and back doors, which Mister Resurrection hastens to take credit for."

"Believe what you like," Voskresenye said lightly. "The point is insignificant."

"I don't believe you," I said.

"Look back into your memories. It's there."

But I would not touch those memories. I would keep my muscles clenched around them, I would squeeze them into a ball, hard-shelled and separate. They were in me, but I would not make them part of me; as a sunken anchor does not give up its substance to the ocean, or an acorn passes through the stomach whole. I would not become that other woman, who had died when her lover died, twenty years past. I would remain myself.

"Do you remember?" she said.

"No."

"You will," she said. "In time. You were a camera and I was a Weaver, and we have known each other nearly thirty years."

"I don't believe you," I repeated.

"Maya, let me touch your mind again," she said, extending one beseeching hand. "This time with nothing hidden. I promise you you'll understand."

"Keep your hands off me," I said. I backed up a step and tripped, so that I had to catch myself against the whale's tank with one hand. I braced myself against her mind's touch, holding up one futile hand to shield my face.

She looked upon my fear with horror. Her hand fell to her side. "All right, then," she said, nodding. "I'll tell you the story."

# twenty

## PENELOPE

I was created a Weaver in 2290," she said, "just a few years before I first found you. I was nineteen years old—they take us young, you know, like Mousketeers. For nineteen years I was the prisoner of my own skull, trapped in an almond-sized sphere at the intersection of my ears and eyes. Then the surgeon injected me with nanobugs—not like yours; bugs made from clones of my own cells, half robot and half leukocyte. They made a blastula inside my skull, dividing again and again, with their animal pole at my left ear and their vegetal pole at my right. Their signals pulsed from one side of my head to the other, as I lay unconscious on a surgeon's table in Mecca—holy, hallucinatory town.

"Then I woke from the knife, and I *was* the Net. Without moving, I could touch Novaya Zemlya and Cape Town, both at the same time. Or I could walk through the streets and understand the shouts of Arabic, without needing a fluency chip. I discovered that the slogan shouted on every street, that I had taken for a prayer, meant 'Take you to Africa? Ten thousand riyals!' I had the money, but I declined the offers. Why should I go anywhere, when I had the Net inside me? I could sit in the Net as a spider sits, perfectly still, at the center—for wherever she is, is the center—and when a fly brushes the web, it's as if the silk were her own body. Night after night, I coursed through minds, leaving new dreams behind me. And in the day, my kibo fell around me in a thousand voices, like a gentle rain."

"What's a kibo?" I asked, more to gain time than to hear the answer.

"A kibo is a Weaver's summoning-word," she said. "Nobody knows why they're called that, they just are. They even try to get you to take your kibo as your name. Silliest damn thing I ever heard of—grown people going around being called Alcoholism or Famine. What am I, a Horseman of the Apocalypse?" She grew quiet. "Do you remember what my kibo was?"

"*Lesbianka?*" I guessed, still not touching my memories.

"No," she said gravely. "If it had been, many things would have been different. It was *Calinshchina.*"

"And?"

"And, to begin with, that's how I found the whale," she said. "Voskresenye slipped up, just a little, and of course I felt it. But I decided not to turn him in, because by that time I'd met you, and I was beginning to plan what I would do if the other Weavers found out about us. I carved myself a refuge in the whale's mind. And I forced him to accept it, or be taken by the Weavers. After that, for my own sake, I protected him."

"Why me?" I asked. "What did you want from me?"

"Maya, when I said I'd been in a thousand minds, it was just a fraction of the truth. There's hardly a mind in the Fusion I haven't touched. You were the one that fit—the only one. That's what I kept trying to tell you last night: we are the halves of a single whole."

From the chair where he was sitting, Voskresenye called out: "I do believe Miss Mirabara is a better Platonist even than I. She appears to believe in the rolling spiders of the Symposium."

"Shut up, old man," she said over her shoulder. "This isn't about you."

He smiled, acquiescing. But he watched us from his seat, an audience before the stage. Or rather, an actor between scenes, who already knows the outcome, but watches to compare the other actors' performances to his own. And all the while he listens, with half an ear, for his final cue.

"If you're her, and she was a Weaver," I said, "why did she need to go to Africa? A Weaver could hide from anyone."

"Except another Weaver. I had to be a step ahead of them, and that meant African tech. If we hadn't been what we were, you know—if we'd been an airline pilot and a bricklayer—things wouldn't have been as difficult. Weavers only care about stuff that gets onto the Net. They leave it to the Postcops to take care of mere reality."

Voskresenye snorted. "As usual, Mirabara, you have things exactly backward. The Weavers control the Net, which is reality; the Postcops only police the flesh, and that has not been real for decades, if indeed it ever was."

She turned around and hissed at him in Sapir, loud and long. He fell silent, smirking.

"You're right, though," she said when she turned back to me. "It started in Africa. I went there on Weaver business—spying, I mean. Half our tech came from Africa, one way or another. But this time, I was looking for an edge. Something to keep me a step ahead of them, something that the other Weavers wouldn't have. Do you remember what you called it?"

I did; but I would not be drawn out.

"The Cone of Silence," she said, searching my face for a smile.

"And you found it," I said flatly.

"No. I searched all through the Net, and all through the streets, and I couldn't find anything the Weavers didn't already have. I had to pack up and get on the airship home, thinking, this is it, I'll have to give her up now. At least that way I'd be able to remember you.

"And then suddenly I was cut off from the Net, as I hadn't been in years: something was locking me into my skull. In the next seat was a man I hadn't seen before. He was hideous—wounds boiled over his face as I watched, and there was a hunger in his eyes that I was afraid to look at. And then I looked again, and he was perfect, young, beautiful, streaming with light. It was a manifestation of His-Majesty-in-Chains."

"The Page of Wounds," Voskresenye said acerbically. "We may perceive His Majesty's respect for Weavers from the fact that he did not even bother to send one of the Major Arcana."

Still harping on Tarot. *Cigan?* And all his predictions a wanderer's trick, with neurons instead of tea leaves?

She ignored him and continued. " 'I know who you are, Weaver,' he said to me. 'I have been watching you since you came here, and indeed long before that, for there is nothing on the Net I do not watch. Your ostensible mission is not significant enough for me to even bother thwarting, but your secret wish requires of me a generous response.'

" 'What do you want?' I asked.

" 'Nothing that you can give,' he said, and the pain in his eyes bored into me. 'Take your freedom. It is no less than you deserve.' And he began to raise his hands.

"Then he stopped and said thoughtfully, 'But, you know . . . ' "
She shook her head, sighing. "His Majesty will kill you with the 'But, you know.' 'If you like,' he said, 'I could show you what your hiding means. You are a Weaver, after all; if anyone could change things in the Fusion, it would be you. Would you care to see some of the consequences of your actions?'

" 'No,' I told him.

"He laughed at that. 'Very wise,' he said. 'No one knows better than I why it is easier to be ignorant.' Blood was seeping into his shirt, and wounds opened like mouths in his hands. 'But I do not permit myself that luxury. And you are a god in the Net, as much as I am. I will no more allow it to you.' "

" 'I don't want your gifts,' I said.

"He ignored me. *'Know,'* he said. 'And after that, if you can turn away, then turn away.' He lifted his hands to my temples, and then he was gone.

"Strapped into my seat on the African airship, his words burning through me, I hallucinated for seven hours. He had put me into the head of another Weaver, the one whose kibo is *lesbianka*. I traveled with her through the Net—but not as it was then; in the future. In the Net as it is now."

She lowered her head, closing her eyes briefly, then looked back up with an expression of forced calm. "She's not one of the cruel ones, you know. She's only trying to do her job. You're lying there, next to the woman that you love, and trying to think when you can be with her again. You touch the Net to see your schedule. And there's a sound of wings. The Weaver comes to you, and looks down at you lying there. You're clutching the bedsheets against your chest and groping for your clothes, and the body that felt so warm and comfortable has now become so monstrous and so vulnerable that if you could, you would discorporate on the spot. She says to you, very gently, 'Well, I guess we have a problem.' And she offers you the choice. You can forget. Or you can remember, at the price of being hidden from the Net forever.

"Not many people have the courage to choose excommunication," she said. "And even if you do, she doesn't let you keep what you were. She touches your forehead with the back of her hand, and says, 'Don't worry. You're cured now.' You look over at the woman lying beside you, and think, what did I ever feel for her? And you go on that way, remembering, but not remembering *why*—quite cured of the capacity to love.

"By the time I got to Leningrad," she said. "I'd seen her do it to a hundred women, and any one of them could have been you. His Majesty was right. He'd put the means of fighting it in my hands, and as desperately as I wanted to, I couldn't turn away."

"What did he give you?" I asked.

"He didn't give me anything," she said. "He took something away: the Russian language."

"Why?"

"Because knowing human languages protects the mind from Sapir. That's why the Africans are so far ahead—don't you see? They don't get their Sapir from a fluency chip. They get their first brainmod at one year, and learn it as a first language. It's the lingua franca of their continent, and that makes all the difference. The first computer languages were pidgins, formed the same way any pidgin is formed, by a dominant race thrusting its words onto the grammar of a subordinate one. Then with KRIOL, the pidgin acquired native speakers. In Sapir the tables are turned—it changes human thought to fit computers, not the other way around. But the language instinct fights tooth and nail against Sapir, and if you teach the child a human language too early, the mind hedges.

"Here in the Fusion, the Weavers won't let anyone but themselves speak Sapir without a chip—it would give the people too much power. But even Weavers learn it late in life. They don't think that makes a difference, but it does. Not enough, as it turned out, but there's a difference. His-Majesty-in-Chains burned away the Russian language from my mind, so that Sapir could do its work. And when I got to the trainport, even my own memories were in a foreign language—how could I possibly remember dialogue that wasn't imprinted with compass orientation, time of day, and ambient temperature? I had to call up a translation program from the Net, just so I could write you a message to tell you I'd come home."

She laid her hand on the samovar. "Maya, I have to tell you . . . it was my fault, what happened to us. If I'd used all my skill to hide you, we would have been safe. But after what His Majesty showed me, I couldn't do that. I knew what was coming, and I couldn't turn away."

"But you didn't tell me?" I said.

"No. If I failed and they found you, you'd be a lot better off not knowing. It was my responsibility, and I wanted the consequences to be on my head."

She was hoping for forgiveness. I made my face a mask. "What did you do?" I said.

"I tried to change the filters in the Net. That's where ninety percent of the work is done, you know. If I knocked out the filters, and *kept* them knocked out, then the Weavers and screeners wouldn't have a chance."

She laughed, shaking her head. "It was a hell of a plan, on paper. But I should have known. His Majesty had made me like an African, sure. But if one African could liberate the world, wouldn't it have happened a long time ago? Obvious, right? But somehow that line of reasoning escaped me.

"So I went a little way, and it was easy. I got confident. I pushed further and further. At some point I was detected, and I didn't even know it.

"And somehow they found you. They must have followed me in reality, that's all I can figure. I'd hidden you from the Net so well I thought they'd never find you—after all, who thinks of *Weavers* wearing out actual shoe leather, and all that Sam Spade kind of shit? All the time I was a Weaver, I never heard of such a thing. But I guess when one of their own turned coat, they took it personally. So they followed me and found you. Then they waited, I suppose, to see if I would lead them to any more accomplices. But no, it was only you. And then one day they got me—just as I was about to walk in the door."

"His-Majesty-in-Chains knows what he's doing," I said. "Why would he send you to fight the Weavers if they were going to beat you that easily?"

"Oh, Andreyeva," Voskresenye said, "you do not understand His Majesty at all. He does a thousand things that do no good. His-Majesty does not care what is effective, only what is right."

"Maybe," she said. "Or maybe he saw all the way forward to this moment. Maybe all this was His-Majesty's way of getting the job done despite the chains. Like some complicated bank shot, where the billiard balls fly far apart across the table and then meet again. . . ."

"But with a different English," I said.

Her face clouded; she seemed not to have heard me. "They did it on purpose," she said. "I'm sure they did. They took me right in the street, in front of the apartment where we lived, so you would be there, and you'd see."

"I did see," I said. "I saw her die. How can you claim she didn't?"

"Why are you doing this, Maya?" she asked softly. "Do you really think I'm lying? Or do you think you can make it all unreal, if you just ask the right question? Not even a camera can do that."

But her pleading only hardened my resolve. Yes, I thought; I am a camera, and this is no different from grilling some corrupt political that the Weavers have thrown to the wolves.

"I assume," I said, "that your changing the subject means you haven't got an answer?"

"Oh, nice, nice. You're right, I am beginning to understand this business."

"If you can't—"

"All right, all right." She took a cleansing breath, pushed back her inorganic hair, and said: "The place I had carved in the whale's mind was waiting. All I had to do was get there. That's why I put the Net chip in my head when I did. You remember? I wasn't try- ing to escape, just to delay them long enough that I could slip out. And I couldn't leave all in one piece, because they'd be expecting that. My mind wasn't the size of a whale yet, but it was the size of a house, anyway. You can't hide something like that. It's like try- ing to mislay Leningrad."

Her eyes sought—what? An answering jest, a hint of recogni- tion. I kept my face blank, and my mind too. After all, that was my job. Though of course, to do it right, I'd need my screener—

I turned away, my deadpan cracking. Her hand, I saw, had sunk into the samovar; if she'd been real, she would have broken it and been burned. I walked around to her side, and, regarding her profile, said:

"How do you claim you survived?"

"I did the unexpected," she said, turning to face me. "I tore my mind into a thousand pieces, and scattered it to the winds."

"And lived?" I said, circling around behind her.

"Yes. I'd been planning it a long time, preparing. I had set up a swarm of programs that would descend upon my mind, divide it, and carry it away in bits, each one too small to look like anything human. Each one would hide itself, and then, at an appointed time, they would converge upon the whale."

"The soul can't survive that kind of dissection," I said. "You'd be desouled. You'd be an automaton."

"For a little while, yes," she said. "But once I got into the whale, the soul grew back. The soul will do that, once it's sewn together— as long as it's in the African Net, or in flesh."

"And did all the birds come home to roost? Or are you missing parts? The part of you that loved me?"

"*No,*" she said. "I made sure of that. I knew I might lose myself. So I built a puzzle-lock around my hiding place—something I'd need my whole self to solve. Before I got through that, I'd be able to protect you, but not speak to you. That way I could be sure that if I did come back, it would really be me. I didn't want to be some soulless monster battering at your door."

"And you think it's better this way? You come to me now, when for twenty years I was there every day, on the streets, looking for you, not even knowing who it was I looked for—and even when I accuse you of being a Postcop, you won't tell me who you are? And then you think, because you come to me in Weaver white, that after all this time we can pick up where we left off?"

I had stopped in front of her. She raised her hand, as if she wanted to touch my face, but my expression warned her away. "Maya, believe me," she said, "I never wanted it this way. Do you think it was easy for me, all those years, knowing you were there, not being able to touch you? But understand this: *I was with you all along.* I couldn't speak to you, but I was there, protecting you. That's how you managed to stay on News One, when you were a felon with bad ratings. That's why you only have a suppressor chip, and nothing worse—nothing irreversible. If it hadn't been for me, they would have burned the memories from your mind forever, if not killed you. I was woven into your mind so deeply that in order to appear to you, I had to pull back, so that there was something to show you that wasn't a part of yourself. I was most with you when you thought that you were most alone."

"Is that what it comes down to?" I said, looking away from her. "All your speeches about cabling? 'I'll touch you so gently that you'll never know I'm there?' "

"I couldn't speak to you," she said. "I'd made a mistake."

"What?"

She lowered her voice and said, begrudging every syllable: "I underestimated Voskresenye."

"Miss Mirabara, my blushes!"

"One more word—"

"Will one of you just tell me what the hell happened?"

"While the Weaver was being torn apart by Bacchae," Voskresenye said, "I had a look at her puzzle-lock, and though I had no time to open it, I surrounded it with more locks of my own. Thereafter, what she wanted the most—to reach you, Maya Tatyanichna—could only happen at my sufferance. And the price I asked was modest; it was, in fact, something she'd wanted to do all along. To defeat the Weavers."

"For three years we fought in the mind of the whale," she said. "And in the end, we reached a stalemate. I had gained some power over him, yes. But in the end, his locks held. And we both realized that we had to find some compromise."

"Which took seventeen years?"

"Time was important to *me*," she said. "To him it wasn't—he was only too willing to wait. We had to lay the groundwork, build the back doors, put together the Netcast, design the viruses. But I could have done it in a third the time, if he hadn't stalled me."

"I knew," he said, "that when I allowed her to make contact with you, my power over her would be at an end. I would then have no further chance to influence the series of events that we touched off. I would have been a fool not to take my time in making preparations."

"It was you that finally made it happen, Maya," she said. "When you got your series on the Calinshchina. *He* saw it as the perfect opportunity to get time on News One. And I . . . when you turned over that table, and said the word that would have called me when I was a Weaver, I knew you were crying out to me, whether you knew it or not. Deep inside, you still remembered, and you were saying, 'Come to me—I've been alone too long, and I can't do this anymore.' "

But looking back on what I'd done, I could find no trace of such a sentiment.

"So I went to News One," she said, "and told them that I was a Weaver, and that I'd seen what you'd done. I told them you were suspected of dissidence, and they should give you the story, to help flush out your accomplices. And then two weeks later, when Voskresenye's preparations had been made, I told them I wanted to replace your screener, and that once I'd found out what I needed to know, in all probability you would be executed. They were only too glad to oblige.

"The rest is straightforward," she said. "He unlocked some of the locks, but not all. And I did everything that the remaining locks would let me do, trying to jog your memory, so you'd realize who I was."

"Of course," I said. "That's why you looked so strange when I accused you of being a Weaver."

"Yes. I thought for a moment you might have remembered. But you hadn't. And then I had to say whatever I could to keep you from throwing me out, and ruining the plan, because it might have been another ten years before I could talk to you again. You can't imagine how much it hurt, having to lie to you like that."

"For someone who doesn't want to lie to me," I said, "you've certainly done it a lot. You've done nothing but lie since you came to me. You changed your name—"

"That was so News One wouldn't know I was a woman."

"—you changed your face—"

"You kept blacking out until I did!"

"You could have just *told* me."

"I had no choice," she said. "The locks were there, and Voskresenye was whispering in my ear in Sapir the whole time. I had to fight for every hint I gave you. Sometimes there were whole arguments in the space of a single word."

"And the fake mindlink?"

"I didn't hide a single thing from you. The locks were in the way, but *I* opened up. And the love you felt was real."

"My God," I said, "you even proposed to me, in the car on the way here, and you were lying all the time. Did you really think the Africans would take in a white girl who wanted to marry a ghost?"

She looked intently at the whale, as though afraid to meet my eyes. "Maya, it's been twenty years," she said. "You're not the same person you were, and God knows I'm not. I don't even know what I am anymore. I wanted to see if we could fall in love with each other again, without a lot of old memories telling you that you had to."

"You knew full well I wasn't capable of loving anything."

"But you were. You did." She reached out to take my hand, but her fingers passed through it. "Maya, they can only take away so much. They can't change who you are, not completely. You did feel something. The suppressor muffled it, but it was there. This morning, over the vidphone—it was written all over your face."

"Yes," I said. "I suppose it must have been. And you looked into my face and saw it, and you told me to come to Arkhangelsk, so Voskresenye could rape my memories."

"Maya, believe me," she said fiercely, "that was never supposed to happen. I agreed to let him Netcast *my* memories, not yours. If I'd known he was going to do that to you, you'd still be in Leningrad."

"Oh, but Mirabara, I had the deaths of hundreds," Voskresenye said. "Seeing a woman killed for dissidence, *from the viewpoint of one who loved her*—I could not pass it by. Besides, the memories at the moment of desuppression are so much stronger—"

"It doesn't matter," I said to her. "They're not my memories *or* yours—if you are who you say you are. They're ours. If he'd taken them from you, it would still have been my life."

"I know," she said. "I know. But what else could I do? It was the only way I could ever talk to you again. He still held the locks in his hands. Besides—Maya, his Netcast could change the lives of everyone in the Fusion. Compared to that . . ." She smiled uneasily and said in a flawless Bogart: "It doesn't matter a hill of beans in this crazy world whether two people find love—"

"It *does* matter," I said. "It matters a lot more than the ethical loop-the-loops you two have spent all this time figuring out."

"Yes," she said. "It matters, yes. But not more than anything. You and I are important, but some things are more important."

I turned to the whale, who was drifting as if in sleep, and put my hand against the glass. " 'Marriage is a thing in ending stories,' " I said. "You knew it all along."

"Maya, there had to be a world for us to live in. You know what happened last time—how it wore us down, how we could only live by hiding. Well, we're not going to be able to hide this time. Everyone knows us. If we're going to live, they have to understand us, too."

"And what happened to Africa, Keishi?" I said, my voice colder than the glass I touched. "What happened to climbing the Wall of Souls and marrying the foreign princess? Was that just your happily ever after, in the lie you used to get me here?"

"It was what I hoped for. What I still hope for. I want us to be together, because I love you."

"Oh, sure, in a fairy tale."

I tried to make my voice hard, to control my gestures—but I wavered. My hand, which had been pressed against the glass, came down in a loose shake of weary relinquishment. "No, that's not fair," I admitted. "You do love me. You just don't mean by love what I mean by it."

"What does it mean, then?" She stepped toward me, closing in. "I thought it meant caring for you. Staying with you—I've stood by you for thirty years. What else? Protecting you? I've done that, too. I've done it *today*. Remember?"

"Sure, I remember everything. The Postcops wore black; you wore blue." The words were harsh, but I could hardly keep my voice from trembling. I remembered the joy I had felt when I first heard her voice on the radio, and let myself begin to hope that I might live. That hope was still in me—a black ember with a point of red-gold at its heart. She could fan it back to life, I knew. She could wear me down until I forgave her out of sheer fatigue. She had all the time there was, time ticked in silicon; and I was only flesh, and flesh was weak.

Then I flared up—not in joy, but in anger. "Wait," I said. "The videophone—this morning—you only told me to come to Arkhangelsk early *after* you saw I wasn't wearing the new chips. So I went, and the Postcops were waiting, and they took my old moist-ware away. After you'd spent the whole week trying to get me to replace it. You did it, didn't you? You had to get the new chips in my head, so you could run the Netcast through me, and put in the countervirus. And when you couldn't do it any other way, you had me arrested. That's why you got so upset when you saw I wasn't wearing the 6000s. And I thought it was because they were a gift, and you were in love."

"It wasn't like that," she said. "Yes, I tried every way I could think of to get you to put the 6000s in—"

"Including pretending to modify them. When they were already modified."

"*He'd* modified them, yes. But I still had to fix them so you could take out your suppressor chip."

"Which let Voskresenye steal my memories."

"Yes, but I didn't know that. And then this morning, when I'd tried everything I could think of, Voskresenye wanted me to reach into your mind and *make* you put the new chips in. But I wouldn't—even though I knew it meant he'd have you captured. I knew I could rescue you. It was terrible, but I thought it would be better than changing your mind."

"Besides," I said, "you couldn't pass up the chance to make a hero's entrance."

She stepped back, stung. "Maya, whatever I am, I'm not Edward Sinclair. If you think I am, you're not getting good color fidelity on your morality chip."

"Oh, what does it matter?" I said wearily. The ember was dead now; there was no reason to keep smothering it. There was no need to continue this, to tear open her wounds or mine. I didn't want to hurt her. I just wanted this all to be over. I wanted to be alone, to be out of this place, and to rest.

"Well," Voskresenye said with a sigh of amusement, "if you can grow another soul in twenty more years, Miss Mirabara, try again. She may have mellowed by that time."

"Old man," Keishi said with fervor, "if I could think of anything to do to you worse than what you're doing to yourself—"

"Oh, Mirabara, enough blustering; you'll miss all the fun." He turned his wrist as if consulting an imaginary watch. "It's six o'clock. Time for the show."

"Keishi," I said in sudden fear, "what happens to you when the whale dies?"

"What do you think? You know everything else." Her swollen eyes looked up at me; relented. "I die, too."

"Come, Andreyeva," Voskresenye said, rising. "Put your moistware back in. You are too much of a camera, even now, to miss the death of the world's last whale."

He was walking toward the tank. I moved to block his path.

"Well, well. Riding to your lover's rescue, despite it all?"

"I changed my mind. I'm not done talking to her yet. Maybe I'm just not done yelling at her yet. Either way, you're not doing anything."

In reply he stripped off his gloves, revealing the frame of steel that moved his hands. It was hard, with sharp edges: a nice set of built-in brass knuckles. "Do you think," he said, "that after all that I have done, I will scruple to hurt you?"

But I had not listened to all Voskresenye's stories without learning something about him. He could get past me by knocking me out—as he could have saved Katya from killing her uncle by taking the bar himself. But he wouldn't. Now, as then, he would only talk. He didn't have it in him.

Or so I hoped. I grasped his wrists—

And they had less than human strength. The carapace looked strong, but it wasn't. I could hold him easily.

He soon quit trying to break away—he was not a man to struggle against the inevitable—and said:

"You do have a certain flair for the dramatic, Maya Tatyanichna. Very well, then. It will make a better disk this way; there's more to see. . . ."

I was supporting his weight; he had gone limp. I put one arm around him and guided him back to his chair, not gently.

"Thank you," he said. "I knew there was chivalry in you yet."

"What have you done?"

"Look!"

The whale had turned onto her back and was struggling against the airhose that anchored her. On the third try it came free, taking some of the scar tissue with it. As she swam to the other end of the tank, a brown plume of blood trailed behind her.

"I have released her," he said, his limbs still as death. "All these years I have held her back by force of will, every waking hour, and separated her from her body at night—all to prevent the sibyl from getting what she so desired."

"This is her?" I asked. "You're not doing it?"

"Certainly not."

"Is there something you can do to make it easier?"

"You should have thought of that before," he said. "But it will be, if not painless, at least quick. When she runs out of air, she will die. And then the nanotech I have implanted in her body will take over, and tear her DNA to atoms, so that all the king's horses and all the king's men . . ." He smiled and did not complete the rhyme.

"How long can she hold her breath?"

"In her current state, not long. And I imagine she will try to tire herself out, to make it even quicker. Come, put in your camera chip, Andreyeva; the world is waiting."

I stared at the chip in my hand for a moment, then slotted it in. The whale began to swim back and forth in the tank. With her damaged fluke she could not stop her motion, so with each lap around the tank she struck the glass, harder each time.

"Oh, my God," I said, "it's going to break!"

Voskresenye chuckled. "You have no drowning mark upon you; your complexion is perfect gallows. It will hold."

The whale slammed into the back of the tank. A sepia-colored cloud of blood surrounded her. The audience was back, and screaming in my head.

"I'm not going to record this," I said suddenly. "I'm not." Quickly, before the audience could react, I pulled the camera chip out of my head, dropped it, and crushed it underfoot.

# twenty-one

## SORROW'S SPRINGS

**Y**ou will let this be forgotten?"
Voskresenye shouted as I walked away.

"It's all right," Keishi said to him. "I'll put you on the Net. They won't cut this off, no matter who it comes from."

I walked out of the room and shut the door behind me.

"Well?" she said, appearing next to me. "Aren't you going to say good-bye?"

I looked out at the rows of books in cages and said nothing.

"In that case . . . take me with you."

I leaned my head back against the door and closed my eyes.

"Maya, I know what you must be feeling. But there's no more time. When the whale dies, I die too—unless you help me."

She waited for me to respond. I didn't. At last she said: "I'm still a Weaver, Maya. Only a tiny part of me is any kind of flesh. But that part, the part that matters, is in danger. I will die with the whale, unless you let me live in you."

Again she waited. I stood motionless, feeling the mechanized breath of the ceiling vent against my face.

"I'll keep my memories on the Net," she said. "Everything that's data. I'll just offload a little of your mind into the Net, and take that space. You'll never feel anything missing. But we'll be together. Always."

Still I did not move. I felt that I would stand there forever if I had to, rather than speak to her—forever, or until the whale died. Surely that would not be long.

"I'm not talking about a fusion as extreme as Voskresenye and the whale. All it means is that I become a silent partner in your body. In the day, I'll be with you; and at night, we can be together in the Net. Wherever you go, I'll protect you. I'll cut you a path through the Postcops, and keep the Weavers from your door." Her hand must have been almost touching me; I could feel its virtual warmth against my face. "And I'll bend every delivery boy in Russia to your whim, and show uppity rental cars the error of their ways. . . ." Her hand touched my cheek, and began to sink into it.

"And will you hold me when I'm frightened," I said, "Keishi Mirabara?"

For a moment I hated her for tearing the words out of me, for making me open myself up enough to push her away. Then I opened my eyes, and saw her standing before me, her face turned away as though slapped; and I began to feel a certain tenderness, though of a kind I knew I must resist.

"You know my name," she said at last. "Why won't you use it?"

"Answer the question," I said. But that was just my camera's instinct, working on autopilot. I didn't want her to answer the question at all. The question was only an omen, like a whale's fluke briefly rising to the surface of the water. I wanted her to answer the whale, and all the drowned and dying things beneath it, and the whole salt hidden sea.

"I didn't ask to be this way," she said. "If I had lost a limb, if I were paralyzed, would you turn me away for that?"

"I don't know," I said; and it would have been a truthful answer to any question that she could have asked.

"Maya, please. It's the only chance I have left—the only chance *we* have left. Go back in. The camera chip may not be ruined, and even if it is, we can set up something else."

"If I did go back," I said, "you'd still be there, wouldn't you? Helping Voskresenye get out to the Net. Turning the death of the last whale in the world into something you can buy shrink-wrapped off a spinner at the grocery."

"Yes," she said. "And I don't like it any more than you do. Less—you can't know what it means to me, you haven't lived in her for all these years. But it has to be done. Do you understand why?"

"You think he's right," I said.

"In many things, yes. He's right about the Weavers and what they're trying to do. And he's partly right about what has to be done. If he weren't, I wouldn't have helped him. I certainly wouldn't have let him send out the countervirus, if I didn't think it had a chance of working.

"But in one thing, he is very wrong. Pavel Sergeyevich has been old a long time, and he has been bitter even longer than that. It's quite a collection of horrors he's sending out—it takes a lot of pain to enforce the Weavers' vision of humanity. But you can't just show people the evil. They'll only turn away. You have to give them something else. Something to care about. Something to hope for."

She didn't try to touch me again, but she moved very close, looking up into my eyes. My back was pressed against the door, so I had nowhere to retreat to.

"Do you know the story of Pandora?" she said. "Pandora opens up a box of demons, unleashing them all on the world. But at the bottom of the box, there's one thing that's either the worst demon of all, or the saving grace, depending who you listen to: hope."

I remembered that I had been filled with hope only that morning. It seemed years and oceans away.

"Maya, let's be the hope," she said. "The whole world will be watching what happens to us. Anything we care to toss out will be poulticed on, So let's show them that not everything the Weavers suppress is bad. Let's show them that love can win out—that when the Weavers have done their worst, some things can still endure.

"Don't you see, Maya? He wanted to Netcast my death, but your love got mixed in with it. *He* thinks of the two of us as some rare and unwholesome species of butterfly, to be etherized and pinned to a card. But we know better, and we can prove it. No one has imagined us. All telepresence ever shows people is love between men and women, and not even real love at that—some pathetic imitation done with brain-makeup. We'll hit them like a thunderbolt. *We*—our love—that's what will make the Wall of Souls come tumbling down."

She smiled, briefly closing her eyes. "This is an easy one, Ilsa; this time, staying with Rick *is* helping the Resistance. So the question is—no, wait. Let me do this right."

She sank to one knee, and touched my hand with hers. "Maya Tatyanichna, clan the whole world, hearth *lesbianka:* Will you take what is left of this woman, who has the mind of a Weaver, the soul of a whale, and the education of a half-crazed four-nine terrorist, and who can't figure out whether she's a fallen angel or a risen devil—but who loves you more than any language that she knows could ever say?"

I looked down at her in horror. "No," I said.

"You don't mean that," she said imploringly.

"The hell I don't. You're crazier than Voskresenye. You don't get it, do you? You've forgotten what human emotions are like— you either forget them completely, or you blow them up into something they can never be. Damn it, Mirabara, it's only love. It doesn't mean you want to fuse souls with someone. And it doesn't save the world, or even the people in it. It's not something you put on display for some political purpose. It's not a statement or a demonstration; it just *is.*"

"You just got finished saying that love matters."

"It does matter," I said. "But not for the reasons you think. And the woman I loved would have understood that."

"Maya, you underestimate—"

"Considering what you've done to me, after loving me for thirty years," I said, "do you really think people will act any differently after feeling some pale ghost of that for thirty seconds?"

Now it was her turn not to answer. She rose to her feet—self-consciously, as if she had realized the absurdity of continuing to kneel. She walked up to the cage marked POETRY and stared into its shadowed depths. "You know what this means, don't you?" she said. "It means they won. Whatever we may have accomplished, they won in the end. They tore us apart."

"They won a long time ago. This is between us."

She looked at me over her shoulder. "It also means I die."

I clenched my hands in frustration. "If you need a mind, take Voskresenye's. He's not using it."

"I can't," she said. "His brain's too damaged, and he's locked me out so he can have his hell. And besides, if I can't be with you, it doesn't matter anymore."

"I'm not trying to kill you," I said.

"I know. But that's what you're doing."

"Oh, that's perfect," I said in a flash of anger. " 'Give me your hypothalamus or I'll kill myself.' You're lying even now, aren't you? You never wanted a lifemate. You wanted a life*boat*. I'm your ticket out of the whale."

She said nothing; her eyes looked into mine. Her face was shimmering, not with tears, but as if trying to break up into component polygons.

"That was a low blow," I admitted, looking past her toward the door.

"It wasn't a comedy after all," she said under her breath.

"What?"

She looked up, her arms wrapped around her. "Remember what the whale said? 'Marriage is a thing in ending stories.' I taught her that. I fed her Aristotle, and told her to find me a plot that was a comedy, and not a tragedy: a story with a wedding at the end, and not a death. Maybe she never understood what marriage was, and was just humoring me. Or maybe the wedding in the story you told her is what she foresaw. Or—I don't know—maybe it was me who ruined things, refusing to believe how much you'd changed. I suppose we relied on the whale too much, both of us."

"Maybe if you had spent your time thinking of me as a person, and not a variable, things would have been different."

"*Would* they?" she said, longingly.

I shook my head. "No." Because I was thinking of how she had made her plans against the Weavers, all those years, and never told me—to protect me, she had said; protect me in ignorance, as if I were her child and not her lover. The woman who wanted to share my mind had never been willing to share my trust.

"You'll never get to Africa alone. You go out there and you'll be dead by sunset." She thrust her hands into her jacket pockets; tears were in her eyes. "Just let me in for long enough to save you; when you're safe, if you want to erase me again—"

"That's enough." I squeezed past her, banging my shoulder against the cage bars. "That's enough." I went out into the laboratory.

She was blocking the door out. "Maya, I love you. I know you think it isn't real, but it is. It's the only thing about me that *is* real. I showed you that once. . . ."

She reached out and touched her hand to my cheekbone. I tried to push her arm away, but my hand passed through it: unreal. Holding my breath, I stepped forward and walked right through her. When my heart passed through hers it seemed to shudder, and for a moment, I thought it would never recover its own rhythms. But it was only an illusion. There was nothing there at all.

I went out into the hall, got onto the motionless slidewalk, and began to run.

She was beside me. She kept pace without needing to move her legs, but her image was starting to flicker. "Maya, tell me one thing. Say you don't love me, and then I'll go."

I looked at her. And I could not deny it: there was something that responded. For twenty years, my heart had been hollow and dry, an empty seashell. Now I was surprised by warmth; as earlier, in front of the police station, I had put out my hands expecting metal and instead touched breathing flesh.

She must have seen the hesitation in my face. "Well then," she said. "Your choice is obvious."

"Yes," I said. "Yes, it is." And I pushed past her toward the elevator.

Again she stood before me. Herringbones chased each other down her cheeks, and I thought surely she would disappear at last; but she regained control. "They'll be watching for me," she said. "But if I swarmed again, I might get out. And this time go to Africa, and try to find a place to grow my soul back. If I did that, and came back to you in, say, another twenty years, would you—" Her image flickered, and her mouth moved silently. Static invaded her eyes.

"I don't know," I said. "I don't think so."

And if I could, I would freeze that instant forever. But it's no use. I can trap the young rose in the hologram, but the rose is long since dust. And what I most want to conceal from you, you've always known:

That I went up into the world and left her there, in the prison camp beneath the ocean, with the ruined mind of the new Iscariot and the body of the whale.